Josephine

Josephine

BEVERLY JENKINS

KIMANI

Recycling programs
for this product may
not exist in your area.

JOSEPHINE

ISBN-13: 978-0-373-83125-8
ISBN-10:   0-373-83125-0

A Kimani TRU title published by Kimani Press/February 2009

First Published by Avon Books in 2003 as JOSEPHINE AND THE SOLDIER

© 2003 by Beverly Jenkins

www.KimaniTRU.com

Printed in U.S.A.

This book is dedicated to my daughter Melaina,
for being the Jojo in my life.

Mama loves you, Baby Girl.

one

June 1864
Whittaker, Michigan

At the age of twelve, Josephine Best had dreamed of being a hairdresser. Now, five years later, her dream had come true. She'd been styling hair since ten this morning, however, and the dream seemed more like a nightmare. Her feet were numb, her shoulders and back ached and the tips of her fingers were singed and tender from handling hot hair and even hotter curling irons.

There was to be a big gathering at the church tonight to raise relief funds for the war effort, and every woman in town wanted her hair done; Josephine had serviced fifteen customers since opening up. Although many of the ladies had made appointments, others had simply rushed in with the hope that Jojo, as she was affectionately known to family and friends, would squeeze them in. In retrospect, Jo wished she hadn't been so accommodating. If she hadn't, she'd be at home now with her feet up, enjoying dinner with her mama, and Jo's sister-in-law, Belle. Jo had planned on spending a leisurely afternoon getting ready for tonight's festivities. Instead, she was putting curls in the sparse, graying hair of her last customer, Mrs. Harriet Donovan, a woman Jo didn't particularly care for because the widow Donovan never had a good word to say about anyone or anything.

"So, Josephine, I hear your friend Trudy's become engaged."

Jo eased the hot curling iron out of the curl and set the iron back on the brazier. "Yes, ma'am. She is. She and Bert are getting married next June. I'm sure they will be very happy." Jo used a comb to section off a small piece of Mrs. Donovan's hair, then fed the lock to the curling iron.

"And what about you?" Mrs. Donovan asked. "When are you going to marry?"

Jo had no trouble hearing the censure in Mrs. Donovan's tone. Jo and Trudy Carr had been best friends since the age of six, and now that Trudy's marriage plans were common knowledge everyone in town seemed to think Jo should be heading to the altar next. Never mind that Jojo had no beau, nor any desire to beat the bushes until she found one. Jo had plans for a career; she wanted to be a woman of business, not a wife and mother— At least not now. But when she attempted to explain her ambitions to those outside her immediate family, all she received in response were pitying looks, as if she were lacking in some way. "I'm not looking to marry anyone right now, Mrs. Donovan."

"Why not? Every other young woman your age certainly is."

Jo bit back her response. She'd been raised to respect her elders, even ones as nosy as Mrs. Donovan. So ignoring the rude question, Jo set the last curl, then put the iron down. After a few whisks of the comb and brush, she had Mrs. Donovan set for tonight's affair.

Jo handed Mrs. Donovan the mirror.

The portly widow turned the mirror this way and that, but instead of admiring what Jo thought to be fine work, the woman thrust the mirror back at Jo. "Surely, you don't expect me to pay for this!" she declared angrily. "Look at me. Why, a beagle could've done a better job."

Jo was so stunned her jaw dropped. She'd been slaving over Mrs. Donovan for more than an hour and the woman hadn't even had an appointment, for heaven's sake. Having never had a customer leave unsatisfied, Jo was at a loss as to how to proceed.

Mrs. Donovan took care of the matter. After gathering up her coat and handbag, she huffed, "I will never patronize you again, and I will be sure to alert my friends."

Jo couldn't believe her ears. "But, Mrs. Donovan, I worked very hard."

The woman waved her hand dismissively. "Goodbye, Josephine."

And she left.

A snarling Jo wanted to fling something across the room. How dare that old bat leave without paying! Jo stomped over to her cash box and counted up the day's receipts. She'd made almost five dollars from the fifteen paying customers; a good sum considering the war and the state of the nation's economy, but Mrs. Donovan should have paid her, as well!

Her face grim, Jo used a towel to shield her hands, then picked up the brazier and went outside to dump its coals. When she returned, she set it off to the side to cool, then swept up all the hair on the plank floor.

Jo's father and her brother, Daniel, were carpenters, and they'd built Jo's shop for her upon her graduation from the Women's Program at Oberlin College two years earlier. In reality, the place was nothing more than a small room with a roof on top, but it was her place of business, and she took great pride in both it and the services she provided. She finished cleaning up. Once done, she put out the lamps, and locked up the place. Still simmering, she headed across the field to her home.

Jo's mother met her at the door. "I was starting to worry."

"I'm sorry I'm late. Mrs. Donovan came in at the last minute."

Jo's twenty-one-year-old sister-in-law, Belle, came out of the kitchen. "Hi, Jojo. We were just getting ready to sit down to dinner. Shall I fix you a plate, as well?"

"I suppose so."

Cecilia Best peered into the face of her daughter and asked, "Why so glum?"

"Old Lady Donovan refused to pay me. She said a beagle could have done a better job."

Cecilia stared. "What happened?"

Jo shrugged. "Nothing. I did her hair, but when it came time to pay, she refused." Then Jo added, "And I did a good job on her, Mama. I truly did."

Jo was so mad she wanted to cry, but because business owners weren't supposed to bawl in their mama's arms, Jo held on to her emotions.

Her mother, not caring about Jo's occupation, came over and enfolded her into a motherly embrace. "You can't please everyone, darling."

Jo's arms instinctively hugged back. She then placed her head on her mother's shoulder. "I wanted to wallop her with the dustpan."

Cecilia chuckled softly, then looked into Jo's face. "The next time she comes in, why not ask her how she'd like her hair fixed? Maybe that will prevent any problems."

"I did that, but it didn't seem to matter."

"Well, some people are born difficult. Don't worry about it. You go get washed up, and we'll eat, then get dressed.

Belle's made some of her biscuits. That should put the smile back on your face."

"And with your brother off fighting for Mr. Lincoln, we should be able to get more than one," Belle quipped.

They all grinned. Everyone knew about Daniel Best's love for his wife's biscuits; he could devour them faster than anyone or anything.

"I really miss Daniel," Belle added wistfully. "When do you think we might get word from our men, Cecilia? I tell myself that Dani and Mr. Best and my papa can take care of themselves, but—"

"I know, dear. I promised William I wouldn't worry while he was away, but I can't seem to help myself. I'll feel better hearing from them also."

Jo could only agree. Daniel, her father and Belle's father, Mr. Palmer, were mustered into the First Michigan Colored Infantry last winter. Their company set out for Annapolis, Maryland, this past April. A few days later, they'd written of their impending move to Hilton Head in the Carolinas, but those letters had been the last. Like her mother, Jo had promised her father she wouldn't fret, but it was hard not to after reading the newspaper reports of Confederate mistreatment of Black Union prisoners of war. Some of those captured had even been sent to the auction block and sold into slavery. Even though President Lincoln had publicly expressed his outrage over the practice and had promised dire consequences if the South didn't change its policy, Jo still worried, mainly because she loved her father and brother so much.

Later, after dinner, Jo was getting dressed in her upstairs bedroom. Her encounter with Mrs. Donovan was continuing to plague her when a knock sounded on her partially closed door.

It was Belle. "Are you ready?" She was dressed in a lovely gray dress with a full skirt and a little white collar.

"Almost," Jo replied. She had chosen a full-skirted blue dress with a black velvet collar. The gown was old and a trifle outdated, but the Bests, like other abolitionists both black and white, practiced Free Produce, a national movement that tried to affect slave owners' profits by boycotting any goods made by slave hands. Since American cotton was on the list of shunned items, women like Jo made do with their old gowns rather than fashion new ones out of fabric made from cotton picked by slaves.

Leaning down into the mirror on her vanity table, Jo hooked the small black earbobs in her lobes, then turned and faced her sister-in-law. "How do I look?"

Belle's affection showed plainly in her dark eyes. "Beautiful as always, Jojo."

"Thanks," Jo responded unenthusiastically.

Belle asked, "Are you still brooding over Mrs. Donovan?"

Jo couldn't lie. "She swore she was going to tell her friends."

Belle cracked, "Since the widow Donovan doesn't have any friends, your business is safe."

Jo grinned. Leave it to Belle to cheer her up. The two young women had been close friends since the day Belle Palmer came to live with the Bests five years ago. At that time, Belle had been a fugitive slave from Kentucky. Jo and Daniel had found her hiding in the brush near the side of the road and had taken her home. Later, the Bests learned that Belle had been separated from her father on the flight from slavery to freedom in Michigan. Many months passed before the two were finally reunited, but in the meantime, Belle and Daniel fell in love. They married August 1, 1860, on Belle's eighteenth birthday.

Jo went to her armoire and took out her good cape. She couldn't get Mrs. Donovan out of her mind. "Do you think I'm abnormal for not wanting to get married?"

"No. Why?" Belle replied.

"Mrs. Donovan said I was."

Belle threw up her hands. "Jo, Mrs. Donovan doesn't know her head from a bucket of paint. Why on earth should you care what she thinks?"

Jo shrugged. "I don't know. Do you think everyone sees me as she does?"

"No," Belle answered firmly. "And I'm not just saying that because you're my sister and I love you. You have plans for your life, Josephine Best. If you wish to be something other than a wife, there's no crime in that. Besides, there's no one around worthy enough for you to marry anyway."

Jo agreed. Even before the war took most of the men away, there hadn't been anyone she'd wanted to spend her life with. Most of the young men were looking for conventional wives, ones who cooked, sewed and had babies. They didn't want a woman who was educated and opinionated. One of her mother's church acquaintances even suggested that men didn't like women with strong minds. Jo knew that to be untrue because her mama had one of the strongest minds Jo had ever encountered, and William Best loved his wife to distraction.

Belle peered into Jo's face. "Forget about Mrs. Donovan. Everyone knows you're a fabulous hairdresser. Promise me you won't let that old sourpuss make you doubt yourself."

Jo smiled, then nodded. "All right." Jo wondered what she would ever do without Belle. Belle could always be counted on to pick up Jo's spirits, no matter what. It was one of the hundred reasons Jo loved her sister-in-law.

Belle asked, "Now that we've settled that, can we go?"

Jo dropped her head to hide her grin. "I suppose so."

Belle gave Jo's shoulders a quick hug. "Then come on. Your mama's waiting for us."

When the Best women got to the church, they were not surprised to find the grounds filled with people. Towns all over the nation were contributing to the war effort and Jo's community was no exception. There'd already been drives to send the troops blankets, socks and toiletries.

Most of the people in attendance at the outdoor affair were women. Jo nodded greetings to the familiar faces, all the while searching the crowd for Trudy. When she spotted her, Jojo waved excitedly, then hastily excused herself from her mother and Belle.

Standing beside Trudy was Trudy's fiancé, Bert Waterman. Jo couldn't help but notice Bert's short, buxom mother, Corinne, at his side. Trudy had nicknamed her future mother-in-law the Dragon Lady. Jo thought *The Shadow* to be a more appropriate name since Mrs. Waterman rarely left her nineteen-year-old son's side. Bert had wanted to sign up for the war like the rest of the men in the community, but his mama had forbidden it.

Jo walked up and greeted everyone.

Mrs. Waterman glanced at Jo from over the lenses of her spectacles and droned, "Good evening, Josephine."

"Good evening, Mrs. Waterman."

Trudy instantly grabbed Jo's hand and exclaimed, "You don't have any punch. Let's get you some."

Bert protested, "Hey, I can get it, Trudy."

Trudy, already leading Jo away, replied hurriedly, "No, Bert, you stay here with your mother. We'll be right back."

Bert's mama gave the young women a look of disapproval. Jo offered a chagrined smile in reply, then let Trudy pull her into the crowd. Jo sensed that going for punch was just a ruse and that Trudy had something she wanted to discuss privately.

Her instincts were correct. Once they were out of earshot, Trudy turned back to Jo and snapped, "If I had had to stand next to Corinne Waterman one more moment, I was going to hurt someone. More than likely it was going to be Bert."

Jo shook her head with amusement.

"It isn't funny, Jojo," Trudy countered. "Bert and I almost didn't come tonight because his mama didn't feel well, and he wanted to stay home with her and make certain she was all right."

By now they were at the punch table. Jo took one of the small cups and handed it to Trudy. Trudy tossed the beverage back like a cowboy with a shot of red-eye. Jo searched her friend's tightly set face. "Are you all right, Tru?"

"No. I feel as if I'm marrying her, not him. I asked him if he planned to let his mama run his life after we married, and do you know what he said?"

Jo shook her head.

"He said, 'I don't know.' Can you believe that?" Trudy asked.

Jo could, but kept silent. She'd had serious misgivings about the engagement from the beginning; Bert wouldn't tie his shoes without consulting his mother first, but, wanting to support her friend, Jo hadn't offered her opinion. "Well, I'm sure the two of you will work things out."

"I hope so, because I love him so much."

Having never been in love, Jo didn't respond. After observing Trudy these past few months though, Jo wasn't sure she wanted anything to do with Cupid and his arrows, especially if being struck addled your brain and made you willing to marry a man who would probably want to take his mama on the honeymoon. Jo kept that opinion to herself, as well.

"My stars, would you look at that?" Trudy exclaimed.

Jo turned to see what had caught Trudy's attention. Coming onto the church grounds were some men dressed in Union blue. The mostly female crowd went silent. Most of the soldiers were on crutches, or walking with a cane, while a few were being pushed along in large, wooden-wheeled chairs by more able-bodied comrades. The uniforms on all the men were frayed and old, but they were clean. Someone in the crowd began to applaud, and soon, the air rang with hand claps, loud shouts and cheers. Jo and Trudy added their boisterous tributes, as well. Both of their families had men in the fight, and it wasn't often that the common folk had the opportunity to express their deep appreciation for the sacrifices the troops were making on behalf of the nation.

Still clapping, Jo asked, "Why do you think they're here?"

Trudy shrugged.

Mrs. Patricia Oswald, a relatively new member of the community, made herself visible to the crowd. She held up her hands and the crowd quieted.

"I'd like you all to meet my son, Calvin, and these are his friends."

Calvin, leaning on his cane, waved. The other men raised their hands, as well. Mrs. Oswald hadn't lived in the community long enough for Jo to know her son, but he appeared to be about Daniel's age.

Mrs. Oswald continued, "He was wounded down in Georgia, and when he came back here to recuperate he invited his fellows to come along." The look on her face made everyone laugh.

"So, I've opened my home to Calvin and to other men of the race who need a bit more care before they can go home to their families. The church has offered to be one of the sponsors of this effort, and that's partly why we're all here tonight. I have enough space for a good twenty men, but the money for none. It would help me and the men if you'd place whatever you can afford in the milk jug that is being passed around. The soldiers and the church would consider it a blessing."

She then added, "The reverend has suggested that the men might benefit from the company of some of the ladies in our community, so if any ladies here tonight have the time to write letters, read or visit with the men, those efforts would be a blessing, as well."

Jo decided she would take Mrs. Oswald up on her offer. Heaven forbid anything should happen to the soldiers in her family, but if any of them were wounded or hurt, Jo knew she would want someone to be kind to them while they recuperated. "I think that sounds like a wonderful way to help out, Trudy, don't you?"

Trudy nodded. "Just as long as I get to help that gorgeous one with the cane."

Jo saw the man in question. He had chocolate-brown skin and a nice face indeed. She laughed. "Aren't you supposed to be engaged?"

"Engaged isn't married," Trudy cracked.

"I think you need to go back to Bert," Jo responded. "A moment ago you were declaring how much you loved him."

"I do, but—don't you think that soldier is handsome?"

Jo worried about her friend sometimes, and this was one of those times. Jo took Trudy firmly by the elbow and steered her back in the direction they'd just come.

Trudy sighed heavily. "I suppose I shouldn't be mooning over strange men. I do love Bert."

"Yes, you do," Jo agreed firmly.

As Jo and Trudy made their way back across the grove to where Bert stood with his mother, Jo nodded and smiled at the people she knew. Most of the women here had known her all of her life, and Jo felt warmth inside at the roles they'd played. There was Mrs. Lovey, Jo's first Sunday school teacher and very first customer at the shop. Seeing another woman she knew well, Jo stopped for a moment to receive a hug from Mrs. Firestone, Jo's old piano teacher and one of her mama's best friends. Last week, Vera Firestone had received a letter from the government notifying her that both her husband and only son had been killed in a battle in South Carolina. Jo hugged her fiercely and felt the tears sting her eyes. Jo had known both men well. It was hard for her to believe she'd never see them again. That someone in her own family could be taken by the war was not something she wished to think about, and at that moment she would have given anything for a letter confirming their safety.

While Trudy went back to Bert, Jo looked around for her mama and Belle. There were so many folks about it took her a moment. She soon spotted Belle by the drape that had been strung between two trees to create a makeshift powder room. Behind the drape were a few chairs and a large standing mirror.

As Jo and Belle spent a few moments talking about the soldiers, a voice drifted out from behind the drape, and both young women went stock-still, hearing, "Ah, yes, Josephine Best did my hair. Isn't it lovely?"

Jo's eyes widened. Why, that was Old Lady Donovan speaking!

A voice Jo didn't recognize responded, "Well, it appears as if she did a marvelous job. Turn, and let me see the back. Oh, it's lovely. I'll bet she earned quite a tip?"

"Of course. A very substantial one, and the girl was most grateful."

Jo started to go charging inside, but Belle reached out and grabbed Jo's arm. "Don't you dare go in there."

Jo was so angry she could spit. "Did you hear that?"

Belle nodded. "I did, but come away. If you start a commotion, it'll draw your mama, then all perdition is going to break loose once she finds out what's going on. We promised your father we'd keep your mama out of trouble, remember?"

Jo knew that Belle was correct. Jo had inherited every bit of her mama's fire, and she'd been working real hard as of late to not be such a hothead. Right now, however, she wanted to explode. That woman hadn't paid her a Confederate cent! How dare she turn around and act as if she had!

Belle steered Jo away from the curtain. "Come on. Let's go sign up to help the soldiers."

"The next time I see her…"

Belle said, "You will say nothing. We both know we have to respect our elders, even the ones who lie through their teeth."

Jo could tell by Belle's tone and glittering eyes that Belle wasn't happy with Mrs. Donovan, either. Jo quipped, "How about I just shave her bald the next time she comes around then?"

Belle tossed back, "Only if you let me help."

Jojo laughed. "I love having you for a sister."

"I love you too, Jojo."

two

On Sunday, after leaving church the Best women joined the small caravan of buggies and wagons traveling to Mrs. Oswald's home to visit the soldiers. There were eight vehicles in all, and Jo, seated beside Belle while Cecilia drove, was extremely proud to be part of such a caring community. "I didn't know so many were coming," she exclaimed, eyes bright with excitement. Jo turned around and waved happily to Trudy and her mother riding in the wagon behind them. "It feels like a parade."

Belle smiled. "Yes, it does. It shows how big all of our hearts are here."

Jo could only agree. Over the years the people of Whittaker had sheltered runaway slaves, donated to abolitionist causes and kept themselves abreast of issues affecting the race and the nation. Volunteering to help Mrs. Oswald and the soldiers seemed the natural thing to do. Jo figured that helping the men might help take her mind off Daniel, her father and Mr. Palmer, too. During this morning's church service, she'd put the Best menfolk in her prayers, then promised the Lord that she would stop pestering Him about their safety, but because she loved Dani and her father so much, Jo knew it would be a hard vow to keep.

The house Mrs. Oswald lived in was an old mansion built

by a now-deceased coal king. In the years since his death, the interior had been sectioned off into smaller areas and turned into a boardinghouse. It was old and desperately needed a new coat of paint, but thanks to the repairs done by Jo's father last year, the roof was sound, a necessity when facing the fierce Michigan winter.

A smiling Patricia Oswald came out onto the porch to greet them. She was short and plump, and wore her slightly graying hair parted down the center and pulled back in line with the current style. The sight of the dozen or so women now gathered seemed to please her. "Thank you all so much for coming. It's such a beautiful day, we decided being out of doors might prove fun. So follow me. The men are in the back and very eager to meet you."

The shady grove behind the big house was all set up for a picnic. There were large trestle tables topped with food, and chairs and benches had been set about. Jo, walking alongside Trudy, roughly estimated there to be about twenty men in attendance. All looked grand in their worn blue uniforms, even the men in the wooden wheelchairs.

Introductions followed, and Jo had to admit that being viewed by so many smiling young men made her a bit self-conscious, but she buried the reaction and concentrated on Mrs. Oswald's voice. One of the last men to be introduced was the soldier Trudy had been so taken with at the church's gathering on Friday night. "That's him!" Trudy whispered excitedly while clutching Jo's arm.

Jo sighed. His name was Dred Reed, and he was by far the handsomest man in attendance. He had dark velvet brown skin and a thin mustache that seemed to add an air of danger to his face. Jo hoped Trudy wouldn't make a fool of herself before the afternoon was over. Better still, Jo hoped

Reed was married. That way Trudy would have to direct her affections back to Bert Waterman where they belonged.

When Mrs. Oswald finished, everyone in attendance was encouraged to chat, eat and become better acquainted. Jo could see a soldier with a cane slowly making his way over to where she and Trudy were standing. For a moment, Jo thought his interest lay in the food table positioned to her left, but then she realized his eyes were on her alone.

Apparently, Trudy spotted him, as well. "Looks like you caught a live one, Jo. Reel him in slow, now."

Jo laughed. "Hush. Can't take you anywhere." But all the while Jo was trying not to acknowledge that his obvious interest had filled her with an uncharacteristic case of nerves. She didn't know what to do with her hands—didn't know if she should look at him, or look away. She finally told herself to relax. It wasn't as if she'd never been approached by a young man before; she had, but something about her always seemed to throw them off.

Trudy said sagely, "And he's not bad-looking, either."

No, he wasn't, Jo admitted to herself. He had beautiful brown eyes and a firm jaw that reminded her of her father. Jo glanced around the grove to see where her mama might be, then spotted her talking with Belle and a small group of men at a table a few yards away. The distance would prevent Cecilia from being privy to any conversation Jo and the approaching soldier might have. Jo loved her mama dearly, but sometimes daughters didn't want their mamas involved in everything.

When the young man finally came abreast of them, he smiled and said, "Afternoon, ladies."

Jo and Trudy responded in kind.

He then asked, "Might I interest you in joining me in some lemonade? My name is George Brooks."

Batting her eyes flirtatiously, Trudy answered before Jo

could speak, "Why, certainly. We'd love to. Wouldn't we, Jo? My name is Trudy Carr, and this is my best friend, Josephine Best. You can call her Jo, everyone does."

Jo wanted to sock Trudy, but thought such an act might make for a bad first impression. "Where shall we sit?" Jo asked George instead.

"I have a friend guarding some chairs over there."

Since his arrival, he hadn't looked away from Jo once. Being the object of such undivided attention made her more nervous and uncertain, but she forced herself to speak calmly. "Then why don't you lead the way."

Once the cups of lemonade were retrieved, Jo and Trudy followed George over to the chairs he had alluded to. The friend turned out to be Dred Reed.

George made the introductions. "Dred, this is Trudy Carr, and this—" he paused a moment and met Jo's eyes "—is her friend Josephine Best."

Jo had never had a young man gaze at her so intently. Heat spread across her cheeks. She forced herself to turn away and concentrate on something else. The terribly handsome Dred nodded a greeting to Jo and Trudy, then graciously gestured them to the vacant chairs. "Welcome, ladies. It's always a pleasure to be in the company of such beauty."

Trudy tittered like a silly adolescent. Jo rolled her eyes.

For the next half hour, the four young people conversed pleasantly. When the subject of hometowns came up, Jo learned that George hailed from Jackson, Michigan. Dred called the small western Michigan town of Niles home.

"I've never been to either place," Jo admitted, "but I know Jackson is the next sizable town west of here."

Trudy was mooning over Dred as if he were a dessert, but she managed to add, "I know that Niles was one of the first Michigan settlements founded by members of our race."

Dred smiled at her and said, "Not only are you lovely, but educated, as well—a rare combination these days."

Jo thought Trudy might swoon from the compliment. Dred reminded Jo of Daniel's childhood friends, Adam and Jeremiah Morgan. The Morgan brothers were born flirts and had never met a young lady whose head they couldn't turn. Dred was definitely turning Trudy's. At the rate Trudy was becoming enamored, Jo guessed that by the time this visit ended Trudy's head would be spinning on her neck like a plate turned on end.

Trudy began telling the soldiers about the years she and Jo spent at Oberlin. Jo pretended to listen but was more interested in taking peeks at George without him noticing her interest. He caught her more than once, though, and when their eyes met, the slight tingle in her blood that resulted was unlike anything she'd experienced before. Jo dropped her eyes shyly.

Trudy went on with her stories. When she started in on the episode about the cow that came to one of their classes, Dred laughed uproariously. Jo noted that Dred seemed to be showing a real interest in Trudy. Just then, Trudy's mother, Barbara Carr, suddenly walked up. Both George and Dred stood politely.

Mrs. Carr inclined her head slightly and said, "Good afternoon."

They responded deferentially.

Mrs. Carr said, "Trudy, there's a young man over there who needs a letter written. I told him you had a beautiful hand."

Jo wondered if Mrs. Carr had seen her daughter flirting with Dred and had come to put a stop to it. Jo knew Trudy didn't want to leave, but the cool look on Mrs. Carr's face was all anyone needed to see.

Trudy stood. "It was nice meeting you both," she said a bit tightly to both Dred and George.

"Nice meeting you, as well," Dred responded, his eyes on Trudy.

Jo could see Mrs. Carr looking between Trudy and the soldier. Mrs. Carr then said, "Come, Gertrude."

Jo winced inwardly. Trudy *hated* being called Gertrude. It was yet another indication that Mrs. Carr knew what Trudy had been up to. Mrs. Carr used Trudy's given name only when provoked. Jo hoped her best friend hadn't landed herself in trouble.

As the Carrs set off across the field, Jo decided that the time had come for her to make a graceful exit, as well. It might have been all right for her and Trudy to be with the soldiers together, but now that Trudy had gone, Jo wanted no questions from her mama.

Jo stood. "I must be going, too." She noted how crestfallen George looked in response, so she added gently, "I'm sure we will meet again soon."

The smile he gave her made Jo's heart beat fast.

"I hope so," he told her. "Thank you for your company, Miss Josephine."

"You're welcome, and thank you for yours."

Smiling, Jo left them with a wave, then walked over and joined her mother and Belle.

On the ride home, Cecilia asked Jo, "Did you have a good time?"

"I did. The men seemed very nice, don't you think?"

"Yes, and I saw those nice young men you and Trudy were sitting with."

"His name is George Brooks. He's from Jackson."

"He seemed polite."

"Very," Jo said in a dreamier voice than she'd intended.

Her mother chuckled. "That polite, huh?"

Jo was immediately embarrassed. "I meant—"

Belle reached over and patted Jo's hand. "You don't have to explain. We understand."

Jo dropped her head to hide another round of blushing. "He's very nice."

Cecilia asked, "And the other one?"

Jo was still thinking about George's smile and didn't respond until Belle elbowed her playfully. "Jo, wake up. Your mother asked about the other one."

Jo shook herself back to the present. "What other one?"

Belle rolled her eyes amusedly. "The other soldier—"

"Oh. His name's Dred Reed."

Cecilia said then, "Trudy seemed to be having a good time with him."

Jo went still for a moment as she tried to gauge her mother's mood. Jo then responded cautiously, "I— Trudy was just being nice, that's all."

Cecilia nodded. "Well, I hope she remembers she's about to marry. Corinne Waterman is just looking for an excuse to cancel the engagement. You might tell Trudy that."

All Jo could say was, "Yes, Mama."

That night, Jo recited her prayers, then climbed into bed. Lying there in the dark, she reminisced on the day. It had begun in church, with her mama and the other choir members singing beautifully, and ended with the visit to Mrs. Oswald's and George. George. She had no trouble conjuring up his smile or his memorable brown eyes. Maybe the next time they met she would ask him how he'd been injured, and how long he planned to stay with Mrs. Oswald, if that wouldn't be considered too forward. According to Jo's mama, not all of the soldiers they'd met today were friends of Mrs. Oswald's son, Calvin. Some of the men had been sent to stay with Mrs. Oswald by the veterans' home in Grand Rapids to recuperate before being ordered back South to fight. Others were on their way home and simply waiting to be retrieved by family members. Jo wondered what category George fit into. She had no plans to fall in love with him or anything like that; she planned to leave such silliness to Trudy, but Jo would be the first to admit that she wouldn't mind seeing George again. Soon.

Jo never opened up the shop on Mondays, preferring to use the day to prepare her business for the week to come. With that in mind, she set about cleaning up. Once that task was accomplished, she checked over her supplies to make sure she had enough of her special hair oil. She made it herself out of bergamot, oils of lemon and orange and a few other secret ingredients she refused to divulge to anyone. Ever the businesswoman, she had dreams of peddling it to women all over America, but with the war on, the dream had to wait.

Satisfied now that she had enough oil, hairpins, ribbons and the like, Jo took a break and settled into one of the chairs to read the latest edition of *Harper's Weekly*. She'd been an avid reader all of her life, but with the war on she devoured every newspaper she came in contact with for reports on the fighting down South. One of the first stories she read today had to do with President Lincoln promoting Ulysses S. Grant to lieutenant general. According to the report, the last military man to be so honored was General George Washington. Another story detailed the dire straits of the Confederacy. Richmond had fallen to the Union on April fourth, and President Jefferson Davis had had no other option but to flee along with the terrified populace. Their troops had no food and their manpower was so depleted that the Confederate Congress was now requiring every able Southern man from age seventeen to fifty to serve in the Army.

Jo put the paper down. She wondered about her father

and her brother. It seemed every adult male she knew was away fighting the war, and she found herself thinking about them all: her papa; her brother, Dani; Belle's papa; Trudy's papa. For the most part, Jo kept silent about her fear for them because she knew her mama was worried, too, and because Jo was supposed to act strong like the rest of the women in the community. Yet, she'd never lived through anything like a war before, especially a war with so much at stake. The child inside Jo wanted the world to be the way it was before, with everyone home and safe, but the young woman she'd become knew that could never be. The country was indeed at war; the Union, and the fate of three and a half million slaves, hung in the balance. Her fears notwithstanding, what her father and the others were doing was right. She'd just have to keep saying her prayers.

A short while later, Jo locked up the shop and walked the short distance back to the house. She decided that tomorrow she would spend her whole day helping Mrs. Oswald with the veteran boarders.

three

TUESDAY morning, Jo dressed herself in a blue skirt and a matching short-sleeved blouse, then walked over to the mirror to see how she looked. After turning so she could view herself from all angles, she decided the outfit met with her approval, even if the cuffs and hem were frayed. She then took a moment to study her reflected image. She supposed the lines of her face were pleasant enough; she couldn't claim to be a great beauty like her mama, though. She had her papa's rich dark skin and her mama's sparkling eyes. Jo had no quarrels with her features; she'd never been one of those girls always wishing this was different or that was bigger. She did consider her hair to be her best feature, though. In keeping with the style of the day, she'd parted her thick black hair down the middle and pulled it back into an elaborately braided coronet that was pinned low on her neck. She had no need for a rat to make her hair long enough. As Trudy once remarked, Jo had enough hair for two people. The only hairpieces Jo employed were the ones she added to the heads of her customers.

All in all, Jo liked her looks, but in keeping with the thoughts of most young women she wondered what a young man would think of her. When she was younger, she'd often dreamed of being swept off her feet the way Dani had done with Belle, but now, at seventeen, she doubted that would ever happen. Not that she really cared. Even though she'd already made up her mind to be an independent woman, all girls wondered, no matter their goals in life.

Declaring such thoughts silly and youngish, Jo set them aside. She took a moment to hook a pair of earbobs in her lobes, then went across the hall to her mother's room.

Cecilia was readying herself for a drive to the Ann Arbor train station with Vera Firestone. The bodies of Vera's soldier husband, Dexter, and her son, Isaac, were due in on this afternoon's train, and Vera had to claim their caskets. Cecilia was going along because she didn't want her dear friend to have to handle the heartbreaking task alone. The funeral would be tomorrow.

Jo asked her mother, "Are you sure you don't want me to come with you?"

Cecilia was standing before her mirror putting the last touches to her hair. She turned and responded somberly, "No, sweetheart. You go on over to Mrs. Oswald's and help the living. I'll help Vera deal with the departed." Cecilia paused, then whispered emotionally, "Lord, I wish I had some word from your father."

Jo walked over and stood behind her mother, then said softly, "If something bad had happened, we would have been notified. Dani and Papa are probably too busy chasing Rebs to write. I'm sure we'll hear something soon."

Cecilia's soft smile was filled with love. "My Jojo has grown up. Who would have ever thought you'd be offering me comfort?"

Jo turned serious. "You've been comforting me all of my life. It's about time I started returning the favor, no?"

Her mother opened her arms and embraced Jo in a hug. Cecilia held on to her daughter for a long moment before saying, "Have I told you lately how proud you make me?"

Jo looked into her mama's eyes. "Yes, but I never get tired of hearing it."

Her mother playfully pushed her away. "Silly girl. Get on over to Patricia's. I'm sure her soldiers will appreciate that wit of yours."

The statement made Jo recall the thoughts she'd had in her room. "Do men like women with wit, Mama?"

Cecilia studied her daughter's face as if trying to determine the cause of the question. "Some men do. Why?"

Jo shrugged. "Just asking."

Cecilia scrutinized her daughter as only a mama can. "Is something bothering you, darling?"

Jo shook her head. "No, Mama. Just a question."

Cecilia looked skeptical. "Are you certain?"

Jo lied firmly, "Yes." Since her mother didn't appear convinced, Jo decided a change of subject was in order. "Is Belle downstairs, or has she gone?"

"Gone. She'll be back later this evening."

Belle was creating a trousseau for a wealthy young woman in Ann Arbor, and for the past few weeks had been driving back and forth in order to complete the fittings. Belle was one of the best seamstresses around. Even with the war on, Belle and her Singer stitching machine were in great demand.

"Will you be staying overnight with Mrs. Firestone?"

"I may. If I'm not back by eight or so, assume I am. I'm taking clothes for the funeral with me just in case Vera doesn't want to be alone tonight."

"Everybody loved Mr. Firestone."

"Yes, they did, but as I recall, you didn't love him much that day he spanked you for climbing his prized apple trees."

Jo met her mother's smile. "No, I did not." Jo remembered the confrontation vividly. She'd been ten years old.

"He told you time and time again not to climb his trees. Your papa did, as well," her mother recalled wryly.

Jo came to her own defense. "But it was the best hide-and-seek place around. Nobody could find me way up there."

"But the man said stay out of his trees."

"I know."

They both chuckled.

Jo said then, "Well, I did love him. Mr. Firestone put up with my terrible piano playing for the three years I took lessons at his house, and never once complained. How could I not love him?"

Cecilia's eyes were misty. "Well, he adored you. He'll be missed."

Jo could only agree. "As will Isaac. I can't imagine never seeing him again. Trudy and I thought the world of Isaac, especially when we were young."

"You two were sweet on Isaac Firestone?"

"No, he would help us bait our hooks when we went fishing—unlike Dani and the Morgan brothers. They would just chase us around with the worms until we screamed. They made us so mad."

Mrs. Best chuckled. "I wonder how those Morgan brothers are doing. Last I heard, they'd both come down from Canada and joined the war. Hope they're all right."

Adam and Jeremiah had lived near the Bests for more than a decade. Right before war was declared, they moved back to their native Canada. Jo hoped they were all right, too. "I should get going, Mama. If you don't return tonight, I'll see you at the funeral in the morning."

"Okay, darling. Give my regards to Mrs. Oswald and the young men. Tell her I'm going to try and get over there by week's end."

Jo kissed her mother's brown cheek. "I will."

Cecilia nodded, and Jo left the room.

Jo's drive to Mrs. Oswald's took less than thirty minutes. After parking her buggy, she walked up and knocked on the front door. To her surprise and delight, George answered the door.

He beamed at her. "Well, how are you, Miss Josephine?"

"I'm well, George. How are you?"

"I'm doing well, too. Thanks for asking."

"Is Mrs. Oswald in?"

"She sure is. Come on in." He hobbled backward on his cane so she could enter. He appeared to be very pleased to see her again. Jo was pleased to see him again, too.

"Is your beau off fighting for Mr. Lincoln?"

The unexpected question caught Jo by surprise. "I don't have a beau."

He looked at her with disbelief. "You're joshing?"

Jo shook her head. "I'm going to be a businesswoman. Well, I am a businesswoman, so I don't really need a beau, at least not right now."

"What do you do?"

"I'm a hairdresser."

He seemed impressed by that. "Do you barber, too?"

"No. I do ladies' hair only."

He looked disappointed. "Oh."

"There's a fine barber over in Ypsilanti, though."

He ran his hand over his hair. "That's good to know. I'll be needing one soon."

Although Jo wouldn't have minded talking the afternoon away with George, that hadn't been her purpose for coming. "I really should find Mrs. Oswald. Do you know where she might be?"

"Kitchen, probably. How about we go and look?"

"That sounds fine."

On the walk through the quiet house, Jo asked, "Where is everyone?"

"Those who were able went to Detroit with Calvin Oswald. Everyone else is either outside or up in their rooms."

"I see."

Mrs. Oswald was indeed in the kitchen and washing the largest stack of dirty dishes Jo had ever seen.

Mrs. Oswald paused in her task to say, "Well, good day, Josephine. How nice of you to come by. Are you just passing through or planning to stay and visit awhile?"

"I came to visit. Thought you might need some help."

"As you can see, I do."

"Well, how about I wash for a while and you dry?"

George said, "I've an even better idea. How about I dry and Mrs. Oswald can turn her attention elsewhere?"

Jo knew he wanted to spend more time with her, and she didn't mind. In fact, she didn't mind at all.

Mrs. Oswald asked, "Are you amenable to that, Josephine?"

"Yes, ma'am. George impresses me as a gentleman." Jo met George's brown eyes and he smiled.

"Then I will let you two get to work. I've laundry boiling outside." She took a quick moment to fetch Jo an apron from a cabinet near the sink, then departed.

Jo suddenly felt shy being in the kitchen alone with George, but swallowed it and dug into the mass of dishes.

Jo hated washing dishes. Only George's presence and the knowledge that she was helping the war effort made the task ahead palatable. Starting in on the plates and cups, she washed them into another cauldron of warm water to rinse. George took a seat on a stool, then with cloth in hand dried each piece and set them on the counter nearby. They soon developed a rhythm and were working and talking away.

Jo learned that George had a mother and sister waiting for him in Jackson, and that his war injury disqualified him from any further combat. "When I saw the doctor last week, he told me I could go home in another ten days or so."

"How old is your sister?"

"Twenty-five. She's married, lives in Lansing and has two young sons."

"Which makes you an uncle."

He grinned proudly. "Sure does."

"And your father? Is he fighting?"

"No. He died last year. Hunting accident."

Jo said genuinely, "I'm sorry."

"Thank you. Do you live nearby?" George then asked her.

"About a thirty-minute drive. How long have you lived in Jackson?"

"Since I was about ten. Man down in Indiana owned us, but one day, my pa got tired of being a slave, so one night he put the family in a wagon, and we got on the Road. Jackson is where we ended up."

Jo knew all about the Road. "Our home has been a station on the Underground Railroad all of my life."

He appeared surprised. "Your parents are conductors?"

"Yes. They're staunch abolitionists."

"Never met a conductor's daughter before. Are they all as pretty as you?"

Jo felt heat creep over her cheeks again. "I wouldn't know."

"You act as if nobody's ever called you pretty before."

"No one ever has."

George dried a saucer, then shook his head with wonder. "The men around here must be blind."

Jo didn't know how to respond to that, so she smiled.

They spent some time talking about the war. Jo told him about Dani and her father. "We haven't heard from them in weeks."

George told her reassuringly, "I'm sure they're well. Last I heard, the Rebs were on the run. Lincoln was smart to let the black men enlist. We've made the difference for the Union."

Jo agreed. Her father, like scores of black men across the nation, wanted to join the fight from the moment the secessionist guns rained down on Fort Sumter in 1860, but because of their race, their enlistment had been forbidden. It had taken three years, many petitions and even more Union defeats on the battlefield to get President Lincoln to change his mind and release the Emancipation Proclamation. Once he did, one hundred and eighty thousand men of color joined the army, and twenty-nine thousand more joined the United States Navy. Now that the South was on the run, even the newspapers were saying that the addition of the black troops and sailors were turning the war in the Union's favor, and Jo was glad the men were proving their worth.

Word must have gotten around the house that Jo was in the kitchen working, because moments later other soldiers began trickling in to say hello and to visit. She smiled a warm greeting to the men she knew and was introduced to the few new faces who'd arrived yesterday.

Dred Reed sauntered in. When he saw Jo his eyes sparkled. "Well, if it isn't the lovely Miss Jo."

Jo wondered if he flirted in his sleep. "How are you, Dred?"

"Fine, but I'd be much better if you'd brought Miss Trudy along with you today."

A smiling Jo shook her head with amusement. It occurred to her that she might do everyone involved a favor by confessing the truth and telling Dred about Trudy's upcoming marriage, but she decided against it. Who knew how Trudy might react, and besides, it was none of Jo's business. She said instead, "I haven't seen Trudy in a few days, but I will let her know you asked after her."

"I'd appreciate that," he said.

For the rest of the afternoon, Jo held court in Mrs. Oswald's parlor, surrounded by soldiers all competing for her attention. She'd never experienced anything like it before, and she had a grand time. They laughed and talked; she wrote letters, sewed on a few buttons and played the piano.

Jo was having such a good time that she shared the men's disappointment when it became time for her to depart. After she said goodbye to Mrs. Oswald, Jo was walked to the door and out onto the porch by George. Both he and Jo ignored the good-natured razzing and teasing George received for his chivalry.

Once the two of them were outside, George said genuinely, "You made us real happy with your visit today, Miss Josephine."

"I had a good time, as well."

"Are you coming back soon?"

"Probably not until after church on Sunday. I have a funeral to attend tomorrow, and for the rest of the week I have appointments to honor at my shop."

"You have your own place?"

"Yes, my papa built it for me a few years back. It's tiny, but it's mine."

"You really are a working woman, then, aren't you?"

Jo smiled. "Sure am."

There was silence for a moment, and he looked a bit odd, so Jo asked, "Is there something the matter?"

"No, not really, just not accustomed to being around a woman who runs her own business."

Jo thought his confession sweet. "Well, it's a new world, or at least it will be once the war's over. Women are going to be doing things they've never done before."

"I suppose you're right. It's just going to take us men some getting used to, I guess." Then George asked, "Who's the funeral for? No one in your family, I hope."

"No. It isn't a family member, but the men being buried are father and son, and they were close to us. Their names are Dexter and Isaac Firestone. They are our first war deaths."

George appeared saddened. "Two deaths? That's a terrible burden for those left behind to bear."

"Yes, it is. That's why my mother went to Ann Arbor with Mrs. Firestone today to claim the caskets."

George said solemnly, "My condolences to Mrs. Firestone."

"Thank you. I'll pass them along."

"Maybe some of the men and I will come to the church and offer our respects."

"That would be a nice gesture, and I'm sure Mrs. Firestone will think so, as well. Service is at ten."

Silence fell again.

George finally said, "Well, if I don't see you at the funeral tomorrow, I'll be looking for you on Sunday. I mean, if that's not too forward of me to say."

Jo shook her head. "No, it isn't."

He smiled. "Good."

For a girl who had no use for a beau, Jo wondered why her heart seemed to be beating so rapidly. "Thanks for the help with the dishes."

"My pleasure."

Jo left the porch and headed for her buggy. She swore she was walking on clouds.

* * *

The next morning, Jo and Belle drove to the church for the funeral. Cecilia had not returned last night, so they would meet her at the church as planned.

Belle was driving the buggy and Jo was on the seat beside her.

Jo said, "I know we're on our way to a funeral, but I need to talk to you about something."

Belle looked over. "What is it?"

Jo paused a moment to try and gather her words. "George."

Belle smiled. "Ah. How is George?"

"He's doing well. I saw him yesterday."

"And what does George do for a living?"

Jo chuckled. "You sound like Mama."

"Just helping you get ready for the Cecilia Inquisition." Jo found the words amusing even though they were true.

"You measuring George for a beau?"

Jo giggled. "No. I barely know him."

"Well, what do you know?"

"That he's very nice."

"And?"

"That he's from Jackson, and his family escaped slavery when he was ten."

"And?"

"His father is dead, but he has a mother and a sister."

"And?"

Jo shrugged. "That's all I know."

"Is he married?"

Jo paused over that question. "I don't think so. He didn't mention that he was." She then stated, "Surely he would have told me, if he were. Wouldn't he?"

Belle shrugged. "I don't know, but I suppose you're right."

Jo raised a fingernail to her teeth. The habit helped her think better. "Now you have me full of doubts, Belle. Thanks."

Belle ignored the sarcastic tone. "I'm just being Cecilia. Better you know the answers now than not."

Although Belle's advice was sound, Jo didn't believe George was married; at least, he hadn't acted as if he were.

Belle said, "Well, now that we've established that George is a fine, upstanding gentleman, and probably not married, what did you wish to talk to me about?"

Jo thought for a moment. "The way I feel when I'm around him."

"How do you feel?"

"Like I'm not me."

Belle glanced over. "Explain."

"Well, I get all tingly inside and I want to spend a lot more time with him."

"Maybe you are measuring him for beau material."

"But I don't want a beau."

"So you say."

"So I know, Belle Best. I'm going to be an independent working woman."

"And there's nothing wrong with that, but sometimes your heart has other ideas."

"You mean, I may fall in love with him?"

Belle shrugged. "Who knows?"

Jo leaned back against the seat. "I'm not falling in love with him."

"No one says you have to, silly, but don't become so set on your life's goals that you shortchange your heart. If George is the one for you, you'll know. If he isn't, you'll know that, too."

Jo thought Belle's advice felt right. "Thanks, Belle."

"You're welcome."

four

The field surrounding the church was filled with buggies and wagons. To Jo, it appeared as if everyone in town had turned out to pay their final respects to the Firestone men. Belle finally found a place to park the buggy, then she and Jo joined the silent procession heading for the church.

Jo and Belle took a seat in the filled-to-capacity sanctuary. When Trudy arrived, she slid in next to them. The air in the church was heavy with grief, the mourners subdued and sitting quietly. Everyone had on black.

Jo could see her mother seated up front with Mrs. Firestone. Beside Vera sat her husband's last living family member, his brother, Carl. Carl and Vera were famous for not getting along, and had never seen eye to eye over anything except their mutual love for Dexter and Isaac, but there would be no arguing today. They'd come to bury two men who'd made the ultimate sacrifice.

A soft rustling in the crowd made everyone turn around to see what was going on. Entering the church was Mrs. Oswald and her veterans. Each man had on a starched clean uniform, and whether on crutches or being pushed in chairs, they exuded a soldierly pride. Jo's heart swelled with pride, and she discreetly attempted to spot George. But Trudy clutched Jo's arm tightly and whispered ecstatically, "There's Dred."

Jo saw him, but she didn't dare tell Trudy that Dred had asked after her, at least not here. Again, there was no telling what Trudy might do or say, and Jo wanted nothing marring the funeral, at least nothing started by Trudy.

Jo found George. Their gazes met, but in keeping with the serious atmosphere, he simply nodded respectfully. Jo nodded a similar response, then turned away.

Belle leaned over to Jo and whispered, "He is a nice-looking man."

Jo simply smiled.

The true purpose of the gathering came back into focus with the appearance of Reverend Harmony standing at the front of the church. He looked properly solemn in his long black robe. The congregation quieted and waited for him to speak.

"Although I did not know Dexter Firestone, or his son, Isaac, the fact that all of you are here today in their honor tells me they were respected and well-loved members of this community."

A few soft amens affirmed his statement, and Jo added one, as well.

The service lasted less than an hour. At the conclusion, the twin flag-draped coffins were wheeled out of the church. The Firestone family exited next. Vera Firestone looked heartbroken. Jo wiped at her own tears. The congregation followed the family's exit, then assembled outside for the traditional walk to the cemetery.

During the wait for the coffins to be hoisted into the hearse, Cecilia came over to where Jo stood with Belle and the cane-clutching George. Mrs. Best stuck out her hand to him. "My name's Cecilia Best. I'm Josephine's mother."

George seemed not to know what to say to the forceful Cecilia. Jo loved her mother but sometimes wished she weren't so diligent. Poor George appeared scared to death as Jo watched him shake her mother's outstretched hand.

"I'm George Brooks, Mrs. Best. Pleased to meet you."

"Pleased to meet you, too. I saw you at Mrs. Oswald's gathering last Sunday."

"Yes, ma'am, you did."

Cecilia added, "The family appreciates your coming."

"Well, Miss Josephine told us about the funeral, and we decided we would come to pay our respects."

Belle asked, "Are you going to the cemetery?"

He raised his cane. "No, this cane and I don't do well on long walks, at least not yet. The men and I are going back to Mrs. Oswald's."

Jo was admittedly disappointed.

Mrs. Best said, "Well, I'm sure we'll meet again."

The coffins were now loaded and the procession was ready to begin.

Cecilia said, "I must go. George, as I said, it was a pleasure meeting you. Jo and Belle, I'll see you at the cemetery." She gave George a parting smile, then hurried off.

Jo quipped, "Now, that wasn't so bad, George, was it?"

George fidgeted with his collar. "Your mother's very forceful. Your father allows it, though, I suppose."

Jo wasn't sure how to take that, but decided to give George the benefit of the doubt. Surely he didn't think there was anything wrong with a forceful woman, but before she could question him further on the matter, Belle said, "Jo, we should be going. The line's starting to move."

Jo saw that Belle was right, so having George clarify his comment about her mother would have to wait until another time. "I'll see you on Sunday, George."

"I'll be counting the minutes," he teased. With a grin and a wave he hobbled off.

Jo watched him for a moment, then she and Belle got in line with the congregation for the traditional walk to the cemetery.

Jo had only a few appointments on Thursday, but by Friday, she had clients up to her ears. She didn't mind the work; the money she earned would help with the family's household expenses. But she did mind that her last customer of the day, Mrs. Waterman, had taken it upon herself to ferret out all she could about George Brooks.

Jo was in the process of fitting Corinne with a long rat so that her hair would coil atop her head, when the Dragon Lady asked, "So, Josephine, who was that soldier you were with outside the church at the Firestone funeral?"

Jo wasn't surprised by the question. The Dragon Lady was known for sticking her long nose in other folks' business. "His name is George Brooks. He's staying with Mrs. Oswald."

"I'd never let a daughter of mine go anywhere near a soldier. I would think your mama would be more discriminating."

"It isn't as if he's courting me, Mrs. Waterman. I met him at Mrs. Oswald's on Sunday along with everyone else from the church."

"All the more reason your mama should be wary. How much do you know about him?"

Jo kept her mouth shut and concentrated on fitting the rat. When it was finally positioned, she pinned it down. A few more touches and she was done. She handed Mrs. Waterman the hand mirror, then stepped back to await her comments.

"This looks very good, Josephine. The color matches very well, don't you think?"

"Yes, I do."

Jo was handed back the mirror. The very short and very wide Mrs. Waterman then stood and picked up her handbag. She took a moment to count out what Jo was owed, and added a five-cent tip. Jo stuck the coins in the pocket of her apron. "Thank you, Mrs. Waterman."

"You're welcome, Josephine. Between you and me, I wish my Bert had fallen in love with you. Granted, you were quite the handful growing up, but now you seem to know where you're going. Sadly, I can't say the same for Gertrude."

Jo came quickly to her best friend's defense. "You aren't being fair to Trudy, Mrs. Waterman. Trudy is an intelligent young woman, and she loves Bert very much."

"She's too flighty for my liking."

"Bert loves her, as well."

Jo dearly hoped Mrs. Waterman wasn't intent upon breaking off her son's engagement because it would break Bert's heart, but Mrs. Waterman had nothing further to say, it seemed, because she put on her coat and walked to the door, saying, "I still don't think you should be seeing a soldier. You wouldn't want folks talking about you and him all over town."

"No, ma'am, I wouldn't." Jo could just about imagine what would happen should Mrs. Waterman ever get word of Trudy's sudden infatuation with Dred Reed. Whittaker was a small town. Gossip was one of the few entertainments offered. In fact, when she and Trudy were younger, gossip had been their whole life, but now that they were older Jo had no desire to be the subject of falsehoods and innuendos.

Mrs. Waterman went to the door. "Remember what I said, Josephine."

"Yes, ma'am. I will."

And she was gone.

After church on Sunday, the Bests once again led the caravan to Mrs. Oswald's. Out in front of the house, Cecilia set the brake, then turned to her daughter and said, "So, tell me about this George."

Jo's eyes shot to Belle, but Belle looked off across the fields. "Well, I don't know much." Jo rattled off the list of "George facts" she'd told Belle previously.

Cecilia listened, then said, "He seems to be a nice young man."

"I thought so, as well."

"All right, then, let's go on inside."

Jo was surprised to have gotten off so lightly. Letting out her pent-up breath, she let her mama and Belle go ahead so she could wait for Trudy.

Once they were out of earshot of their mamas, Trudy whispered excitedly, "Do you think Dred is still here?"

Jo shrugged. "What about Bert, Tru?"

Trudy waved her hand dismissively. "He and his mama went to Ypsilanti to have dinner with one of the Dragon Lady's friends."

"Trudy, why are you flirting with Dred when you have Bert?"

"I'm not flirting. I'm just being nice." Trudy then asked, "Wouldn't it be something if he remembered me long after he left here? You know how in the novels the soldier always remembers the young woman he met during the war and spends the rest of his life pining for her? Just imagine, I could be the last thing Dred thinks back upon right before he dies."

"Trudy!" Jo had heard Trudy spout some ridiculous notions over their lifetime, but this one had to be the worst.

"Don't you think that's romantic?"

Jo threw up her hands. "No. You're supposed to be thinking about Bert and only Bert."

Trudy's chin rose and she sniffed, "Well, I think it's very romantic. Just because you've decided to put business before matters of the heart doesn't mean I have to, too."

Jo snapped her mouth shut. She wanted to shake Trudy

from now until Christmas Day, but knew it wouldn't do to have a fight here, nor would it matter. Trudy had always been stubborn and rarely took advice that didn't suit her purpose. Jo supposed some folks would describe Jo in those same terms, but she wasn't silly enough to think she would be the last thing George would think about on his deathbed. Lord, it was a good thing she loved Trudy.

Jo and Trudy spent the first part of the day's visit writing letters for the men who could not do it for themselves. Some were hampered by injuries to their arms or shoulders, but others were hampered by their inability to read or write. One man wanted a letter written to his mother in Ohio, so she would know he'd been injured. Now that he was recovering he would be unable to visit her as he'd planned because he'd been ordered to rejoin his unit in three days' time. Jo found the news sad but knew his mother would be happy to hear from him in spite of the spoiled plans. Having received no word from the men in her own family, Jo thought the soldier's mother a lucky woman indeed.

After all the letters were written, Jo rejoined her mother, who was seated on a bench stitching up the torn shoulder of a Union jacket. "Mama, would it be all right if I spent a few minutes talking with George?" He was over at a table playing chess with the Reverend Harmony. Jo had been keeping a discreet eye on his location since her arrival.

Cecilia looked up from her needle. "I don't see why not, but do me a favor first, if you would. My scissors must have fallen out of my sewing basket on the trip over. Would you go out to the wagon and see if you see them anywhere?"

"Sure. I'll be right back."

Jo hurried out to the wagon, and after a short search found the scissors beneath the wagon seat. After hopping back down to the ground her intent was to head back to her mother, but Jo stood there a moment to enjoy the silence and the gentle June breeze. She looked out over the fields toward the horizon and drank in the green, lush countryside. Michigan was so lovely in the spring, Jo could never imagine living anywhere else.

She was just about to head back when the sight of a rented hack pulling up to the front of the house made her stop. The driver, a short, gnarly old man, hurried around to open the door. Out stepped a light-skinned man on crutches. One leg was heavily bandaged from his knee to his toes, so she assumed him to be another veteran coming to stay with Mrs. Oswald. He hopped around a bit to get himself steadied, then said something to the driver. Jo watched the driver firmly drop a valise at the feet of the crutch-bearing man. The men spoke for a moment. Their voices rose. She was too far away to hear the entire argument, but it seemed the man on the crutches wanted the driver to carry the bag to the door, but the tight-jawed driver climbed back into his rig and drove away. The man didn't appear able to pick up the valise and handle the crutches, too, so she went to his aid.

As Jo neared, however, she realized that she knew him. Although she hadn't seen him since she was thirteen, Jo was ready to bet every hair iron she owned that the golden-skinned man with the golden brown eyes was her brother's friend Adam Morgan. Happiness and surprise filled her. What was he doing here?

"Hello, beautiful."

Jo stopped, then stared up into the handsome, sculpted face of Adam Morgan. *Beautiful?* When she was young, her brother and his friends called her nothing but "Pest."

Adam regained her attention by adding, "I lived in Whittaker for ten years. I don't remember ever seeing you back then."

Jo blinked. He didn't recognize her? She almost burst into

laughter but decided to play along. She'd tease him later. "I've lived here all of my life."

"Really? I would remember someone as lovely as you."

"I bet you say that to all of the girls."

He clutched his heart. "You wound me, *mademoiselle*. Weren't the Rebs enough?"

Jo giggled in spite of herself. He was as silly as ever.

He then introduced himself. "I'm Adam Morgan."

"Pleased to meet you, Adam."

Silence.

"Now you're supposed to give me your name," he pointed out.

Jo replied with sparkling eyes, "I don't think I will."

"Ah, a woman of mystery. I like intrigue."

"Do you?"

His voice softened. "I do."

Jo felt something come over her that she'd never felt before. George made her flutter, but this feeling was deeper, stronger somehow. It was like comparing the wind from the wings of a butterfly to that from the mighty wings of a red-tailed hawk.

"How old are you?" he asked.

It took Jo a moment to answer. "Seventeen."

"You've a mama nearby, I'm betting?"

Jo nodded. "Yes."

"Does she let you have dinner with soldiers?"

"No."

"Smart woman," he offered in tandem with his heart-melting smile.

As an adolescent, Jo never understood why girls swooned every time Adam or his brother, Jeremiah, walked by. Now she did. Shaking herself free of his spell, she said, "I came to help you with your bag."

"Thanks."

Jo picked up the valise. It was heavy, but not so much so that she couldn't lug it the short distance to the porch. When they reached the door, Jo set it down. "I'll go and find Mrs. Oswald for you."

His eyes were all she could see. She seemed to be drowning in them. It was an oddly pleasant feeling. Then remembering that this was Adam Morgan, she shook herself free again. "Nice meeting you, Adam."

"Nice meeting you, as well, beautiful. You aren't going to tell me your name." It was a statement, not a question.

Jo smiled secretively. "No, but I'm certain you'll learn it soon."

Trudy had apparently come looking for Jo, because she suddenly appeared at Jo's side. Jo sensed Trudy was about to say something, but upon seeing the man Jo was talking with, Trudy offered nothing but a look of utter surprise. Jo assumed Trudy recognized him, too. He didn't seem to recognize Trudy though, if the polite but distant nod he sent Trudy's way was any indication. Jo supposed she and Trudy did look different from the short, skinny, ringlet-wearing adolescents they'd been the last time he'd seen them. They were both taller and no longer skinny. Trudy was a bit more round than Jo, but they were young women now.

Before Trudy could open her mouth and ruin Jo's game, Jo told Adam, "You go on inside and take a seat. I'll fetch Mrs. Oswald. That is who you're here to see?"

"Yes, the hospital in Detroit recommended I stay here until I recover." But he seemed more intent upon Jo, and she could feel the interest as well as she could feel the breeze on her cheeks. She grabbed the still-staring Trudy's arm. "Come on. Let's get Mrs. Oswald."

Once they got around to the back of the house, Trudy finally found her voice, "Jojo, that was Adam Morgan!"

"I know."

Trudy then gushed. "Lord, did you ever see anyone so handsome?"

Jo had to admit she had not. "He doesn't recognize either of us, though. He called me beautiful."

Trudy stopped dead in her tracks. "He did?"

"Yes." And as Jo recalled the incident now, she could still feel her insides shimmering like sun on the lake.

Jo and Trudy found Mrs. Oswald. She'd joined Cecilia, Belle and the other women sewing beneath the trees. Before Jo could say a word, Trudy announced quickly, "Mrs. Best, Adam Morgan is here!"

Cecilia and Belle sat up in surprise.

Trudy added, "He didn't recognize us. He called Jo beautiful!"

Jo wanted to bop her friend in the head for revealing that, but nothing could be done about it now.

Cecilia echoed skeptically, "Beautiful?"

Jo waved her hand dismissively. "Mama, you remember how Adam and Jere were? No female was safe from their silver tongues. Well, apparently, nothing's changed. Trudy's right about him not recognizing us, though. He didn't."

Cecilia smiled. "Adam and Jere were handfuls. Always respectful, but they lived for turning a young lady's head. Won't he be surprised when he finds out who you two really are!"

Once he did, Jo doubted he would call her beautiful again, and for some reason that knowledge didn't sit real well with her. Jo, however, thought it wise not to put any stock in whatever Adam had to say. She'd seen the Morgan brothers work their magic on young ladies for many years, and she personally had no desire to be put through her paces by a café-au-lait Casanova. Besides, she was supposed to be starting up with George. She wondered where he'd gotten to. She glanced around the grounds and saw that he was still engrossed in his chess game.

Mrs. Oswald rose to her feet, saying, "I should go and meet the young man and assign him a space."

Cecilia and Belle got up, as well.

"You know, Patricia, I loved those Morgan boys as if they were my own," Cecilia said to Mrs. Oswald. "Depending on how long Adam's going to stay and what his plans are, I'd be willing to take him into my home. We've the room. Haven't we, ladies?" Belle nodded enthusiastically. Jo wasn't so sure about having the blarney-filled Adam Morgan under her roof.

Cecilia studied Jo for a silent moment, but Jo responded with a smile she hoped would allay any concerns. "That might be nice, Mama."

Cecilia nodded. "Good. Then let's go and see him."

five

---

seated in the parlor alone, Adam Morgan glanced around at the room's well-worn furnishings and threadbare rugs. The house wasn't fancy, but it was clean and smelled pleasant. Having to recuperate here might not be too bad, he mused, then cast his mind back to the intriguing black-eyed beauty he'd just encountered. Why wouldn't she reveal her name? Had she chosen to remain anonymous because she was married or perhaps engaged? Adam didn't remember seeing any rings on her fingers, but knew that meant nothing. Many married and engaged women didn't wear rings. No matter, though, he found her stunning and vowed to ask Mrs. Oswald about her as soon as possible.

Adam heard someone coming, and hoped it would be the young woman returning to tell him her name. Instead, Cecilia Best and Belle entered the room. The sight of their familiar faces filled him with such happiness and joy, he snatched up his crutches and struggled upright.

Cecilia came to him with open arms. "Oh, Adam. It's so wonderful to see you."

Adam embraced her as best he could and felt her love flow through him with such force it put a sheen of tears in his eyes. When she finally let him go, he said emotionally, "It's good to see you again, as well."

Then Belle stepped forward. She gave him a strong hug too. "Welcome home."

Adam couldn't believe they were here. The last time he'd seen the Best women had been more than five years ago. He and his older brother, Jeremiah, had been half in love with Belle back then, and she was still as lovely as he remembered. She'd been a fugitive slave living with the Bests. Thoughts of her resolve and spirit were what kept Adam and his brother Jeremiah from giving in to despair when they were illegally kidnapped by slave catchers and temporarily sold into bondage. He turned his mind away from that dark peroid in his life and back to the now. His family and the Bests had been close friends in those days. He, Jeremiah and Daniel had attended Oberlin together. Adam had planned to pay the Bests a visit just as soon as he was able to do so, but being surprised like this was better.

Adam's thoughts then moved to Daniel's little sister. What a little hellion she'd been. Everyone had lovingly called her Pest.

Adam turned to Cecilia and asked, "Where's Jojo? Is she back at the house?"

Cecilia smiled. "No, this is Jo, right here."

Jo stepped to her mother's side and let him get a good look.

Adam blinked.

Jo smiled smugly.

Adam studied her as if he'd never seen her before. "You can't be Jojo."

He had such conviction in his voice, Jo was almost offended. "Why can't I be?"

"Because—" Adam had trouble finding the words he wanted to say.

"Good answer. Where did you say you went to school again?"

His eyes sparkled, and he tossed back, "Pest." The nickname came out so effortlessly, Adam had to laugh, as did Cecilia and the rest.

Jo said, "Adam Morgan, I want you to meet Trudy Carr."

Adam's eyes widened. "Pest Two!"

Trudy cut him a look, but she was smiling. "Welcome home, Adam."

"Thanks. Lord, Trudy, you're all grown up."

His attention settled on Jo again. That she was who she claimed to be was mind-boggling. "Are you all sure this is Jojo?"

Jo, who had tried to make everyone stop calling her Jojo when she reached the age of fourteen, rolled her eyes.

Cecilia laughed. "We're sure, Adam."

Adam could not get over what a beauty little Josephine Best had blossomed into. The upswept hair, the soft, clear ebony skin. She'd gotten taller, as well, and he doubted there wasn't a young man alive who wouldn't be drawn to her. Were she anyone else, Adam would be doing his best to get her to agree to have dinner with him, or go on a picnic, or any other outing that would allow him to spend the day in her company. She was Daniel's baby sister, however, and Adam thought it best he direct his interests elsewhere, even if he couldn't keep his eyes off of her loveliness.

Jo could see Adam watching her. Even as Mrs. Oswald quizzed him on his injury, his gaze kept straying Jo's way. Jo tried to be nonchalant, but his interest in her was plain to see.

When Mrs. Oswald finished her questions, she said to him, "Well, Mrs. Best has offered you a room in her home. Would you prefer to stay there?"

Adam was elated. He was sure Mrs. Oswald ran a good establishment, but being with the Bests would be like being home. "May I?" he asked Cecilia.

"Of course. We've room. You can stay for as long as you need to."

Adam looked to Jo. "Do you mind having me underfoot for a while?"

"No." Jo was lying, of course. He was handsome and gorgeous and all that, but she wasn't certain she wanted him under her roof mesmerizing her with that smile of his. She sensed she was susceptible to it, and in spite of the interest he seemed to have in her now, Jo doubted it would last very long. Once he recovered, he'd be casting his net for prettier fish. She didn't want to have to hit him over the head with a hair iron for breaking her heart.

The group spent a few more moments talking over the arrangements, then Jo asked, "How's your brother, Jeremiah?"

"Faring well, I hope. I say that because I haven't heard from him since April."

"What unit is he with?" Belle asked.

"We were both with the Fifth Massachusetts Cavalry, but I was injured before they rode into Virginia. The newspapers said the Rebs and the rest of the unit are all right. Have you heard from Dani?"

Mrs. Best shook her head sadly. "Not in some time."

Jo added, "Their last letter was from the Carolinas."

Adam echoed Jo's earlier advice. "If there was something wrong, you would have been notified. You'll hear from them soon."

"I pray you're right, Adam," Belle said softly.

Mrs. Oswald asked Adam, "Are you hungry? There's plenty of food outside."

"I'm famished, but I don't wish to impose."

"You aren't imposing. The ladies from the church brought enough food to feed General Sherman's troops. You can also make the acquaintance of my other boarders, even if you won't be staying here with us."

Adam looked over at Jo just long enough for her to feel touched by his gaze, before he replied to Mrs. Oswald, "I'd be honored to meet them."

Outside, the visiting was still going on. Jo said to her mother, "I'm going to talk with George for a while."

Before Mrs. Best could respond, Adam asked in an amused tone, "Who's George?"

Trudy told him, "One of the soldiers. He's sweet on Jo."

Jo couldn't believe Trudy. She shot her friend a look.

Adam raised an eyebrow as he asked Mrs. Best, "Have you properly quizzed this bounder about his intentions toward our Jojo?"

Jo's mouth dropped at his words.

Mrs. Best laughed, however. "I have indeed, Adam. Now leave Jo alone. Run along, dear. We'll take care of Adam."

The soft devilment lighting Adam's eyes made Jo inwardly fume. Pledging to ignore him for the rest of her life, she took Trudy firmly by the arm, and announced, "We'll be back in a bit."

Adam called out to her, "Jo?"

Grabbing hold of her last bit of patience, Jo turned back. "Yes?"

"It's good to see you again."

The sincerity in his velvet voice made her heart flip and flop. Her own voice came out softer than she intended. "It's good to have you home, too."

She and Trudy headed across the yard. Jo sensed Trudy was about to say something, so Jo said warningly, "Don't say a word, Trudy. Not one word."

Trudy didn't, but she did smile.

Jo put Adam out of her mind as she and Trudy walked

over to where some of the soldiers and a few of the other young women from the church were gathered. They joined the group just in time to hear Dred declare, "I have a riddle."

Trudy said, "Then let's hear it."

Dred's deep, dark eyes met Trudy's, then he began, "A soldier gets married. Now, before he marches off he promises his bride he'll write to her every day. He keeps his promise. He writes her every day. Well, six months pass and he gets a letter from her saying she's married someone else. Who'd she marry?"

Jo and Trudy turned to each other. Neither had a clue. Jo looked around and saw that most of the soldiers had knowing smiles on their faces.

Jo asked, "Are we ladies the only ones who don't know the answer?"

The men nodded. Jo met George's eyes. He gave her a smile, but her heart's reaction to it seemed surprisingly tame in comparison to the heady reaction she'd had with Adam. Jo hastily set that observation aside and brought her mind back to the present just in time to hear Trudy say, "All right, we give up. Who did she marry?"

The men's voices rang out in unison, "The mailman!"

The young ladies laughed. Jo made a note to pass it on to her mother and to Belle.

As the laughter faded, George asked, "Miss Josephine, we've carried the piano outside. Would you play for us?"

Trudy dug her elbow into Jo's ribs. Jo tried to ignore her. "I'd be happy to play."

When Jo was young, she hadn't enjoyed playing the piano. Piano lessons took her away from climbing trees, fishing and trailing after Dani and the Morgans. Her mother refused to let her quit the lessons, however, insisting the musical skill would come in handy one day; Jo supposed those days were here. She enjoyed being able to play for the men.

Jo sat down upon the piano stool and placed her hands on the keys. She played a few simple pieces to warm up her fingers. George came over to stand by the piano. She acknowledged him with a smile, then asked, "What would you like me to play?"

One of the men called out, "How about, 'When Johnny Comes Marching Home'?"

"Good choice."

Jo dove into the keys. The song, a favorite of the Union soldiers, was sung aloud and boisterously by the men, especially the "hurrahs." After the song had been sung a few times, Dred asked her to play "Tramp, Tramp, Tramp," another popular war tune. Its lyrics centered around a soldier writing to his mother from his prison cell.

Soon, they were singing "Oh Susannah," "Pop Goes the Weasel" and "Jimmy Crack Corn." The program ended with the spirited verses of "The Battle Hymn of the Republic."

When the piano quieted, Jo could see tears standing in the eyes of nearly everyone: the soldiers as well as the women who'd gathered. Over the course of the war, the hymn had become a rallying cry for those fighting and for their loved ones waiting at home. Many of the men commented on how they'd sung the hymn in the heat of battle, and how much strength they'd drawn from its words. Jo thought about her father and brother somewhere singing the hymn, and hoped it would give them strength, too.

Trudy, like Jo, must have sensed the melancholy in the air because she stood and clapped excitedly. "Who wants to play checkers with me?"

Her question broke the mood. Jo could've kissed her. The checkerboards were brought out, and the men were now all jockeying to see who would play first with Trudy and the other young ladies from the church.

George, however, stayed where he was. "You play very well, Miss Josephine."

"Thank you, George."

"Nothing better than a pretty girl behind a piano."

Jo grinned.

"Do you cook as well as you play?" he asked.

Jo laughed. "No, I'm a terrible cook."

"You are?"

"Honestly, yes. My mother has all but given up on me ever learning to do it properly. I suppose I shall have to learn someday, but now I'm rarely allowed to do anything in the kitchen besides reheating leftovers."

He was staring at her as if she had suddenly started speaking in Greek. "All women can cook."

"No, George, they can't." Jo studied his face. "Is that all the women do where you come from, play the piano and cook?"

"There's nothing wrong with that."

"I never said there was, but women have other options also."

"But a woman's place is in the home."

Jo felt some of the air going out of the balloon she'd been floating for George. She sighed. "So in your world, women don't attend college?"

"Not women who want to be wives."

Jo shook her head.

George asked, "Don't you want to be a wife?"

"Maybe after I get my business going in the direction I've envisioned, but being a wife is not my only goal. It wasn't how I was raised."

"I see."

He looked disappointed, but no more disappointed than Jo, who said, "Maybe we should talk about something else?"

He appeared relieved. "Sounds like a good idea."

Jo cast around for a safer topic. "Do you play an instrument?"

"Nope. I like music, though. Maybe sometime you could teach me a few tunes."

"I'd be happy to."

An awkward silence settled between them. George said finally, "I'd like to get to know you better, Miss Josephine."

"Even though I went to Oberlin," Jo teased.

He had the decency to drop his head. "Even though you went to Oberlin."

Jo felt the earlier tension dissipate. "I think I'd like that, George."

"Do you think your mama would allow me to call on you?"

Jo shrugged. "She commented on how nice you seemed."

He let out a breath. "That's great news."

Jo grinned. "Were you worried?"

"I was. Had I a daughter as pretty as you, I'd be protective."

"She is that, but she has had only kind things to say about you."

"Well, do I have your permission to approach her about visiting you?"

Jo had never had anyone ask her that before. "Yes, you have my permission," she replied quietly.

"Good. We'll see what she says."

Jo nodded, then said, "I should join the others."

His face was understanding. "All right. I'm going to find a few strong backs to help take the piano back inside, and then gather my courage to talk to your mother. Wish me luck?"

"I do."

He hobbled off on his cane. Jo stood and watched him depart. That had certainly been an eye-opening conversation, she mused. Surely he couldn't be that old-fashioned in his views on women. Jo was confident she could change his outdated thinking, so she hoped her mama would let him visit. Jo did enjoy George's company.

Jo looked around the grove in an effort to locate Trudy, but didn't see her anywhere. There were duos still dueling at the checkerboards, but none included Trudy. Jo wondered where she might be. It occurred to her then that she didn't see Dred Reed, either. Oh, Lord! She hastily but discreetly located Trudy's mother, Barbara, who was now sewing with the others. Jo hoped Mrs. Carr didn't suddenly look up and start to wonder where her daughter had disappeared to. Jo prayed that Dred's absence was simply coincidental and that he and Trudy hadn't slipped off somewhere. Jo then decided she wasn't being much of a friend by imagining the worst. Trudy could have a perfectly legitimate reason for being out of sight, such as— She suddenly saw Trudy coming from around the back of Mrs. Oswald's barn. The privy! Jo smiled with relief, then chastised herself again for being so disloyal.

Trudy walked over and asked, "What are you grinning about?"

Jo fell into pace by Trudy's side. "Nothing."

"You're pleased about something, Josephine Best, so out with it. What did I miss? Did Adam Morgan call you beautiful again?"

"I'm just glad to see you, is all."

Trudy stopped. Her face was puzzled. "But I've been here all day."

"I know, but when I didn't see you just now, I thought maybe—"

"Maybe what?"

Jo threw up a dismissive hand and resumed walking. "It was nothing."

"Jo, what did you think?"

"Oh, all right. I thought maybe you and Dred had snuck off."

Trudy laughed. "Me and Dred." Then she went all dreamy again. "Oh, wouldn't that be exciting, Jo, a secret moment with Dred?"

Oh, Lord! Jo moaned to herself. "Never mind. Forget I even mentioned it."

"Do you think he knows how to kiss?"

"Trudy!" Jo said. This was not the place to be discussing such a topic. "Do you want somebody to overhear?"

"No, but do you think he can?"

"Aren't Bert's kisses the ones you're supposed to be dreaming about?"

Trudy sniffed. "Bert knows less about kissing than I do."

Jo shook her head with amusement.

"What?" Trudy asked.

"Nothing. I am so glad you're my best friend, Tru. I really and truly am." Jo doubted any other friend would make life so lively.

In an effort to keep Trudy on the straight and narrow and away from Dred, Jo steered their walk over to where their mothers sat sewing. As they neared, Jo noticed Adam eating at a table a few feet away. Several young ladies were buzzing around him like bees to honey. He was smiling up at them and they were tittering and giggling in response. Granted, Adam had known most of the girls growing up, and they were no doubt renewing old acquaintances, but for some reason the sight didn't sit well with Jo. Then, as if he sensed her attention, Adam met her gaze. His eyes sparkled a greeting that seemed reserved for her alone. At that moment, Jo had no name for how he made her feel, but it was almost as if a part of herself took wing and flew over to him before she could stop it or snatch it back.

Trudy said softly, "Lord, if Bert ever looked at me that way—"

Trudy's voice broke the spell. Jo turned to her and asked, "What?"

"Nothing. Just a comment."

Jo had no idea what Trudy was referring to. "You're not making sense, Tru."

"I know. It's all right though."

Jo shrugged and they resumed their walk. "I wonder if George has had a chance to talk to Mama yet?"

"What about?"

"Calling on me."

Trudy's voice rose excitedly, "Really?"

Jo nodded, pleased. "I hope she says yes."

Their eyes met. Trudy asked, "So you like him?"

"I do. But I'm not looking for a beau, of course."

"Of course not."

SIX

when Jo and Trudy reached their mothers, the women were folding the garments they'd been mending for the soldiers and placing them in a pile on the table. Later, Mrs. Oswald would make certain the items were returned to the proper owners.

Barbara Carr, a taller, older version of Trudy, had a smile on her face as the girls walked up. "Well, we're all heading home. You two ready?"

Trudy and Jo nodded that they were. Jo didn't want to look in Adam's direction but couldn't help herself. His eyes were waiting. His gaze was so direct it put a weakness in her knees. Startled by her response, she hastily looked away from him only to see George walk up.

Mrs. Best greeted his presence with a cheery, "Well, hello, George."

George nodded, then said quickly, "Mrs. Best, before you leave, I've something I need to ask."

Cecilia eyed him. "Yes?"

George looked around at the small group of people. He seemed to see Adam for the first time. "Have we met?"

"No. I'm Adam Morgan."

George stuck out his hand. "George Brooks."

Adam leaned over his crutches and shook George's hand. "Pleased to meet you."

Cecilia asked, "George, you had a question? Adam's tired and I need to get him home."

"Home?"

Adam explained. "Yes. I'm moving in with the Bests for a while."

George seemed taken aback by that. His eyes swept to Jo's face for a moment before refocusing on Adam. "I'm assuming you're a friend of the family, then?"

"I am."

Cecilia's voice had just a touch of impatience in it now. "George? Your question."

George looked away from Adam, who appeared slightly amused by the whole affair. "Yes, well, I'd hoped to do this in a more private setting, but—" George glanced over at Jo once more, then as he began to speak to Mrs. Best, his nervousness was plain. "I'd like your permission to call on your daughter. If I may, of course."

Cecilia studied him, then asked Jo, "What should I say, Josephine?"

Jo smiled. "Yes would be fine, Mama."

Cecilia nodded. "Then I suppose my answer is yes."

George broke into a grin. Jo grinned, too, but when she happened to glance at Adam, his coolly raised eyebrow made her own eyebrow raise. She asked him, "Is something wrong?"

Adam gave George a quick, dismissive look, then said, "No. Just waiting for you and your beau to finish so I can get to the house." Adam then asked, "Belle, do you still make those great biscuits?"

"Sure do," she responded proudly. "Would you like some with breakfast in the morning?"

"Is Jeff Davis a Reb?"

They all laughed.

Her mother then asked, "So, George, when may we expect you?"

"I'm not sure, ma'am. But I'll come as soon as I can."

"Well, you will be welcome at any time."

"Thank you."

George then asked Jo, "May I walk with you to your wagon?"

"Sure."

Feeling Adam's eyes on her back, Jo walked off with George.

Once they were out of earshot, he asked, "Did I sound nervous?"

She chuckled. "A bit, but it was sweet. Mama must like you."

"I like her, too, I think."

They laughed.

George then asked, "How long have you known that Morgan fellow?"

"Most of my life. He and his brother, Jeremiah, are my brother's best friends."

"I see. Your mother doesn't have any worries about him being in the house with you?"

"No, of course not. Why do you ask?"

"He's unmarried?"

"Yes, but there's nothing improper about him moving in. Adam is like a brother to me."

"There was nothing brotherly about the way he was looking at you."

Jo sighed. "George, what are you talking about?"

"He was looking at you the way a man looks at a woman."

"He's just trying to get over the fact that I'm no longer twelve. He didn't even recognize me at first."

"Well, I still say you need to be careful."

Jo shook her head, but said nothing. How did one explain that Adam Morgan was harmless? Well, sort of.

"You probably think I'm being foolish, don't you?" George asked.

"No, but you don't have to concern yourself with this."

"If you say so."

"I do."

He looked into her eyes. "You're pretty headstrong, aren't you?"

Jo searched his face. She wondered if this was more of his outdated thinking. "Yes, I am. It's in my blood. Does that bother you, too?"

He gave her a brief smile that appeared forced. "No, it doesn't. Just never been around a woman who knew her own mind like you."

"You have to thank my mama for that, as well." Jo decided that since she hadn't had ample time to influence George's outdated thinking, she shouldn't let him upset her. George seemed to be an intelligent man and Jo was certain it wouldn't be long before he learned to appreciate all aspects of the free-spirited, free-thinking young woman she'd been raised to be. With that in mind, she thought a change in conversation might serve them well. "So, what's the most important thing I should know about you, George?"

He pondered that for a bit, then offered in a genuine voice, "You should know that I'm a straight arrow. When I give my word, it can be counted on."

Jo liked that. "No skeletons hiding in your closet?"

He grinned. "No, ma'am. I'm just George Brooks from Jackson, Michigan, and I'm very taken with you, Josephine Best."

The way his voice softened made Jo feel very special. "I think I'm taken with you, too, George."

He reached out and gently took her hand. She'd never held hands with anyone before and was unprepared for the happiness it gave her.

"Ahem!"

Jo and George jumped apart. They turned to see a grinning Trudy.

An embarrassed Jo scolded her good friend. "Trudy Carr, you scared us to death. I thought you were my mama."

"I thought you might need a chaperone, and I was right."

Jo laughed. "Go away."

The tight-lipped George said nothing.

Trudy strolled off in the direction of the wagon, saying, "You two better hurry it along. The mamas will be here shortly."

Jo ignored Trudy for the moment. "I had a nice time today, George."

"I did, too. I'll call on you soon, all right?"

Jo nodded.

"Well, guess this is goodbye for now," George said with regret.

"Guess it is. Take care of yourself," Jo responded.

"I will and you do the same." With that, he reluctantly headed back toward the house.

After he took his leave, Trudy and Jo sat on Trudy's wagon and waited for their mothers and Belle and Adam. They chatted as they waved goodbye to the other women from the church who were also heading home.

"You know, Jo, if you and George were to be married, you wouldn't have to change your embroidery because his name starts with a *B*," Trudy pointed out.

Jo chuckled. "Only you would come up with something so practical."

"That's why you keep me around. Now I have a question for you. What do you think of Dred Reed?"

"He's very handsome."

"Very. I'm thinking of breaking off my engagement."

Jo stiffened. "What! Why?"

"Dred is handsome and exciting. Bert is, well, Bert."

"Trudy, you can't be serious! You *love* Bert."

"Do I?"

Jo couldn't believe her ears. "What's come over you?"

"Dred's asked if he could write me when he returns home to Niles. I told him yes."

Jo was so flabbergasted she couldn't speak.

"Jo, he's everything a woman could want. He's strong, intelligent, and his form…"

"His form? You've known the man less than two days."

"You haven't known George very long."

"No, but I'm not acting as if I want to bear his children. What's come over you?"

Jo knew that no one in the world would ever describe Bert as exciting, but his love for Trudy was true. Breaking off the engagement would devastate him. "I think you need to sleep on this before you do anything rash."

Trudy did not care for Jo's advice, apparently. She puffed up as if she were offended. "As if you wouldn't drop George like a hot yam if Adam looked at you twice."

"I would not!"

"Oh, you would, too. You went all parfait inside when he called you beautiful."

"I admit that, but it doesn't mean I'd toss George in the dustbin."

"You're lying, Josephine Best. I saw the way you were looking at Adam, and he was looking back. I'll bet my corset that you and George will be history before the end of July."

"Nobody wants your corset, Trudy Carr, and I don't want to talk about this anymore."

"Fine."

Jo hopped down off the wagon and strode off toward her own, only to hear Trudy add, "You just wait until Adam kisses you. George won't stand a chance."

Jo ignored her, or at least tried to.

When the rest of the family arrived, Jo tried to hide her bad temper. The ride home was uneventful. No one knew she was simmering inside over what had taken place between her and Trudy. Although Adam was seated in the wagon bed and Jo could feel his eyes on her back, she participated in the small talk flowing around her, but she didn't look back at him once.

After Adam was settled in, Mrs. Best retired to her room to write yet another letter to her beloved William. Jo, simmering over Trudy again, wandered into Belle's room. Belle took one look at her sister-in-law's face and asked, "Whatever is the matter?"

"Trudy and I had a fight." Jo plopped down onto Belle's bed.

Belle went back to hemming a skirt for the trousseau she was making for the woman in Ann Arbor. "Oh, I thought something was really wrong. You and Trudy fight all the time—that's what best friends do."

"Not like this."

"What did you and Trudy fight about?"

"Adam."

"Adam?"

"Well, in a roundabout way. It was mainly over Trudy wanting to toss Bert over for Dred Reed."

Belle's eyes went wide. "What?"

Jo shrugged. "That's what she said. Bert is too dull for her liking now. She wants strength, intelligence and a finely made form."

"None of which Bert has, in her opinion."

"Correct."

"So, how did Adam figure in all of this?"

"He didn't. Trudy was being Trudy and spouting nonsense about me preferring Adam to George. Silliness."

Belle studied Jo for a moment.

Feeling somewhat guilty, Jo looked away.

Belle said finally, "Well, I'm sure the two of you will make up. You always do."

Over the years, Jo and Trudy had fought over everything, and yes, they'd always made up. This skirmish seemed different, however; Jo wanted to shake Trudy until her teeth rattled for acting like the flighty young woman Mrs. Waterman thought her to be—shake her until she turned back into the Trudy Carr Jo had always known and loved.

Cecilia came in then and the conversation quickly ended. Jo didn't want her mother to know what had happened, or what Trudy was contemplating. Like most mamas, Cecilia would run right to Trudy's mama, Barbara, and then all perdition would break loose.

Jo asked, "Is Adam settled in?"

"Yes, he's sleeping and I doubt he's going to awaken anytime soon. He was asleep as soon as his head found the pillow."

Jo was grateful for small favors. A sleeping Adam Morgan couldn't cause trouble.

That evening, as the sun went down, Jo sat outside on the big, rail-backed swing her papa had built for his wife right after Jo's birth. It was hung from the sturdy limbs of one of the largest elms on the property. The spot was so peaceful and tranquil, everyone in the family enjoyed sitting here when the opportunity presented itself. Even during the hottest days of July and August, the elm's leafy green canopy kept the spot shady and cool.

Jo had come out to the swing to think and to watch the sunset. The sky had taken on the mauves and oranges that heralded the end of another day while the sun slid below the horizon in a blaze of fiery reds. Trudy's situation continued to worry Jo. Bert certainly didn't deserve such shabby treatment, but when Jo put in her two cents, Trudy had smacked it away. Jo decided she was done trying to make Trudy see reason. If Trudy wanted to mess up her life, so be it. Jo just hoped Trudy didn't come running to her expecting sympathy when everything blew up in her face.

When Adam Morgan awakened the next morning, it took him a few moments to remember where he was. Although he'd never been in this room when it belonged to Belle, he had when its first occupant, Daniel's grandmother, had been alive. In fact, Adam and his brother and Daniel had assisted Mr. Best in constructing the small walk-out porch that was connected to the room.

Adam looked at the sunshine streaming in through the windows. He still found it hard to believe that he'd left the war behind. During his stay here, there'd be no bad food, thundering cannons or sleeping on the hard, cold ground. He wouldn't have to fight anyone, or kill anyone or listen to the moans of the dying. War was a terrible and frightening place; the tranquility of the Best home was like heaven.

Adam slowly swung his leg free of the sheets and sat up on the edge of the bed. A little over a month ago, the bone in his ankle had been shattered by the burst of a cannon shell. The doctors weren't sure how it would heal, or even if it would. The dull ache of the injury plagued him night and day, but he'd gotten accustomed to it. The pain seemed to be growing stronger as of late; not a good sign, he was sure, but he hadn't mentioned it to the doctors for fear they wouldn't have permitted his discharge from the hospital.

Adam picked up the crutches he'd left within easy reach and hobbled over to the screen to take care of his morning needs. When he was done, he came back to the bed and sat down. He'd slept like a rock last night; he didn't remember dreaming at all. He did remember Mrs. Best leaving a clean shirt and a pair of trousers for him on one of the room's chairs last night. Getting up, he retrieved them and made his way back to the bed. Both garments belonged to Dani but because Adam and he were similar in height and build, the red flannel shirt Adam slipped into fit reasonably well. The pants were another story. Pulling the leg up over his swaddled ankle caused him so much pain, tears wet his eyes. Taking a moment to draw in a shaky breath, he waited until the wave of agony passed before continuing.

Finally dressed, Adam ran a hand over his hair. It had been a while since it had been cut; he and it needed a thorough wash, but right now he wanted to eat. Fixing the crutches into his armpits, he slowly made his way to the door. The ankle was still beating out a fiery rhythm but he forced himself to ignore it.

He smelled bacon as soon as he got out into the hallway. It made him smile. Jo came out of Belle's room just then, dressed in a wide navy skirt and a lighter blue short-sleeved blouse. Her hair was done, her eyes bright. Adam thought her dark beauty a lovely complement to the morning. "Morning, Jo."

Jo hadn't expected to see him, and his presence caught her by surprise. His gorgeous brown eyes and bone-melting smile made her heart flutter. She quickly willed it to stop. "Morning, Adam. Did you sleep well?"

"Yes, and you?"

"I'm a little sleepy. Belle and I were up late."

"Doing what?" he asked as they moved to the stairs.

"Telling ghost stories."

He grinned. "Ghost stories?"

"Yep."

At the top of the stairs, Adam paused. Yesterday, it had taken him quite some time to maneuver his way up to his new room. He doubted this morning's descent would be any faster.

Jo could see the concern on his face. "Are you going to be able to go down on those crutches?"

"Yes, but it may take me a while. You go on ahead."

"And have Mama fussing at me for not helping you? She'll have my head if you fall and go tumbling down the steps like a log."

Adam chuckled. "All right, but don't blame me if that bacon I smell is cold by the time we get to the table."

Jo waved off his concern. "No matter."

Adam maneuvered his way to the railing. He handed Jo his crutches, then slowly and carefully hopped his way down, one step at a time. "Good thing your house isn't any bigger," he said as he went.

Perspiration began to shine on his forehead and his breathing had shortened to pants. Jo was concerned. "Is the ankle paining you?"

"No," he lied.

Jo could see the cringe that flared over his features every time he gained a step. He was in pain whether he wanted to admit it or not. "Bea Meldrum is coming by later today. Maybe you should have her take a look at it." The aged Mrs. Meldrum wore many hats, including that of community healer.

"I'm fine."

Jo didn't believe him, but she didn't argue. If he wanted to play the big brave soldier so be it, but she was going to talk to her mama about him anyway. His distress was quite obvious.

By the time Adam made it to the bottom of the steps, his breathing was labored. His face was so dewed with perspiration, Jo offered him a handkerchief to wipe his brow. "You're not fine, Adam Morgan."

He grinned through the pain. "No?"

She shook her head and sighed impatiently.

"Please don't make a fuss," he pleaded.

Jo handed him back his crutches. "I won't. I'll leave that to Mama." With that, she strode off.

"Jo!" he called, wanting to stop her. "Come back here!"

But Jo didn't turn around.

seven

AS it turned out, Jojo didn't have to say a word to her mother about Adam's condition. By the time he made his way to the table, he was so winded and pale, Cecilia took one look at his face and declared, "You look terrible, Adam. Aren't you feeling well?"

"I'm fine." He took the empty chair at her side.

Viewing him skeptically, Cecilia reached over and placed a motherly palm against his forehead. "You're on fire. Is it the ankle?"

"I'm all right, Mrs. Best."

"No, you aren't. Bea's coming by this morning. We'll have her give that ankle a look-see."

Adam didn't want to be fussed over. "But—"

"No buts. You're under my roof and my care. I'd dishonor your mother if I did anything less."

The mention of his late mother made Adam instantly contrite and he mumbled, "Yes, ma'am."

Adam looked over at Jo and saw the concern on her face. In an attempt to allay her fears, he threw her a quick wink. That turned her look just as unsympathetic as her mother's, so Adam helped himself to the breakfast offerings.

Once the meal was finished, Adam sat back satisfied. It had been quite some time since he'd had a real meal. Belle's biscuits tasted as if they'd been made in heaven. He'd had eggs and Canadian bacon. The only thing marring absolute contentment was the pain in his ankle. It was now singing like an opera star, and no matter how hard he tried to ignore it, the searing increased.

Mrs. Best must have sensed the rise in his discomfort, because she said, "As soon as Bea gets here, you are going to be her first order of business."

"I'm fine."

The three Best women shook their heads at his stubborn claim.

When Mrs. Meldrum stopped by later to drop off the eggs Mrs. Best had ordered, Cecilia brought her into the parlor to see Adam. Mrs. Meldrum had known his family before the war, too. "Good to see you, Adam. Sorry to hear about your ma's passing."

"Thanks, Mrs. Meldrum."

"Cecilia says you're in quite a bit of pain. Let's see that ankle."

Adam sighed. It was plain he was not going to win this war, so he pushed his chair back and stuck out his leg so that Mrs. Meldrum could evaluate him.

While the other ladies looked on, she began to undo the swaddling protecting his ankle. She asked Adam, "When were you injured?"

"About six weeks ago, but I haven't seen a doctor in two."

As Bea gently removed the bandages, Jo could see the lines of pain crossing Adam's face. Just having the wrappings taken off made him stiffen and bite his lip. Her heart went out to him. Fueled by nothing but concern for this old friend, Jo went to his side, and said, "Here, hold my hand. Squeeze if you need to."

He smiled through the beads of sweat pouring down his face, but took her hand. "Thanks."

She nodded.

The wound was infected, so much so that the putrid smell of the flesh permeated the room. Bea noted, "You must have the constitution of a horse, Adam Morgan. This would have felled a lesser man."

Jo took one look at the swollen, discolored flesh and quickly averted her eyes; she doubted she'd ever make a good nurse.

Bea said, "This is going to have to be drained, I'm afraid. It looks as if it didn't get cleaned out very well before it was bandaged."

Adam had no trouble believing that. He was sure the doctor had done all he could, but with the war on, the conditions in the field hospitals were neither sanitary nor comforting. On top of that, many of the black soldiers were the last to receive care; Adam had lain on a cot for three days before being treated.

Bea looked over to Cecilia. "He needs to be in a bed so that when I'm done cleaning the wound, he can go right to sleep."

Cecilia asked Adam, "Do you think you can make it back upstairs?"

"Sure," he gritted out.

Jo released his hand and gave him the crutches. All of the women hovered, showing worry and concern.

Adam struggled to get himself upright. The ankle was throbbing as if an elephant had stood on it. Gathering his strength, he forced himself across the room.

Bea said, "I'm going to need lots of hot water. Belle, can you put some on to boil?"

Belle hastened to the kitchen.

"And I'll need thread, Cecilia. Thread, and your sharpest knife."

"Knife?"

"Yes." She said no more.

Cecilia went to take care of the requests while Jo and Bea accompanied Adam to the stairs.

As Adam slowly maneuvered his way back up the steps, he tried to maintain a humorous air. "The next time I go up these steps, I'll do it riding a horse."

But by the time he reached the top, the tremendous pain in his foot and ankle had reduced him to a stoic silence. He stopped to catch his breath.

Jo asked him in a voice softened by concern, "How are you doing?"

"Almost to the finish line. Do I get to kiss the girl if I take first place?"

She smiled. "Let's just get you to bed. We'll talk about kisses once you're better."

"I'm going to hold you to that, Jo."

"I don't doubt that for a moment." Humor tinged her voice.

He gave her a lopsided grin then hobbled into his room.

Jo and Belle waited tensely downstairs while Bea, assisted by Cecilia, worked on Adam. A few moments later, the sound of him roaring like an injured mountain lion shook the house and Jo, as well. A shaken Jo turned to Belle. "What do you think has happened?"

"Mrs. Meldrum probably had to cut open the flesh to let out all the poisons. Poor Adam."

Jo wanted to go up and see for herself how he was faring. She didn't though; she didn't want to be in the way, so she waited, and paced, and waited some more. Thirty minutes later, Mrs. Best came down.

The anxious Jo asked, "Is he going to be all right?"

Her mother nodded reassuringly. "Bea seems to think so.

There was dirt and pieces of shrapnel left in the wound, but it appears to be cleaner now. He's going to be off his feet for a while. Adam's very lucky. Another week or so and he might have lost his leg."

Jo shuddered in reaction. She was glad to hear he would recover, however. "Are you still going down to Toledo for your lecture?"

Cecilia Best was a well-sought-after speaker on both abolitionist and women's issues. One of Toledo's Women's Societies had invited her down to speak at their Founder's Day celebration.

"The speech isn't until Saturday, so I'll wait and go later in the week. I want to make certain Adam is healing."

Jo thought that a good idea.

"Is Mrs. Meldrum done?" Belle asked.

"Almost. She was finishing up the last of the stitches when I left her."

"May we go up and see him?" Jo asked.

"I don't see why not, but don't stay long. He'll need his rest."

"All right, Mama."

Jo and Belle hastened upstairs. They reached the room just as Mrs. Meldrum was exiting. She was carrying a basin filled with the soiled bandages and other items she'd used to help Adam. "How is he?" Jo asked her.

Bea smiled. "He's doing well. I gave him something that will help him sleep. He's asking for you, Josephine."

"Me?"

"You're the only Jojo here."

Jo turned startled eyes to Belle, who gave her a knowing smile in response. Mrs. Meldrum headed for the stairs and Jo and Belle entered the room. Even though it was early afternoon now, the drawn drapes had plunged the room into shadows.

Jo advanced slowly over to the bed. "Adam?"

He turned his curly head to her and gave her a sleepy smile. "Hello, beautiful."

Embarrassment burned Jo to her toes. "You must stop calling me that."

"Why?" he teased softly. "You are, you know."

Jo saw the smile on Belle's face and said, "It's the medicine talking, Belle, not him."

Adam shook his head slowly. "No, it isn't. You've grown into a very lovely pest, Jojo. Hasn't she, Belle?"

Belle shook her head. "We came up here to ask how you're feeling."

"Sleepy. Felt that knife, too, but now I feel like I'm floating away."

Belle told him, "Well, you talk to Jojo for a moment, then go on to sleep."

"Yes, Miss Belle," he murmured, then corrected himself. "I guess that should be *Mrs.* Belle, now."

Belle grinned and shook her head. "I'll come back and check on you later." She turned to Jo. "Don't stay too long."

"I won't."

Belle's departure left them alone.

Adam looked at Jojo's increasingly hazy features, and asked, "Will you come and sit?"

Jo took the few steps to the big overstuffed chair beside the bed and sat down.

When she was settled, he said faintly, "Good. Now your face will be the last thing I see before I doze off."

"You're lathering it on rather thick, aren't you?" Jo cracked.

"Am I?"

"Yes."

His eyes drifted shut for a moment, then he added, "I forget that you've known me most of your life."

"Yes, I have, and I am therefore not susceptible to your Canadian charm."

His smile wobbled. "Pity. I'd hoped to turn your head."

"You have. Watch."

Jo slowly turned her head back and forth.

He grinned. "Pest." His voice then took on a serious note. "I'm glad I'm here."

"We are, too. You should sleep now."

He reached out and took her hand. "Stay until I do?"

Jo nodded.

After he fell asleep, Jo gently freed her hand. Because she was alone and no one would know, she leaned down and gave him a soft kiss on his cheek before tiptoeing out. Little did she know that in the silence that followed her departure, Adam Morgan smiled.

Two days later, Mrs. Meldrum thought Adam's wound had healed well enough for Cecilia to travel to Toledo without worry. She'd also promised to stop by every few days and check on Adam's progress. Vera Firestone would be accompanying Cecilia on the train ride, and the two friends planned to return Sunday afternoon. Since Belle had to travel to Ann Arbor that day, she drove the older women to the station, leaving Jo alone to look after the house and Adam until evening.

Once Cecilia and the others were gone, Jo ran over to her shop to put a note on the door notifying her customers that all appointments would have to be delayed until tomorrow. Jo didn't want to leave Adam in the house alone. He'd been forbidden to attempt the stairs, and with Belle gone for the day, he'd need Jo's assistance with meals and such.

After posting the note, Jo returned to the house. She went

up to his room to retrieve his breakfast dishes and knocked softly on the closed door. "Adam?"

"Come in," he called out.

Jo entered to find him seated in a chair with his back to her, enjoying the sunshine pouring in through the porch's open French doors. This was her first visit with him today. "Morning. How are you feeling?"

He swiveled his head around so he could meet her eyes. "Not bad."

For Jo, the intensity of his gaze was like staring up at the sun; both were blinding. "I...came up to get your breakfast dishes. Are you done?"

"Yep." They were piled on a tray on the bed.

Jo retrieved the tray. "Do you need anything?"

"How about some company?"

Jo paused. There would be nothing improper in saying yes; Adam was family, but there was something building between the two of them that was still too unclear to see, and too unfamiliar to name. "Okay. Let me take this tray down, and I'll be right back."

Downstairs, Jo told herself that his request for company had nothing to do with his supposed attraction to her; he was simply lonely. Finding a logical explanation for her pounding heart proved more difficult, however. Willing herself to calm down, she went back upstairs.

When Jo returned, the way Adam looked at her made her wonder how any young woman alive kept her faculties in his presence. He told her, "I was thinking of moving out onto the porch. Join me?"

"Sure."

Jo watched him prop himself up on the crutches.

"Ladies first," he said gallantly.

Jo walked over to the French doors and he followed.

Outside, she sat down on the smooth wooden bench positioned next to the porch's railing, then moved over so he could sit, too.

"Beautiful day," he remarked.

"Yes, it is."

Jo could feel the warmth of him next to her, and found it hard to be nonchalant. His presence made her very self-conscious.

Adam sensed her nervousness and searched for a way to set her at ease, but she asked first, "Would it be rude of me to ask how you were injured?"

He shook his head. "No. We were about to go on patrol and were surprised by some Rebs. A cannonball exploded about a foot from where I was standing saddling my mount. I remember being blown over and hitting the ground—that's all. When I awakened I was in the field hospital with most of the flesh of my ankle gone."

Jo shuddered. She thought about her brother and father and prayed they weren't in a field hospital somewhere. "You were lucky."

"Very. The man standing to my left was killed." Adam suddenly found he didn't want to talk about the war any longer. He'd had enough experience with it to last a lifetime. "So tell me. What do you do when you're not coddling injured soldiers?"

"Hair."

"Hair?"

"Hair. As in hairdresser."

He threw back his head and laughed.

Finding his reaction infectious, she asked humorously, "What's so funny?"

"It's just—I remember that's all you did when you were young. You and those hair irons were closer than some siblings."

"Well, we still are. In fact, Dani and Papa built me a shop a few years back, and I have a clientele and everything."

Adam was just beginning to realize how much he enjoyed this grown-up version of Josephine Best. Beneath the ebony beauty lay the saucy, uninhibited Jojo he'd known when she was twelve. She'd been a pistol back then; now she was a polished one.

Under his silent regard, Jo fought to keep her hands still. "You know," she told him, "Dani would be very upset if he knew you were here sharpening your wiles on his baby sister."

"Is that what I'm doing?"

Jo met his eyes. Her heart began flipping and flopping. "Yes. And once you've gotten your wiles back up to snuff you'll be off to conquer some other poor, unsuspecting beauty."

"I'd never conquer you. Your brother would roast me like a Christmas goose. Your mother, too."

Adam was mesmerized by the intricate way she'd braided, then coiled her gleaming black hair into the chignon pinned low on her neck. She smelled good, too. He detected just the faintest scent of—oranges? "Is it my imagination or do you really smell like oranges?"

"It's my hair oil."

He leaned close and placed his nose near her hair. "Ah, it is, isn't it?"

He was so near, Jo had to force herself not to fly up out of the seat. "I make it myself," she explained inanely, trying not to look into his eyes for very long.

Adam was drawn by the shyness she sometimes showed. "Do you?"

She nodded like a horse. "Papa has a friend in Florida who owns orange orchards. He sends us a big crate every winter, and I use the oil from the rinds in my hair dressings." Jo could hear herself babbling, but couldn't stop. "I want to market it after the war. All my clients rave about it."

Jo clamped her mouth shut. She was determined not to say anything further, lest he think her an absolute ninny.

Once again, Adam found himself wishing Jo was someone else. That way, he'd be free to explore the strange new feelings that being around her were creating. But she wasn't; she was the sister of his best friend. A sister who as a child had been the bane of their boyish existence with her tattling, pesky ways. She was all grown up now, and the tattling pest had been transformed into an exquisite young woman he'd like to know better.

Jo didn't know how to respond to his silent but intense scrutiny. "What are you thinking, Adam?"

"Truthfully?"

"Yes."

"That I wished you were someone else."

Jo was confused by the admission. "Why?"

"Because you're Dani's little sister."

"And?"

"And I shouldn't be starting something with you that I maybe can't finish."

Jo studied him. She understood.

Jo thought she heard the door pull. She sat up and listened hard. There, it sounded again. "I think someone's at the door. I'll be right back."

Glad for the distraction, she hastened out and down the stairs. When she pulled open the door, there to her surprise stood George Brooks. "George? Hello!"

"Hello, Josephine. How are you?"

Jo was still trying to get over the shock of his visit. "I'm well. You?"

He nodded. "No complaints to speak of. May I come in?"

She looked up the steps to see if Adam had come to investigate. "My mama's not at home. Neither is Belle."

"I see. Well, then, how about we sit on the porch for a spell? Nothing improper in that."

"Well—" She thought about Adam being upstairs alone, and then about George, who'd come all this way. Jo had no experience juggling suitors. "I—"

Adam called out, "Jo, who's at the door?"

Jo looked up to see him on his crutches at the top of the stairs. "It's George."

"What's he want?"

George spoke up for himself, "I came to call on Josephine."

Adam said, "Well, call back some other time. She's not available until her mama comes home."

Jo told Adam, "Will you go back to your room, please? You're not supposed to be up and around."

"And you're supposed to be keeping me company."

George didn't appear to like the sound of that. "Josephine, are you alone here with him?"

Jo sensed that Adam was being difficult on purpose. Turning away from Adam and back to George, she responded, "Yes. Why?"

"That's not real proper, you know."

"Adam is family, George. I'd trust him with my life."

She glanced back up at Adam and found herself held prisoner by his eyes.

Adam said in turn, "And I'd trust her with mine, as well."

She forced her eyes away from his and said to George, "I don't see why we can't spend a few moments on the porch, George."

Adam broke in and declared, "I'll have to come down and play chaperone, then."

Jo's hand went to her hip. "You will not."

"Yes, I will. I'm family, remember, and as family, I'm the only one here able to chaperone. Your mother will have my hide if she finds out I let you sit on the porch without proper supervision."

Jo could feel steam pouring out of her ears. "I don't need a chaperone, Adam Morgan."

"All right. Then Brooks can come back when your mama's here."

"Go back to your room," she gritted out.

He stood silently, as if challenging her.

Jo didn't like Adam's high-handedness one bit, but she knew she was defeated. "It's really up to you, George. We can include him, or you can come back another day."

George scowled up at Adam. "I'm willing to put up with his presence if you are."

Jo smiled at him. "Then let's go out to the porch."

She didn't smile up at Adam when she said, "You win. Try not to break your neck coming down the steps."

Then she stepped outside to join George on the porch.

eight

when Adam joined Jo and George on the porch, she did her best to ignore him. Even though he had the decency to choose a seat a bit away, he was still too close for her liking. Out of the corner of her eye she watched him set his crutches within easy reach and unfold the newspaper he'd brought along. The sheen of perspiration on his forehead and his very labored breathing were evidence that the trip had cost him much in the way of energy and strength, but she didn't let her concern for his health override her irritation. If he keeled over it would be his own fault. She was perfectly capable of keeping company with a gentleman without Adam Morgan hovering over her like a disapproving maiden aunt. She had hoped he would be more understanding about her situation, given he was only a few years older than her, but no, Adam wanted to lord over her as if she were a child. She was not pleased.

George told her, "I'm thinking of settling around here someplace once the doctors discharge me."

Jo set aside her pique and concentrated instead on George's easygoing company. "Really? You aren't returning to Jackson?"

"It depends."

"On what, if you don't mind my asking?"

His eyes twinkled. "Oh, maybe on how things go with a certain hairdresser that I know."

Adam rustled his newspaper loud enough for the conversation to pause. Jo glared his way. He gave her an inscrutable look from over the top of the paper, then resumed reading.

Jo took a deep breath and prompted, "Go on with what you were saying, George."

"Well, I thought I might be able to find work here."

From behind his newspaper, Adam asked bluntly, "As what?"

Jo gritted out, "Adam Morgan, mind your own business."

George placed a calming hand on her arm. "It's all right, Josephine. I don't mind answering."

George directed his response at the raised newspaper. "I'm a farmer by birth, but I do odd jobs on the side. I'm real handy at fixing things."

Adam lowered his paper. "Good." The paper went back up.

Jo wanted to sock Adam in his nosy nose. There was no way she and George were going to have a pleasant visit with him around. "George? How about you come back when Mama's here? This is not working out well."

"I don't mind him looking on."

"I do."

Adam rustled the paper again.

Jo sighed with frustration and impatience. "The next time I come to Mrs. Oswald's we'll set a date. Is that all right with you?"

"That sounds like a well-thought-out plan, Josephine," Adam declared.

"Will you stay out of this?" she shot back.

Behind the paper, Adam grinned. *Yes, she was still a pistol.*

George stood, albeit reluctantly. "You're right. This isn't working. I'll see you on your next visit to Mrs. Oswald's."

"Yes, you will."

George looked over at the man behind the raised newspaper and said, "I'd be lying if I said, 'Hope to see you again, Morgan.'"

Adam countered, "So would I. Have a safe drive back."

A tight-lipped George nodded at Jo. "Goodbye, Josephine."

"I'll see you soon, George. Thank you for the visit."

"You're welcome." George gave Adam one last glare, then stepped off the porch. With the assistance of his wooden cane, he headed back to the buggy he'd rented to make the ride over. He waved at Jo. A smiling Jo waved goodbye.

Once George was out of sight, she wheeled on Adam. "I hope you're satisfied."

He put down the paper and folded it slowly. "I am. Your father and brother would be satisfied, as well."

"I am not a child."

"Precisely why I needed to be out here. George doesn't think you're a child, either."

"George is a gentleman."

"Oh, I don't doubt that, but Dani would have wanted me to be sure."

"Dani has nothing to do with this and you know it."

"No? Then what does it have to do with?"

Arms folded firmly across her chest, Jo replied, "I don't know. You tell me."

Adam knew he had no business becoming involved with this black-eyed firecracker, but he couldn't seem to help himself. "Suppose I said it has to do with me not wanting you keeping company with anyone but me?"

"Then I'd say I may have been born at night, but not *last* night, Adam Morgan."

He chuckled. "You doubt my sincerity."

"Yes, because I don't believe you have a sincere bone in your body where young women are concerned," Jo declared.

"Suppose you're wrong."

"I'm not."

"Suppose you are?"

Jo had her hands on her hips. She had nothing more to say.

"You always were too stubborn for your own good," he told her.

"I'll take that as a compliment," she replied fiercely.

He dropped his head in amusement. When he raised his head and met her gaze again, he said softly, "Look, Jo. There's something growing here, I feel it and you do, too, but like I said earlier, I don't want to start something I maybe can't finish, at least not right now."

"Because?"

Adam didn't like being put on the spot. "I'm twenty-one, Jo. I'm young. I don't know if I'm ready to stop picking flowers."

"In order words, if something better and prettier comes along—"

"That's not—"

"Yes, it is. Boys can be so selfish sometimes. If you want to pick flowers, then go and pick flowers, Adam Morgan. Just leave me alone while you do."

That said, an angry and hurt Jo turned on her heel and marched back into the house.

Adam knew he'd injured her feelings and he wanted to kick himself. He'd not explained himself very well, or maybe he'd explained himself too well. Either way, Jo was mad and would probably stay that way for some time. A part of him was relieved because he had no business dallying with Dani's sister in the first place, but another part of him was saddened by the knowledge of what would clearly never be.

Up in her room, Jo chastised herself for having any hurt feelings at all over Adam's confession. She'd known all along that he'd meant nothing by his actions toward her; the Morgan brothers lived to turn the female head. Luckily, she'd made him tell her the truth early enough in the game not to be seriously affected, but for some reason, she didn't feel lucky in the least.

Jo was subdued for the rest of the morning. Around noon, she ventured down the hall and knocked upon Adam's door. "Do you want luncheon?" she asked him through the wood.

"Come on in, Jo."

"I can't, there's no chaperone. Do you want something to eat or not?"

For a moment there was silence, then she heard, "Yes, I do."

"I'll be back then," she told him. She turned away from the door and headed downstairs. *Take that*, she declared inwardly.

Adam was amused but not surprised by her attitude; Jo had always given as good as she got. He'd hurt her, and now she was punishing him. He had no recourse but to take his comeuppance like a man.

Jo made Adam a large sandwich out of some leftover roast beef and slices of Belle's rye bread. She added a hearty wedge of last night's apple pie, and a cup of coffee to round out the fare.

When she reached his room the door was open. He was seated outside on the porch. She called out, "I'm leaving your tray here on the dresser. If you need anything more, just yell. I'll be downstairs."

By the time Adam grabbed his crutches and hobbled in, she'd already gone.

Belle came home late that afternoon. Jo was in the kitchen putting the last touches on dinner. In reality, she'd done nothing but reheat last night's leftovers, but leftovers were what her mama had instructed her to prepare, so that's what Jo did. She gave Belle a smile of welcome. "Did Mama and Mrs. Firestone make the train?"

Belle took off her hat. "Yes, they did. How's Adam?"

Jo snarled.

"That well, huh?"

Jo then explained how Adam had ruined George's visit.

Belle couldn't control her chuckle. "He actually sat on the porch with you two?"

"It wasn't funny, Belle."

Belle was instantly contrite. "Of course it wasn't. I'm sorry, Jo."

"He could have stayed upstairs. Nothing was going to happen. George is a gentleman."

"He certainly appears to be. Adam was just being over-protective."

"He was being nosy, that's all." Jo didn't tell Belle about the flower-picking part of the conversation; she wasn't ready to reveal that yet. "Nosy and meddlesome."

"Well, how about I take over the care of the nosy and meddlesome Mr. Morgan for the rest of the day?"

Jo smiled happily. "The smartest thing my brother ever did was marry you."

Belle said, "I love you, too."

Jo said, "I'm going over to the shop to make sure I'm ready for business when I open up tomorrow."

"All right. I'll keep your dinner warm."

Jo left with a wave.

Jo didn't really have anything to do at the shop; she was always very organized. Her supplies were up to snuff, her irons and combs were clean and a stack of towels was waiting at the ready. She'd come over here to think more than anything else, so she took a seat on one of the stools. In a perfect world, everything and everyone would be just that—perfect. Trudy wouldn't be contemplating breaking off her engagement, Jo and George would be getting to know each other better without outside interference, her menfolk wouldn't be off at war and Adam Morgan would be gone wherever flower-pickers go. But the world was an imperfect one, one filled with war, and uncertainty, and a young woman's inability to control anything in it. Being melancholy was uncharacteristic for Jo; she could usually ride out whatever life threw her way, but she didn't feel like riding anything right now.

She supposed it had to do with Adam's confession and how it made her feel. She didn't deny she'd been hurt by it, but she should have known better. Girls like her had no business even contemplating someone like Adam; she had neither the experience nor the dash necessary not to be left flat as yesterday's flapjacks when he moved on to another flower. She was going to have to buck up, though; there was no telling how long he would be staying with them, and if she spent the whole time moping, her mother would want an explanation. Jo was no longer twelve years old. She was a seventeen-year-old owner of her own business, and such women did not let themselves become distracted by light-skinned Canadian Lotharios.

Jo spent the entire next day doing the heads of her customers. By the time she got home late that evening she was so exhausted, even walking was a tremendous chore. She fell into one of the parlor chairs and moaned to Belle, "Tell me again why I want to be a hairdresser."

Belle smiled. "I have some water heating on the stove if you'd like to take a long hot soak."

"Oh, I love you more each day. That sounds perfect. How's our guest faring?"

"Coming along. He asked after you. He says he hasn't seen you since yesterday."

"Another few days won't hurt him."

Belle acted surprised. "Jo?"

Jo waved her hand dismissively. "I'm sorry, Belle. After I'm done with my bath I'll stop in and say hello. I'm just tired now, is all."

Belle nodded understandingly. "Well, I already pulled the tub into the room for you. The water should be hot enough shortly."

The room Belle was referring to was a bathing room built off the kitchen. It was small but served its purpose well. Jo couldn't wait to bask in the big, claw-foot tub.

After Jo had her bath and dinner, she put on an old skirt and blouse, then went down and knocked on Adam's door.

He called out, "Come on in."

When she entered, he nodded slightly. "Evenin', Jo."

Her reply was distant. "How are you, Adam?"

"Fine."

Adam surveyed her and wondered what he'd have to do to restore the sparkle he'd become accustomed to seeing in her eyes. He asked in serious tones, "How long are you going to punish me?"

The question caught Jo off guard. "Who says that's what I'm doing?"

"I do. You didn't come to see me today."

"I had appointments to honor. I've been home only an hour or so."

"I want us to be friends again, Jo."

"I don't see why we can't."

Adam noted that in spite of her conciliatory words, her frosty manner could chill ice cream. "Then can I convince you to play checkers with me?"

"Sure," she replied. "I'll get the board."

She turned to go. His voice stopped her. "Jojo?"

She faced him. She waited.

"I'm sorry for hurting your feelings. Truly. Please forgive me?"

Emotion swelled in Jo. The honesty in his eyes and the sincerity in his voice touched her deep inside. "I shouldn't speak to you ever again, Adam Morgan, but you're forgiven."

"Thank you."

"You're welcome."

Jo went downstairs to retrieve the checkerboard and pieces; she felt much better.

Jo won the first game, hands down.

An impressed Adam asked, "When did you learn to play so well? I remember being able to beat you with my eyes closed."

"I was twelve at the time."

"Oh, that's right. A twelve-year-old pest."

"Don't start," she warned him, smiling.

"Sorry."

She then asked, "Was I really that bad?"

He set his pieces up for another game. "Yes."

"No, I wasn't."

His voice was lit with humor. "If you don't want to hear the truth, don't ask the question."

"Well, all I remember is how rotten you, Dani and Jeremiah were to me when I was small."

Adam looked offended. "I beg your pardon! We treated you like a little queen."

"You don't tie a queen to a tree and use her as bee bait."

Adam threw back his head and laughed. "I'd forgotten all about that."

"I haven't. Nor have I forgotten the serious whippings Papa gave out on my behalf after you all brought me home that night."

Adam rubbed his hip at the memory. "Ouch. It was memorable, all right. It was your brother's idea to smear that honey all over you."

"Whose idea was it to tie me to the tree?"

"Jere. He wanted to know if the honey would protect a person from bee stings."

"So you all used me."

Adam grinned and nodded. "You were available, but boy, when Jere whacked the hive with that stick and those angry bees came pouring out loaded for bear, I never ran so fast in my life."

"I thought you all were going to get stung to death and die, and I was going to be tied to the tree forever."

"But we came back for you."

"Yes, only to take me down to the creek and rub my skin raw trying to remove the honey."

"You were screaming bloody murder, too."

"I wanted to shoot the three of you."

"How old were you?"

"Six."

"And we begged and pleaded with you not to tell."

She chuckled. "Dani promised me all of the money from his newspaper deliveries."

Adam laughed. "He wanted you to say you'd accidentally fallen into the honeycomb barrel at my parents' store."

"As if Mama would have believed such a tale. But he promised me ice cream, trips to the circus, anything my heart desired as long as I didn't tell the truth."

"All of which you turned down."

"Of course. I was six, not stupid. I knew the three of you were going to be in so much trouble that not even the angel Gabriel could save you, so the minute we turned up the walk, I started screaming like I'd been run over by a train."

He began to laugh. "Your mother took one look at you all wet and sticky and crying and I knew she was going to fry us until we burned. In a way, we were real glad your papa was home."

"Why?"

"We knew that after he punished us, we'd still be alive. We weren't so sure about your mother."

Jo laughed. "Mama is something, isn't she?"

"Mrs. B. is one of a kind."

"I want to grow up and be just like her."

"Heaven help us. I don't know if the world is ready."

"Well it won't have to be for a while. I have a lot more living and learning to do before I can equal my mother, but that's my goal."

"Not a bad goal. Bad news for your husband, but not a bad goal for you."

"Hey, what are you saying about my mama?"

He laughed. "I mean it in a good way. A man who marries you will have to have patience, a strong mind and an even stronger wit. Your father does pretty well with your mother because he has all those things."

"And he loves Mama more than anything."

"Yes, he does. The man you marry will probably love you that way, too."

Their eyes met for a moment, and Jo asked, "You think so?"

He nodded. "I know so." He then added softly, "You're a beautiful, headstrong woman, Josephine Best. Don't settle for less. You hear?"

She nodded. "I hear."

"Good. Now, back to these checkers. I owe you a whipping, I believe."

Jo laughed and rolled her eyes. "Let me feel your forehead. Your fever must have returned."

He grinned. "Pest."

She grinned right back.

nine

when Jo awakened in her bed on Friday morning, the first thing she thought about was how much she'd enjoyed Adam's company the past few evenings; they'd played checkers, done more reminiscing and, all in all, had a good time. He hadn't flirted once, and she hadn't succumbed to his charm. The second thing she thought about was how much she missed Trudy. They hadn't spoken since last Sunday's spat, and even though Jo was convinced Trudy's brain had lost a wheel, they were still best friends—no matter what. Jo decided that after work she'd drive over and see Trudy.

As Jo headed over to her shop, she was surprised to see a hack pull up and her mother step out. Jo's face split into a grin. She watched her mother pay the driver, and after he drove off, Jo hurried over to help carry the small cache of luggage to the house. "What are you doing back so early?"

"The festivities were canceled."

"Why?"

"They had a contested election, or some such nonsense. It seems the last elected president of the society refuses to relinquish her position, and so after listening to them argue and fuss for the past few days, Vera and I decided to pack our bags and come home. How are you, darling?"

"Fine, Mama."

"How's our patient?"

"Doing well, actually. He's able to get around much better, but he still tires easily."

"Has Bea stopped in?"

"Yes. She says he's progressing."

"That's good news. Are you on your way to work?"

"Yes, ma'am."

"All right, then, I'll see you later on."

Jo smiled and headed over to her shop.

It was six o'clock by the time Jo was done for the day and had everything cleaned up and put away. She was tired but still determined to go by Trudy's after supper and attempt a reconciliation.

When Jo got home, Cecilia and Vera were in the process of heading off to the church for the weekly Friday-night choir rehearsal. Jo ate a hasty dinner, then, having received her mama's blessing, rode her mare the mile and a half to the Carr home. Since Trudy's mama, Barbara, was also a choir member, her absence would guarantee Jo and Trudy plenty of time to talk freely.

Jo dismounted and walked up the gravel path that led to the door. Trudy's house was small and painted green. It was a nice spring evening and the air was fragrant with the smells of Mrs. Carr's prized roses.

Jo knocked on the screened door and called out in a singsong voice, "Trudy! It's Jojo."

Silence.

Jo knocked again, harder. "Trudy!"

Nothing.

Perplexed, Jo walked to the edge of the porch and looked out toward Mrs. Carr's greenhouses that lay a few yards from the house. Barbara Carr grew flowers for pleasure and profit, and her daughter and Jo, too, on occasion, had often been pressed into lending a hand in the business. Jo saw no sign of Trudy, however.

Jo went back to the door. She pulled on the handle and when it opened, she stepped inside the silent front room. "Trudy? Are you here?"

Jo looked around the room and her eyes widened. The place was a mess. Furniture was knocked over. China plates and broken crockery littered the rag rugs. One of the beautiful oak sideboards her papa had made for the Carrs many Christmases ago lay facedown on the floor. The shattered glass from its windows lay around it like tears. Jo got a sick feeling. Something was wrong. Terribly wrong.

Fighting her fear, Jo began running from room to room, calling Trudy's name. Nothing. She did find Trudy's handbag on her bed in her bedroom. The contents were strewn all over the yellow quilt. Trudy's collection of little elephants that usually sat on the mantel above the fireplace was all over the floor; one, made out of blue glass that Jo had given to Trudy on her fourteenth birthday, lay in pieces as if it had been stepped upon. *Where was Trudy?*

"Trudy!" she yelled again.

Jo ran back outside and searched the barn. The buggy Trudy had been given by her papa was gone, but Jo knew Trudy would never leave the front door wide open nor go anywhere without her handbag.

Jo searched the greenhouses, but found only flowers. The only place left was the cellar. Jo held on to her hope. Like other cellars in the area, the Carrs' underground room also served as a storm shelter. Maybe Trudy had hidden herself there.

Jo pulled up on the heavy wooden door, then let her eyes follow the beam of light down into the darkness. "Trudy!"

A soft, muffled sound rose from the depths.

Jo backed her way down the earthen steps as quickly as she could, then peered round in the half light. Jo gasped. Trudy lay trussed and gagged on the floor.

Jo moved to her side and Trudy moaned happily through the red handkerchief tied between her lips. Jo hastily undid the knot, and a grateful Trudy cried, "Oh, Jo, I knew you'd come. I knew it."

They hugged each other emotionally. Jo was glad to have found her. Trudy was even gladder to have been found. Only now did Jo acknowledge how scared she'd been; her heart was pounding like war drums. "Are you all right? Are you hurt?"

"No, he didn't harm me."

"Who did this to you?"

Trudy guiltily dropped her eyes.

"Trudy?"

Silence.

Jo's first instinct was to shake her—after all, finding the Carr house torn apart and Trudy missing had scared Jo half to death—but she chose another tack. They were supposed to be best friends. "Trudy?" she asked gently. "Who did this?"

"You're going to think I'm so stupid."

"No, I'm not. Tell me."

"It was Dred Reed."

Jo's mouth dropped.

"Oh, Jo, he robbed the house. He made me show him where Mama kept all of our valuables—the good silver, all the money she's saved, Papa's gold pocket watch."

"How on earth did he get in?"

Trudy dropped her eyes again, then confessed in a tiny voice, "I invited him over. I...knew Mama was going to be gone all day delivering flowers and wouldn't be back until after choir rehearsal, so I thought we could just sit on the porch and talk."

Jo shook her head. "Oh, Trudy."

"Only he didn't want to talk. He had a knife, and the first thing he asked was how much money Mama kept in the house. When I wouldn't tell him— Oh, Jo, I feel so stupid. Mama's going to kill me."

Jo agreed. She and Trudy had been in some serious scrapes in the past, but nothing of this magnitude. "We have to alert the sheriff. Maybe Dred can be waylaid."

Trudy wailed again, "Mama's going to kill me."

Again, Jo had to agree.

Jo went to work on the ropes tied around Trudy's legs, ankles and wrists. The knots were all good ones, so it took some time. When Trudy was finally freed, she and Jo climbed the ladder back up into the evening light. "Are you sure he didn't hurt you?"

"I'm sure. He called me a silly little girl not worth a real man's attention. It was humiliating."

Jo shook her head sadly. Poor Trudy. What an awful lesson she'd just learned.

They were walking back to the house when the sight of Bert Waterman and his mama standing on the porch froze Jo and Trudy in mid step.

Trudy wailed quietly, "Oh, Lord. I forgot I was to have dinner with them this evening."

Jo felt her pain. "Oh, Lord, is right."

Mrs. Waterman appeared very perturbed, and as Jo and Trudy approached the porch, the Dragon Lady asked, "What has happened? The house looks like it has been ransacked."

Bert moved quickly to his intended's side, asking with concern, "Are you hurt, Trudy?"

"No, I'm fine." Trudy shook her head stiffly. "A little shook up, but I haven't been harmed."

Trudy opened her mouth to say something else, but closed

it at the sight of her mother driving up. Following Mrs. Carr were buggies and wagons being driven by other members of the ladies' choir, including Cecilia Best. Jo didn't think this could get any worse.

Mrs. Carr stepped down from the wagon. She took one look at her daughter's tear-stained face and asked with concern, "Tru, what's wrong?" Had the situation not been so awful, Jo would have jumped right in with a plausible lie to help explain away Trudy's appearance, but Jo didn't say a word.

Mrs. Carr walked closer to Trudy and peered into her face. Trudy said, "Hello, Mama. Why's the choir here?"

"There's a skunk loose in the church. The reverend made us all leave until he can get someone in there to catch it. So we came here. Now, what's this all about?"

Jo went and stood beside her mother. Everyone, it seemed, was waiting for Trudy's explanation.

"Mama, I didn't know he was going to do this!" Trudy wailed pitifully, then threw herself into her mother's arms and wept like her heart was broken.

A very bewildered Barbara Carr held her daughter while she cried. Jo had no idea if Trudy's tears were sincere or not, but it was certainly buying her more time.

Mrs. Carr comforted her with the nonsensical words and phrases mamas often employ at such times, then said, "Who is *he,* and what did *he* do?"

"He robbed us," Trudy said and began to cry again.

Mrs. Carr's eyes widened. "Robbed us?"

Jo doubted she'd ever seen an adult woman run so fast, but Mrs. Carr was up the walk in a flash. She went inside, and then her scream of disbelief shook the silence.

Jo's mother hastened up the walk to see if help was needed, only to be stopped by the sight of Mrs. Carr barreling out the door.

She walked over to her daughter and asked in a shaken voice, "Who did this?"

Trudy tried to forestall the eruption. "Mama, I didn't—"

Mrs. Carr cut her off. "Gertrude Carr. For the last time. Who did this?"

"Dred Reed," Trudy replied.

"Who?"

"One of the soldiers staying with Patricia Oswald," Cecilia reminded her.

Mrs. Carr turned back to her daughter. "That soldier? Did he force his way in—"

"Mama, he tied me up and put me in the cellar. Jojo found me."

Trudy hastily went on to tell that Dred has stolen all of their valuables, and again how she'd been trussed and gagged and stashed in the cellar.

Bert stepped up and said, "I'll ride for the sheriff, Mrs. Carr."

"Thank you, Bert."

His mother called out, "Hold on a moment, son. Mrs. Carr, Trudy never explained how this soldier came to be in the house."

Trudy shot her future mother-in-law such an ugly look, Jo cringed.

Mrs. Carr said, "She's right, Tru. Did he force his way inside?"

Trudy, who must have known her goose was cooked, sighed and said, "No. I—I let him in."

The choir ladies gasped collectively. Jo knew this story would be all over town before nightfall.

Mrs. Carr studied her daughter. "What do you mean, you let him in? Why?"

Trudy looked up into her mother's eyes. "I...told him he could call on me."

"All the while knowing I'd be away for the day?"

Trudy nodded sadly.

Mrs. Waterman sneered. "Well, there's no way my Bert is going to marry a girl like that. Who knows what she and that soldier might have engaged in before he robbed you, Barbara. The engagement is off. Come, Bert."

Mrs. Carr wheeled on Mrs. Waterman. "How dare you slander my girl!"

Mrs. Waterman chuckled bitterly. "I don't need to slander her. She's doing just fine on her own."

Bert looked heartbroken but agreed. "Mama's right. The engagement's off, Trudy."

"But, Bert, I—"

He was tight-lipped. "Goodbye, Trudy. Mrs. Carr. I'll stop by and alert the sheriff on my way home."

Trudy was crying for real now. "Bert, I'm sorry. I—"

Bert gave Trudy a final stony look, then followed his mother back to the carriage. They drove away.

After the departure of the Watermans, Mrs. Carr said softly but firmly to her daughter, "In the house, Trudy. We'll talk in a while."

"Yes, Mama." Trudy ran inside, crying. Jo felt like crying, as well.

Mrs. Carr said to the choir members, "Under the circumstances, I don't think we'll be having rehearsal here tonight, ladies." She turned and walked stiffly back to the house, then went inside and closed the door.

The choir members were whispering and nudging one another as they dispersed.

Jo asked her mother, "Do you think we should offer to help Mrs. Carr put the house back in order?"

Cecilia hugged her daughter's waist. "Not today. If they need us, they'll let us know."

Jo felt so sorry for Trudy.

Cecilia must have sensed Jo's concern. "Come on, darling, let's go on home. Trudy and Barbara will work things out. It'll be all right."

Jo nodded, but took one last longing look at the closed door and silently sent Trudy a prayer.

Later that evening, Cecilia stopped by Jo's room and asked, "Did you know about Trudy inviting Reed over to the house?"

"No." On one level the answer was a lie, but on another, Jo had answered truthfully. Trudy had only been thinking about ruining her life when Jo last spoke with her on Sunday.

"It's certainly a mess," Cecilia offered sadly.

"It certainly is. I hope the sheriff finds him."

"I do, as well."

"Do you think Bert will ever forgive her?" Jo asked.

"I don't know. Our Trudy has created quite a scandal. No one would blame Bert if he never spoke to her again."

Jo sighed sadly. Her mother was right. A young woman's reputation was all she had, and Trudy had shattered her own in the blink of an eye—for what? Jo dearly wished to go to her friend and offer what comfort she could, but doubted Mrs. Carr would allow any visits in the foreseeable future.

After Cecilia's departure, Jo left her room and knocked on Adam's door.

He called out in response, and when Jo entered, his eyes lit up. "Well, hello, beautiful. I was wondering if you'd ever grace me with your lovely presence today."

Jo put her hand on her hip. "Adam, you promised not to call me that."

Looking puzzled, he asked with sparkling eyes, "I did?"

Jo shook her head. Despite herself, she could feel him lightening her mood. "Yes, you did. Are you so old and decrepit that your mind's going?"

"Decrepit? Hey!"

She grinned. "I stopped in to say hello and to give you something."

"What, a hard time?"

"Would you stop? This is serious."

"All right, the serious Adam is here. What do I get?"

Jo walked over to where he was seated. When she was standing in front of him, she said, "Close your eyes."

"You aren't going to hit me over the head with something, are you?"

She giggled. "No."

"Good." He closed his eyes.

Once he did, Jo leaned down and gave him a soft kiss on his golden cheek. She whispered, "Thank you, Adam."

He opened his eyes and studied her slowly. "What was that for?"

"For being you."

He studied her again. "I'm not complaining, but I'd like to understand."

"Trudy let a man into her house while her mama wasn't home today, and he tied her up and robbed them."

"What!"

"Yes."

"Was she hurt?"

"Just her dignity."

"Did someone get the sheriff?"

"Yes."

"Maybe he'll be caught, then." Adam asked, "Is that why you looked so sad when you came in?"

She nodded. "She is in so much trouble." Jo added,

"And Mrs. Waterman was there and told Trudy the engagement was off."

"Trudy's engaged to Mrs. Waterman?"

Jo rolled her eyes. "I can't believe you asked that with a straight face."

He grinned. "Well, is she?"

"No, you woodenhead. Trudy's engaged to Bert Waterman."

"Little Bert Waterman who used to cry all the time?"

"Yes."

"Then Trudy *is* engaged to Mrs. Waterman. I remember her. Never had a kind word to say about anyone but her son. Didn't Bert enlist?"

"No. Mrs. Waterman wouldn't let him."

Adam whistled. "Trudy may be better off without those two."

"But she loves him, Adam. Or at least she did before she met Dred Reed."

"Dred Reed. Why is that name familiar?"

"He's one of the soldiers staying with Mrs. Oswald. You were introduced to him on Sunday."

"Ah." Adam remembered. "And that's who robbed the Carrs?"

Jo nodded.

He shook his head sadly. "Did he know Trudy's mother wouldn't be home?"

"Yes, because Trudy told him."

Adam stared at her in disbelief. "Trudy told him?"

"She invited him to the house. She just wanted to sit on the porch and talk."

"But she got trussed up and robbed instead."

"Yes."

"She was lucky to have gotten off so lightly. The results

could have been far more disastrous. Do you understand now why I insisted on playing chaperone?"

"I do. That's why I kissed you."

"Well, you're welcome."

The moment lengthened and suddenly Jo thought it best she get going. "Well, I'm going to go to my room, write to Papa and Dani, then go to sleep. My first appointment tomorrow is at seven."

"A.M.?"

"Yes. Some of my clients like to get their hair done early so they can get on with their day."

"Well, I won't be up at seven. Your mother has been encouraging me to be a lazybones and I'm taking full advantage of it."

"Enjoy it while you can because once you're up and around, she's going to work you like she works everyone else who lives here."

Jo went to the doorway, then looked back and said, "Thanks again."

"Anytime. Get some rest."

She nodded and left him alone.

Adam sat there for a moment. The effects of Jo's softly bestowed kiss continued to touch him like sunlight. The brief brush of her lips against his cheek had been innocent, yet so stirring. Adam realized he had a serious problem; in spite of his wishes to the contrary, his feelings for Josephine Best were growing stronger by the day, and he had no idea how to stop them.

Jo finished her letters, then put them away. She'd take them to the post office on Monday. Readying for bed, she changed into her nightclothes and put a mobcap over her hair. She then doused the light and fell back onto the bed. The darkness was calming, comforting. She could feel all the tension drain away. What an evening! Poor Trudy would probably never be allowed out of the house again until she turned thirty-five. The gossip was sure to be hot and thick, and by the time the story reached its zenith, who knew how inaccurate the details would turn out to be? Once again, Jo thought back on how she and Trudy once thrived on gossip, and the glee they'd always derived from gloating over someone else's misery. The shoes were on the other feet now, and they pinched mightily.

Jo's thoughts slid to Adam. That little spark of attraction she had for him hadn't gone out. The way he looked at her sometimes made her think he had a tiny spark burning for her, as well, but with him it was hard to tell. Who knew how the mind of a Casanova really worked? Because Jo had no answer for that question, she thought it best to continue to look upon Adam as a friend; that way, her feelings wouldn't be put at risk.

ten

———————————————————

Bea Meldrum stopped by late Saturday morning to check on Adam's ankle. She had him sit on the bed in his room so he could be comfortable, then carefully began undoing the bandages. "Let's see what we have here," she said as she worked.

She had packed the wound with a mixture of herbs to aid the healing. They formed a thick green patch over the wound. Bea touched the skin gingerly, trying not to disturb the herbs. "Well, Adam, I think you're healing nicely."

Adam thought so, too. To his untrained eye, the wound and seared flesh around it appeared no healthier than before, but the fire in the ankle had lessened considerably and the swelling in his foot and toes had started to subside. "How long before I can stand on it again?"

The white-haired Bea shrugged. "A week? Maybe two. It's hard to tell. You'll know when it's time. Could be months before it heals all the way through, though."

"The doctors thought they were going to have to amputate some of my toes."

Bea shook her head. "Toes look all right to me." She then studied the greenish-black herb mixture spread over the wound again. "We'll change the paste in a few days."

She gently rewrapped the ankle with a clean white rag.

When she was done, she gathered up everything and headed to the open door. "I'll stop by next week and see how things are doing with you then."

Adam nodded. "Thanks, Mrs. Meldrum."

"You keep resting yourself."

"Yes, ma'am, I will."

Adam lay back on his pillow. His wound had been serious enough to get him discharged from the Army. As a result, his future rested solely with him. Returning to Canada was an option; he had extended family there, and the war had no major impact on their everyday lives. Yet there was no real reason to return. His mother had died two years ago; Jere was still riding with the cavalry, and until the war ended, no one could make firm plans about anything. If the truth be told, he'd rather stay here and help Mrs. Best. He knew she was perfectly capable of running her household without the benefit of a man's help or interference, but he also knew that Daniel and Mr. Best would rest easier knowing their ladies had a man about the place, even one who couldn't walk without the aid of crutches. Another factor to consider: in spite of the war, and Lincoln's Emancipation Proclamation, slaves were still being sold in the South and fugitive slaves continued to stream north. Wherever fugitive slaves fled, slave catchers followed. Adam assumed Mrs. Best still had her Underground Railroad station open, so the danger of slave catchers showing up at her door remained a real threat.

He wondered what she would say to such a proposal. Soon as he healed, he'd be able to earn his keep by doing whatever chores she needed a hand with. He and Jere had inherited quite a sum of money when their mother died, and both shares were sitting in the bank in St. Catharine's, Ontario, waiting to be withdrawn. The funds made finding employment unnecessary for now and would enable him to contribute to the Best household, as well. Of course he didn't imagine Mrs. Best would actually take any money from him, but as a gentleman, Adam was duty bound to make the offer.

Becoming a temporary member of the Best family presented one problem, though: Jo. How was he going to keep his feelings from growing if he was living under her parents' roof? But then again, daily contact might make the novelty of a grown-up Jojo wear off, thus placing her back into the role of Daniel's little sister where she rightfully belonged. Adam thought the plan sounded good on paper. But on paper, men could fly.

That afternoon, when Mrs. Best brought up Adam's lunch, he used the visit to talk with her about extending his stay.

She heard him out, mulling over his reasons for a moment, then nodded. "I think that's a wonderful idea, Adam. Although we Best women are a fairly resourceful group of females, men do serve a purpose, so it never hurts to have one around."

Adam chuckled. "Thanks. I think."

Her dark eyes twinkled. "You're welcome. I think Jo and Belle will be pleased that you're going to be with us for a while, as well."

Adam was certain Belle would be, but he thought Jo might be a bit more wary. In spite of their mutual pledge to become friends again, he knew that their real relationship was still forming. "I'd like to contribute in any way I can. Once I heal, I can work on the property, do the planting."

She held up her hands and laughed. "Hold on a moment. Your eagerness is appreciated, but let's get you well first."

Adam dropped his head. "Yes, ma'am."

"Once we get you back on your feet, you may regret all that offering."

"I doubt that. I can't wait."

"Well, don't rush matters. Let yourself heal."

"Yes, ma'am."

Cecilia went to the door.

His voice stopped her. "Mrs. B.?"

She turned back. "Yes?"

"Thanks."

"None needed. You've been a son to me most of your life, Adam, and I loved your mama very much. She's up in heaven smiling down knowing she raised such a fine young man." She smiled softly. "I'll check in on you later."

Adam nodded; his heart was full knowing he'd made the right decision.

At church on Sunday, everyone was whispering about the absent Trudy and her mother, Barbara. Some had the decency to shut their mouths when Jo came near, but others like Mrs. Waterman seemed to relish relating what she'd witnessed at the Carrs' house on Friday night to anyone who would listen.

Jo walked by the Dragon Lady during the fellowship time after the service and heard her exclaim to a small group of women, "The little ninny actually invited the bounder in! Can you believe that? I, of course, put my foot down about my Bert marrying her. Who knows what really happened before he robbed her."

Jo's temper simmered, but before she could defend Trudy's honor, Cecilia Best and Vera Firestone stepped forward.

Cecilia said, "Corinne, you're not being very Christian."

Mrs. Waterman sniffed. "Being Christian has nothing to do with this. If it had, Trudy would not have done something so disgraceful and outrageous."

"We were all young once," Cecilia countered. "Who here didn't make a mistake during those years?"

The gaggle of women surrounding the Dragon Lady appeared visibly uncomfortable and Jo wondered what secrets they were harboring. She also applauded her mama for taking Trudy's side, but Jo wondered if Cecilia would be quite this understanding had Jo been the one in the middle of this mess instead of Trudy. Jo didn't want to think about that.

Cecilia continued, "Now, I think it best we support the Carr family during this ordeal, not gossip about them."

Mrs. Waterman drew herself up. "Who do you think you are, trying to lord over us?"

Jo could see the anger flash across her mother's face. *Uh-oh,* Jo said to herself and quickly looked around the church grounds in an effort to locate Belle just in case reinforcements were needed to keep Mrs. Waterman from being turned to stone. Vera Firestone, however, placed a restraining hand on the volatile Cecilia's arm before asking Mrs. Waterman, "Corinne, you and I grew up together, and I seem to remember a certain disheveled young woman whose daddy caught her on a hayride with a young man her family didn't approve of. The incident caused quite a bit of gossip back then. Do you remember that young woman's name? Didn't she have to go and stay with her grandmother or some other relative until the talk died away?"

Corinne went stiff as a post.

From the quiet knowing burning in Vera's eyes, everyone knew that the hay-riding young woman had been Mrs. Waterman. Jo wanted to cheer from the rooftops but knew better than to make a sound.

When Corinne finally spoke, she snapped, "No. I don't recall such a girl." Then she stormed off, yelling, "Bertram! Let's go!"

Watching her leave, the still-simmering Cecilia snarled under her breath, "Fat old bat!" Then she said to Jo, "You didn't hear that, Josephine."

Jo smiled. "Hear what, Mama?"

Cecilia turned to the women who were still standing there stunned, and said to them, "See you next week, ladies. Come, Josephine."

The grinning Jo followed her mama to their buggy.

The sniffles Belle had contracted a few days prior prevented her from attending church, so only Jo and her mother were able to visit with Mrs. Oswald's soldiers. When they arrived, Dred Reed's thievery and flight were the main topics of conversation; all the men were upset by his actions and were concerned the community's good will toward the soldiers might now be withdrawn.

George, seated beside Jo in the parlor, spoke for the other men gathered around when he said, "If we could catch that bounder and bring him back we would."

The men mumbled agreement.

Jo asked, "Did the sheriff come here?"

"Yes," George replied. "He asked several questions, but we could answer only those that pertained to Dred's stay here. None of us knew him before we arrived."

"Well, I hope they do catch up with him, and soon," Jo said.

As the afternoon visit with the soldiers lengthened it became apparent that Dred's actions had changed attitudes. According to Mrs. Oswald, none of the young women who'd been visiting the men on a regular basis had shown up since the robbery, and none showed up today. The loss of their company saddened Mrs. Oswald and her charges, but they all understood.

As Jo and her mother were leaving, George stepped out onto the porch with them. He said to Mrs. Best, "I'd like to pick a time to call on Josephine."

"When would you like to call?"

"Tomorrow?"

Mrs. Best chuckled. "Why not? You can come to dinner." She then looked to her daughter. "Is that all right with you, Jo?"

"Yes," Jo said. She truly wanted to change George's thinking. "That would be fine."

Cecilia declared, "Then dinner it shall be. We'll expect you around, say, four, George?"

George, who couldn't seem to take his eyes off Jo, replied, "Four is just fine."

Once they were back home, Mrs. Best started dinner. Jojo went to her room and changed out of her Sunday clothes and into an everyday skirt and blouse. After giving her hair a final pat, she left her room and went next door to check on Belle.

Jo knocked.

A hoarse-voiced Belle called back, "Come in," then broke out into a loud series of coughs.

Jo opened the door gingerly. "I don't know if I want to come in. I've no desire to catch whatever you have."

Belle, lying in bed, cracked, "I thought sisters were supposed to share everything."

"Almost everything," Jo countered sagely. She stepped inside, however, then took a seat on one of the overstuffed chairs. "How're you feeling? Can I bring you anything?"

"No, I'm fine. I'm going to wallow a bit more today, then tomorrow, it's back to work. I'm almost done with the Ann Arbor trousseau. I can't afford to get behind now. How was church?"

Jo told her all that happened, including the startling piece of gossip about Mrs. Waterman. She said to Belle, "You should have seen the Dragon Lady's face. I thought she was going to drop her teeth. She went so stiff you could've used her for a shovel."

"Well, good. Maybe she'll keep a civil tongue in her head from now on."

"Mama called her a fat old bat."

Belle's laugh was cut short by another bout of coughing. She blew her nose on a handkerchief, then said, "Your mother is both descriptive and correct."

Jo changed the subject then. "Guess what?"

"What?"

"George is coming to dinner tomorrow."

"We're not going to have to hide the valuables and the silver, are we?"

Jo rolled her eyes. "That isn't funny, Belle Best."

"I'm sorry. I couldn't resist. I'm sure George is the complete gentleman he appears to be. Does Adam know?"

"No. I haven't spoken with him yet."

Belle took a moment to study her young sister-in-law before asking, "How are you and Adam getting along?"

"We're fine" was all Jo would say. She didn't elaborate further because Belle knew Jo too well, and Jo didn't want to talk about Adam or the muddled feelings he evoked. At least not yet.

As if to prove the point, Belle said with all sincerity, "When you're ready to talk, I'm here. All right?"

Jo didn't feign ignorance, or try to deny Belle's insightfulness. Jo simply replied, "Thanks."

Jo left Belle to her sniffles, then went across the hall and stuck her head in Adam's open door. He was reading. "Hello," she called cheerily.

"Well, hello to you, too. How're the soldiers?"

"They're all well."

"Any word on that bounder, Reed?"

She shook her head. "Nothing so far. Everyone at church was gossiping about Trudy, though."

"It's to be expected. It is news in this little bitty town."

Jo sighed. "I know."

Adam had noted how lovely she looked this morning in her purple gown with the white lace inset. Her thick hair was done up elaborately but fashionably, and her dark unblemished skin glowed with health and beauty. She was by far the most radiant young woman he'd ever had the pleasure of knowing.

"George is coming for dinner tomorrow."

Her voice broke Adam's trance, and he responded testily, "Why?"

Jo's hands went to her hips. "Because he likes me and I like him."

"How much do you really know about him?"

Jo's jaw tightened. "We are not going to have this conversation, Adam Morgan."

"Just asking."

"And I expect you to be nice to him."

"Bea's confined me to my room, remember? I doubt you'll have to worry about me spoiling your fun."

"That didn't stop you last time."

And it probably won't again, he said to himself. "What time is he coming?"

"Around four."

"He won't be after the silver, will he?"

Jo wanted to sock him. "You are a cad."

"But a handsome one, don't you think?"

Jo threw up her hands, turned on her heel and stormed off.

Adam smiled, but as soon as he was alone, the smile faded. George coming to dinner was not the best news he'd heard today. Was Brooks seriously pursuing Jo, and if so, to what end? Marriage? Adam couldn't see her marrying such a provincial fellow. The man for her needed to be well educated, well traveled and able to walk proudly at her side.

But stranger things had been known to occur. The idea of Jo being some other man's sweetheart didn't sit well, though. Not at all. By all rights, Adam should be the one keeping her company; he'd known her first and had the stronger claim, even if he hadn't known she'd grow up to be so fetching. No, he couldn't have her, but the male in him didn't want her sharing her smile with anyone else, either.

On Monday afternoon at four o'clock, George arrived. He was dressed in a nice brown suit and had a bouquet of violets in his hand.

Jo ushered him inside. She was happy to see him.

He handed her the flowers. "These are for you."

Jo took the bouquet. "Thank you." She brought the fragrant blooms to her nose. They smelled wonderful. "Come on into the parlor and have a seat. I want to put these in some water."

Jo went into the kitchen where her mama and Belle were finishing up the dinner preparations.

Cecilia remarked, "My, what lovely violets."

"They're from George."

Her mama grinned. "They're beautiful. I like George, even if he does act as if I terrify him."

Jo said, "You can be very intimidating, Mama. Especially to someone who doesn't know you very well."

"Me? Really?" Cecilia replied innocently.

Belle and Jo laughed.

"Is dinner almost ready?" Jo asked. They were having roast chicken, potatoes and Belle's wonderful biscuits. Belle was feeling much better.

"Almost," her mama replied. "You go sit with George and we'll let you know when it's time."

Jo left the kitchen and placed the vase of violets in the center of the already set dining table. "This will make a beautiful centerpiece, George. Thank you."

"You're welcome. They're almost as lovely as you are."

Jo smiled.

"How's your friend Trudy?"

Jo shook her head. "I haven't spoken with her since the incident. She's probably too embarrassed to leave her house. I don't much blame her. Everyone's gossiping about her."

"That's too bad. She seems like a nice young woman."

"She is."

Jo came over and took a seat beside him on the settee.

"I've been asking around about employment," George said meaningfully.

"Anything promising?"

"So far no. The war's making it hard to find anyone willing to hire, but I'm determined to find something."

His eyes met hers and Jo could see all of his feelings. She said, "It would be nice if you could find work here."

"I know. Then you and I could get to know each other better."

Whatever George planned to say next was silenced by the sight of Adam Morgan slowly crutching his way down the staircase. "I see he's still here," George cracked.

"Yes, he is."

Jo watched Adam's progress with her arms folded and her lips pursed. He was coming to make trouble. She just knew it.

By the time Adam made it into the parlor he was so winded he immediately took a seat.

"I thought you were going to stay in your room," Jo said.

"Didn't want to miss all the fun. How are you, Brooks?"

"I'm well, Morgan. You?"

"Oh, I'm all right, be better in a week or so. When are you going home to Jackson?"

Once again, an inwardly simmering Jo longed to sock Adam.

George shrugged. "Don't know yet. May stay around for

a while. I like the scenery." He smiled at Jo, who was so mad with Adam she could spit fire.

George asked Adam, "When are you going home?"

"Not until the Best men return. Mrs. Best decided she needs a man about."

Jo stared, then asked, "You can't be serious?"

Adam smiled her way. "She didn't tell you, I take it?"

"No, she did not."

"Well, I'm here for the duration."

Jo couldn't believe her mother had made such a decision. "When did this come about?"

"A few days ago. Guess she forgot to mention it to you."

"I guess she did." Jo didn't know how to react to such potentially troubling news. According to the newspapers, the Union armies now held the upper hand in the conflict with the Confederacy, but who knew how long the war would continue? Adam Morgan could be in her hair for years!

Apparently, George was thinking the same thing. He looked appalled. "You're going to be here until the war ends?"

"Appears that way." Adam gave them both that patented Morgan smile, then settled into his seat as if he were very pleased with the world and everything in it.

Cecilia came out of the kitchen carrying the plump golden chicken on a platter. "Well, hello, George."

"Hello, Mrs. Best."

She placed the platter on the dining table. "And Adam? What brings you downstairs?"

"Tired of being cooped up. Thought I'd come down and join the festivities."

"Well, good. You didn't hurt yourself on the stairs, did you?"

"No, ma'am."

"Mama," Jo said, "Adam just informed me that he'll be staying on until Papa and Dani return."

"Yes, he will. Isn't that nice of him? Now, he may regret his offer once he recovers and I put him to work, but by then, it'll be too late."

Adam grinned at Jo. She almost stuck out her tongue in response but caught herself.

Belle entered then. She had a bowl of potatoes and a plate of biscuits on a tray. "Hello, George."

"Hello."

Upon seeing Adam, she said, "Well, hello to you, too."

"Came down to eat Dani's share of those biscuits."

Belle chuckled. "I'm sure he won't mind. Although if I don't hear from him soon, he may never get biscuits again." In contrast to her sassy words, she had a slight sheen of tears in her eyes.

Mrs. Best gave Belle a reassuring pat on the back. "We'll hear from them soon. Mark my word. Let's take our seats."

Once everyone was settled, Mrs. Best looked over at George seated next to Jo and asked, "George, will you bless the table, please?"

To Jo's delight, he didn't hesitate. His prayer was appropriate, and when he was done speaking, Mrs. Best said in a pleased-sounding voice, "Thank you, George."

"You're welcome."

Jo's insides were beaming with pride. Adam did not look impressed, but Jo was determined to ignore him even if the roof fell on his head.

eleven

After dinner ended, Mrs. Best and Belle cleaned off the table while Jo and George went out to the front porch. Adam hobbled over to a chair so as to not be in Belle or Mrs. Best's way. He forced himself to sit even though he would have preferred to go out to the porch and spy on Jo and George Brooks. Doing so would only relight Jo's fuse and Adam didn't want to risk that. Telling himself that Brooks's intentions toward Jo were none of his business made no difference to Adam. He wanted to know what they were doing and what sweet nothings Brooks might be whispering in her ears.

Mrs. Best's voice broke into his reverie. "Adam, you're scowling. Is your ankle paining you?"

"Uh, no," he answered hastily. "I'm fine."

"Are you sure?"

"Yes."

She didn't appear to believe him, but went ahead and removed the last of the dishes from the table, then disappeared back into the kitchen. Adam resumed scowling.

Meanwhile, outside on the porch, Jo was listening to George's vision of his future. He said, "I wouldn't mind having a passel of children and a wife who was devoted to them and to me."

"But not a wife intent upon her family and a business enterprise?" Jo asked.

George said, "That would be fine for a while, but after the children are born, I'd expect her to focus on being a mother."

Jo felt that familiar deflated feeling return. "It isn't fair to your wife to make her choose, George."

"I don't agree."

"I think a woman can do both," Jo insisted.

He shook his head. "Maybe some women can, but I wouldn't want my wife to. The family should be her business, and she should let her husband guide her future."

Jo couldn't help herself. She giggled.

George eyed her curiously. "What's so funny?"

"I'm sorry. I just— George, this is the nineteenth century. How can you be so—"

"Traditional?"

Backward had been the word Jo would have used, but decided his choice to be more diplomatic. "Yes, traditional."

"I feel very strongly about the roles in a marriage."

"As do I, and as an Oberlin graduate with my own business, I doubt I need my husband telling me what I may or may not do. My mama would have a fit if Papa tried to direct her life."

"Then maybe your papa should put his foot down."

Jo cocked her head his way, then said flatly, "Papa doesn't want to put his foot down. He's very proud of Mama and her accomplishments."

"Women were created to be a helpmate to their husbands."

Jo found this conversation maddening. "Women are more than just helpers, George."

"Not where I'm from."

"And you expect your wife to defer to you in all things?"

"I do," George said with a confident smile.

She shook her head and chuckled. "Well, be prepared to have your mind changed."

"There's nothing to change. A man is the head of his house." His smile remained steady.

"George, who on earth is going to marry you under such antiquated circumstances? It's a new world. Women are studying to be doctors. They own newspapers, they're going to colleges. What if you and your wife have daughters? Are you planning to let them grow up ignorant and—" She noticed that he'd gone silent. "George?"

"If a woman loves a man, she will defer to him." George wasn't smiling quite so hard now. It was clear he meant every word he was saying to her.

Jo found his stubbornness very disappointing. Both her papa and brother firmly believed in a woman's ability to know her own mind and make her own way. In reality, there were many progressive men around, but apparently George couldn't be counted among them. Or at least not yet. "Do you mind if I attempt to change your thinking?" Jo asked bluntly.

He responded with a twinkle in his eye. "Only if you afford me the same opportunity."

Jo had never backed down from a challenge in her life. "You have a deal."

They grinned at each other, then settled back onto the bench to talk about something else.

Jo asked, "What's your favorite dessert?" She was hoping to find something they had in common.

"Blueberry pie."

Her eyes widened with glee. "Mine, too. Oh, my."

He asked, "What's your favorite color?"

"Violet. And yours?"

He shrugged. "Don't have one really."

Jo chuckled. "Then why'd you ask?"

"Because most girls have a special color and I wanted to know yours."

Jo felt warm inside. "That's sweet."

"So, those flowers were a mark in my favor?" he asked.

"Yes. Violets were the perfect choice."

"Good. I'm glad."

They spent the next few hours talking about everything and nothing, but as dusk fell, Jo knew it was time for George to go. Except for their earlier debate over a woman's place, they'd gotten along rather well. Jo felt as if she knew him much better now. Her first dinner with a gentleman caller had been a success, if one didn't count his stubborn, outdated thinking. "I enjoyed your company, George."

"I enjoyed yours, Josephine. I'd like to do it again, real soon."

She looked over at him. "So would I."

"I heard Mrs. Oswald's planning an ice-cream social on Saturday. Do you think your mama might let you attend?"

"I don't know, but I will ask."

"Good."

He stood then. "I should go in and say goodbye to everyone, then get going."

"I'll come in with you."

Inside, Adam and Belle were playing checkers in the parlor. Cecilia was seated at the dining table penning a letter.

Adam looked up from the board at their entrance and asked, "Brooks, do you play checkers?"

"Sure. Can't beat Miss Belle though. She's whipped every soldier around."

Adam said, "I had hoped her skills had diminished with age, but I guess not."

"How dare you call me old," Belle tossed back. "Just for that, I'm going to beat you until we're seventy-five."

Adam said, "I don't doubt that. She's been beating all comers since she was sixteen. She's even taught the pest here to play well enough to trounce me."

Hearing herself called by her old nickname made Jo's mouth drop. Did Adam not see George standing here? Or had he done it on purpose just to embarrass her?

Adam took one look at her face and knew he'd stepped into a bear trap. He was instantly contrite, "I'm sorry, Jo. I didn't mean to call you that. It just slipped out."

George, studying the two of them, asked, "What's the matter?"

Cecilia eyed her daughter and said gently, "Nothing, George. Nothing at all."

A perturbed Jo turned away from Adam and said, "Mama, Mrs. Oswald is having an ice-cream social on Saturday. George wants to escort me. May I go?"

"We'll talk about it later," Cecilia promised. "How about you walk George out to his carriage?"

Jo shot Adam another deadly glare, then escorted George out of doors.

He climbed up on the wagon's seat and picked up the reins.

"You seem to be moving much better, George," Jo noted.

"I am. The doc comes on Tuesday. I'm hoping I can put this cane away for good after he sees me."

"That would be nice."

"Yes, it would be. It would also mean I'd have to find another place to stay. Mrs. Oswald houses only the injured."

"Well, there are at least two boardinghouses nearby. Maybe one of them would be amenable."

"Mrs. Oswald gave me a few names. I'm going to drive over tomorrow and talk with the landladies." He then added, "In the meantime, I had fun with you this evening, Josephine."

Jo smiled. "I'll see you on Saturday."

"You bet. Take care now."

"I will."

George drove off with a departing wave. Jo waved back, fighting against the notion that it might be harder to change George's thinking than she'd first assumed and that in the end, he might not be the man for her. Once he'd driven from sight, though, she headed back to the house to confront Adam.

Adam hoped Jo had forgiven him for calling her by her childhood name, but the look on her face when she came barreling back inside plainly showed she hadn't. In fact, the first terse words directed his way were, "Thank you very much, Adam Morgan."

"Jo, I really am sorry. I did apologize."

"Do you have any idea how embarrassed I was?"

"Jo, I'm sure Adam didn't mean to embarrass you on purpose, dear," her mother put in.

Jo longed to tell her mother to mind her own business, but knew better than to voice such disrespect. Instead, she said, "I'm going to my room. I'll see you all later on."

And on that note, she left the parlor.

Had Adam not been crippled by his ankle injury, he would have gone after her, but—

He looked over at Mrs. Best, who seemed to be eyeing him closely. She asked, "It was an accident, wasn't it, Adam?"

"Yes, ma'am. I swear it was. The last thing I want is to have her angry at me."

Belle was already upstairs, so Adam and Cecilia were the only people in the room. "May I ask you a frank question?" Mrs. Best asked him.

Her tone made Adam a bit wary, but he nodded. "Yes."

"Do you have feelings for my daughter?"

Adam very much wanted to duck the question, but he

knew better than to try and pull the wool over the eyes of a woman everyone knew could see through walls, so he confessed truthfully, "Yes. I believe I do."

"Does Jo return your feelings?"

He shrugged. "Not really. We talked about it briefly, but I wound up mucking things up."

"Josephine is a very headstrong and determined young woman."

"I know."

Mrs. Best studied him for a few moments before saying, "Truthfully, if you and Jo were to iron out your differences and declare for each other, I'd be as happy as I was when Dani and Belle fell in love. It would please me no end to have you for a son-in-law. However, your reputation with the young women is well known, Adam, so I'm warning you right now, if you break my daughter's heart, I will roast you like a piece of pork. Do you understand me?"

Adam didn't hesitate. "Yes, ma'am. That was one of the reasons Jo and I decided to just be friends for now. I'm not certain I'm ready to settle down."

"I appreciate your honesty."

"Well, Jo didn't." Adam scowled.

"If you aren't sure about how you feel about her, Adam, you have no reason to scowl when she is with someone else."

"I know, but— Oh, I don't know, Mrs. B."

She nodded understandingly. "Give it time, Adam. Even if you and Josephine decide to remain just friends, you will always be welcomed here as long as you don't break her heart."

"May I have George kidnapped and sent to Siam?"

She chuckled. "No, you may not. I won't be interfering in my daughter's life and neither will you."

Adam shrugged. "It was worth a try."

Cecilia's smile broadened. "If I were you, I'd be trying to

come up with a way to get back into Jo's good graces. You stepped into quite a bog calling her Pest."

"Don't remind me." Adam could only speculate how long it would be before Jo smiled his way again. "Any suggestions?"

"Nope. As I said, I'm not meddling, nor will I be promoting one suitor over another. Now, if George turns out to be someone other than the man he's presented himself as being, that changes things, but unless that happens, I'm content to sit back and watch."

"Thanks," Adam said glumly.

Amused, she told him, "You're welcome." She resumed her letters.

Adam resumed his brooding.

In the days following George's visit, Jo and Adam saw very little of each other. She spent most of her time doing heads at her shop. It seemed every woman in town planned to attend the social at Mrs. Oswald's on Saturday, and because everyone wished to look their best, Jo and her irons worked from sunup to sundown.

Adam spent his time recovering in his room. Bea Meldrum stopped by and removed the herbs from his ankle. The paste had worked remarkably well. The skin had begun knitting itself back together and the pain and swelling were no longer an issue. Bea was so pleased by his progress she gave Adam her permission to graduate from his crutches to a walking stick. Adam responded with a grateful "Hallelujah!"

On Thursday evening, a knock sounded on Jo's closed bedroom door. "Come in," she called back. She was in the process of going through her wardrobe in search of something to wear to the social that George hadn't already seen her wear. The visitor turned out to be her mother.

She asked Jo, "What are you doing, dear?"

"I'm trying to find a gown that everyone in town hasn't already seen me in two dozen times." Jo had been given permission to attend the social with George. He'd sent a note around to let her know what time to be ready. Belle would be going with them, as well, but Jo didn't mind having her sister-in-law tag along.

Cecilia took a seat on the end of the bed. "The war will be over soon, and once it's done I'll have Belle treat you to a new gown or two."

"That would be wonderful. I can't wait to finally say goodbye to the Free Produce tenets." None of the Best women had had new gowns in years. "In the meantime, I guess I'll have to make do with this old green one."

"It's still in good shape, Jo. No one else will be sporting anything new, either."

Her mother was right, of course. Most of the families in town adhered to the Free Produce edicts. Still, Jo dearly wished the war would end, not only for the freedom it would bring to the three and a half million enslaved souls in the South, but for the freedom from worry it would bring to all who had soldiers in the South. She thought about her father and brother but didn't mention them in an effort not to make her mother sad.

After resigning herself to the fact that the green gown would have to do, Jo took a seat on the bed and said to her mother, "May I talk to you about something?"

"Sure."

Jo took a moment to think over what she wanted to say, then began, "George doesn't think a woman should own a business after she has babies."

Mrs. Best studied her. "Why not?"

"He says a woman should devote herself to her family, and be guided by her husband."

"Having babies doesn't make a woman feeble-minded, Josephine."

"I know, Mama. I tried to explain that to him, but his thinking seems set on the matter." Jo looked over at her mother to gauge how she might be taking the conversation. Jo didn't put it past her mother to forbid her daughter from ever seeing the wrong-thinking George Brooks again.

Cecilia asked instead, "So, what do you want to discuss?"

"Do you think he'll change, is what I'm asking, I guess."

"A better question is, do *you* think he will change?" her mother replied. "You've always been a good judge of character, dear, but I believe all men can be put into two categories. There are the intelligent ones who have no quarrel with the free-thinking and free-acting women like the ones you've been raised around. Then there are the ones who will go to their grave still believing they've a God-given right to lord it over the so-called weaker sex."

"Do you put George in that second category?"

"I have no way of knowing where George fits. That's why men and women court, so you can have these thorny questions answered *before* you decide to embark on a life together."

Jo understood. "Well, I like him very much, I think, but—"

"You have your doubts?"

"I do, but I'm hoping he might be one of the intelligent ones, Mama. Maybe being around you, me and Belle will change his views."

"You may be right." Mrs. Best smiled at her daughter. "If anyone can change his mind, you can, dear."

"I hope so. Oh, and thanks for letting me go to the social with him."

"I trust you two will behave yourselves."

"You won't have to worry. With half the town in attendance, I'm certainly not going to do something that will probably get back to you before I even get home."

Mrs. Best chuckled. "You always were a smart girl."

"I wonder if Trudy will be there," Jo mused aloud.

Her mother shrugged. "No one has seen her mother."

"I haven't seen Trudy, either. Maybe I'll drive over there after work tomorrow. It has been nearly a week since they were robbed, so maybe Trudy's off punishment."

"Well, go by and see. I hope everything is all right over there."

"Me, too."

Cecilia got up and walked to the door. "I'm going to bed now, dear. I'll see you in the morning."

"Good night, Mama. Thanks for listening."

"You're welcome. Oh, have you and Adam made up?"

"I haven't seen him. I've been too busy."

"You've been too busy being mad, isn't that what you mean?"

Sometimes, Jo hated having a mother who was so wise. She sighed. "He thinks I'm still twelve, Mama."

"Then stop acting as if you are."

Jo came to her own defense. "What do you mean?"

"A mature young woman accepts a sincere apology. She does not walk around the house holding her breath like a six-year-old. It's neither Christian nor becoming, Josephine."

Jo listened, but she didn't want to, mainly because she knew her mother was right. Again. "I'll talk to him."

"Good. We're supposed to be fighting the Rebs, not each other."

"Yes, ma'am."

Mrs. Best smiled her love. "Get some sleep, sweetheart."

Jo nodded.

Her mother slipped out and closed the door softly.

Alone now, Jo supposed she had been acting like a child. She'd been purposefully avoiding Adam simply because he'd accidentally called her a name she'd grown up under. In hindsight, she admitted that he had used the nickname affectionately, as always, but she certainly hadn't responded in kind. She initially chalked up her tantrum to George's presence; no woman wants a suitor to know she once answered to the name Pest! Now, however, she wasn't sure what had triggered her reaction. Being angry at him certainly kept her other feelings for him buried and at bay. Maybe staying mad would be a perfect cure-all; not that her mama would allow it. The soft-spoken lecture her mother had just issued might have been a gentle one, but the meaning was clear. Cecilia Best expected Jo to make up with Adam, and soon.

Deciding she'd best get it over with, Jo left her room and knocked upon Adam's partially opened door. "May I come in?"

He set aside his book. "Sure."

"I...just stopped by to say hello."

"Hello," he said to her. Out of all the young women he'd met, he wondered why this one would affect him so. Just the sight of her made his insides grin. "I haven't seen you in a few days. All the ladies must be after you to get them gussied up for the social."

"Yes, I have been swamped, but...I've been mad at you, as well."

"I know."

"I've come to apologize for not accepting your apology in the spirit in which it was given. Mama says I've been acting like a six-year-old holding her breath."

"There's no way you're going to get me to even discuss that, let alone agree with your mother."

Jo smiled.

"But I accept your apology, and once again, I'm sorry."

"Thanks." Jo could feel herself getting all confused inside again, a common affliction when she was around him. "Well, I'm going to bed. I'll see you tomorrow."

"Good night, Jo."

"Good night, Adam."

As darkness fell, Adam and Jo crawled into their separate beds and they both slept soundlessly for the first time in many days.

Jo confessed because deep down in her heart she knew it to be true. Trudy loved Bert; always had, always would.

"Why would she do such a thing?"

Jo shrugged, then said softly, "I don't know. Sometimes people don't think, and this seems to be one of those times."

"But we were engaged to be married," he pointed out emotionally.

"I know."

He stayed quiet for a few moments. The soft singing of the birds was the only sound. "I doubt I'll ever love anyone as much."

That gave Jo hope. "Have you talked with her?"

"No."

"Do you plan to?"

"I don't know. One minute I want to ride over and tell her I forgive her, but the next minute I want to leave town and never see her again."

He met Jo's eyes. "And I know you've heard all the gossip."

She had.

"I'm a laughingstock, Jo. If folks aren't laughing, they're looking at me with pity."

Jo reached out and put a hand on his arm. "Maybe you and Trudy need to talk this out. I'm sure she's as miserable as you seem to be."

"I'm not miserable. I'm angry, dammit! Sorry."

Jo smiled softly. She'd never seen Bert riled up.

He told Jo tightly, "I know I'm not the handsomest man around. I know that I'm not terribly exciting or glib, but Trudy knew that when I gave her my heart. She's always looking to get swept off her feet by some mythical daredevil, and I was willing to put up with it because that's Trudy—it's how she is. But for her to actually act on something as hare-brained as this? She could have been hurt, Jo. Very badly."

twelve

It was just past dawn when Jo quietly slipped out of the house and headed off to work. The air was fresh, the birds were singing and the sun was bright orange in the light gray sky. As a child, Jo had detested rising early. Had her mama allowed it, Jo would have slept in every day until noon. Older now, she'd begun to appreciate the peaceful serenity of a beautiful morning.

The sight of Bert Waterman sitting on the ground in front of the door of her shop brought her up short, though.

Bert nodded tersely. "Mornin', Jo."

Jo approached slowly. "Mornin', Bert." She wondered how long he'd been waiting and why he'd come.

"I need to talk with you, if I might."

"Certainly." Jo fit the key into the lock. "You want to come inside?"

"No. Having one compromised girl in town is enough. How about we talk out here?"

It pleased her to know he still had his dry sense of humor. "All right." She smoothed her skirts beneath her, then sat on the ground in front of him.

"Do you think she still loves me?"

Jo didn't have to ask to whom he was referring. "I do,"

"I know, Bert."

"But does *she* know? Should I go out and slay a bunch of bears to make her believe I'm exciting enough to be her husband? Do I have to go and find Dred Reed myself to prove to her and the town that I don't have oatmeal for a spine?"

Jo didn't like the sound of that. "Now, Bert. I—"

"My mother is already planning who I'm going to marry next. Can you believe that?" He rubbed his hands over his short hair. "Lord, I should have gone to the war. Fighting Rebs has to be easier than this."

Jo's heart went out to him. "So what are you going to do?"

"I've been asking myself the same question for the past few days, and I've decided to do two things. First, I'm going to move out of my mother's house. I love her very much, but I can't stomach it one more hour."

Jo fought to keep the smile from showing on her face. "And the second? You're going to talk with Trudy?"

"No, I'm going to find Dred Reed."

Her eyes widened with alarm. "You can't be serious."

He stood. "I've been tied to my mother's apron strings all of my life. I'm twenty-one years old—it's time I started walking on my own. Part of being a man is protecting the ones you love."

Jo scrambled to her feet. "But, Bert—"

"Look, Jo. The sheriff has men watching the train stations, and so far Reed hasn't shown himself, nor has he been spotted on any of the main roads. The sheriff is pretty certain Reed's still in the area."

Jo didn't like the idea of this at all. "Cutting your mama's apron strings and confronting a criminal are two different things, Bert Waterman."

"I know, but Trudy is my intended and it's my job to protect her, especially with her father away fighting."

"You should let the sheriff handle this."

"No. It's my responsibility."

"That doesn't make sense, Bert."

"Do you think your father and brother would stand around if Dred had done to you what he did to Trudy?"

She had to answer truthfully, "No."

"Well, neither will I."

Jo could not believe this. "You are not to go after Dred Reed."

"I'm going, Jo, and I'm going to find him and bring him back to face the law, and when I do, you tell Trudy I expect her to have on her wedding dress. We're getting married and I'm having no more of her foolishness."

That said, he mounted his horse and rode away. Jo was so astonished she couldn't move.

Jo worried about Bert for the remainder of the day. What if he really did stumble across Dred? Jo applauded Bert for wanting to free himself from his mother's yoke, but this mess with Trudy was having repercussions no one had foreseen. Jo had known Bert her whole life and she could never remember him being this upset. She knew that people could be changed by events in their lives, but she never imagined it would happen to someone like Bert. Bert seemed to have been transformed by the firestorm surrounding Trudy's actions, and in place of the agreeable, boring old Bert stood a confident and assertive Bertram Waterman. She saw this new version giving Trudy fits. She smiled to herself at the idea of Trudy being given a run for her money, but Jo's amusement was tempered by her worries over Bert's safety. Jo had to talk with Trudy as soon as possible—maybe she could make him see reason—but Jo had so many customers, it was impossible for her to get away until the last head was done.

And that last head belonged to Mrs. Corinne Waterman. Accompanying her was a tall and beautiful dark-skinned young woman Jo had never met.

Mrs. Waterman made the introductions. "Josephine Best, this is my niece, Libby Spenser. Libby, Josephine."

Libby looked to be about Jo's age.

Mrs. Waterman continued, "Libby will be staying with us for several weeks. Her parents thought she might find the country air pleasing."

"Welcome to Whittaker, Libby," Jo said genuinely. "And country air is about all we have around here, so be warned."

Libby looked amused. "Thanks. I'm from Chicago. A place this small will take some getting accustomed to."

"Well, if you need any help adjusting just let me know."

"I'll hold you to that."

On the surface, Libby seemed nice, which made Jo question the Dragon Lady's claim that the two were related.

As Jo began on Mrs. Waterman's hair, Libby looked around and asked, "Is this your mama's shop, Jo?"

"No, it's mine."

Libby appeared surprised by the answer. "Really?"

"Yes."

"I'm impressed. I wish I could own my own business. Quite a few women in Chicago do, but I have neither the smarts nor the desire."

Jo set the cooled-off curling irons on the brazier to heat again before picking up one of the hot ones. "You can be whatever you want to be, Libby."

Libby shrugged. "Oh, I know, but all I want is to marry a man who won't want me to do anything but look beautiful and grace his table."

Jo stared at her. "Really?"

"Yes, I'm very traditional."

George came to Jo's mind. She wondered if the two would hit it off. That Jo had considered fixing George up with someone else spoke volumes about her own commitment to him, but she chose not to admit the obvious to herself, at least not yet. Instead, she refocused her attention on Mrs. Waterman's hair.

While she worked, Jo wondered if Bert had informed his mother of his plans to move. She assumed not since she hadn't arrived spitting fire. It was quite possible that after Bert went home, he had calmed down and changed his mind, Jo reasoned. She hoped he had, but she still wanted to talk with Trudy about him. Jo also wanted to see Trudy to make certain she was all right.

Mrs. Waterman asked, "Josephine, how is Adam Morgan getting along?"

"He's well. He's now walking with a stick instead of the crutches."

"I'm thinking of introducing Libby to him."

"Aunt Corinne says he's very handsome," Libby said, looking pleased. "Is he wealthy, as well?"

Jo was so taken aback by the blunt question, she didn't quite know how to respond. "Well, I'm not sure."

Libby replied, "It would be nice if he were. There's nothing better than a handsome and wealthy young man, don't you think?"

Jo changed her mind. Libby was indeed related to the Dragon Lady.

Jo closed the shop after Mrs. Waterman and Libby departed, then headed across the field for home. Libby Spenser was still on Jo's mind, however, having replaced Bert for the moment. Would the Waterman niece really train her sights on Adam? Jo couldn't see Adam being attracted to such a potentially predatory female, but Libby was very pretty, so who knew? Adam had never impressed her as being susceptible to shallow girls, though. He'd detested Francine, the wealthy, snobbish girl Dani had been sweet on before Belle came north. Libby reminded Jo of Francine quite a bit. Jo then chastised herself for even being concerned about whether Adam would like Libby or not; after all, Jo and Adam were nothing more than friends.

After hastily consuming her dinner, Jo rode her mare over to Trudy's house. Upon seeing Trudy sitting on the porch, Jo waved happily and Trudy waved in reply. Jo was glad to see that Trudy's mama had decided to let Trudy live.

Barbara Carr stepped out onto the porch just as Jo walked up. Mrs. Carr had never been a smiling woman, so Jo found it hard to gauge her mood. "Evening, Mrs. Carr," Jo said politely. "I came by to see if Trudy can have company."

Mrs. Carr scanned her daughter's face. Jo could see the hope in Trudy's eyes. Apparently Mrs. Carr could, too. "I suppose. No more than an hour though."

"Yes, ma'am, and thank you."

Mrs. Carr stepped off the porch and walked slowly in the direction of the greenhouses. Watching her depart, Jo let out a sigh of relief.

Jo joined Trudy on the porch and the two shared an enthusiastic hug before they each took a seat on the steps.

"I'm glad you came," Trudy said. "I've been so lonely cooped up here."

"How's your mother treating you?"

"Well, she's not as mad as she was, but I've been walking on eggshells trying not to set her off again."

Jo nodded sympathetically. "I've been worried about you."

"Thanks, but if I had known this was going to happen, I never would have looked twice at Dred Reed."

Jo thought about Bert. "As my papa likes to say, you live and you learn."

"Oh, I've learned my lesson well. No more adventurous males for me. If I could turn back time, I'd take my bland, boring Bert Waterman and count myself blessed."

"That's one of the reasons I had to see you. Bert stopped by my shop this morning."

Trudy asked quietly, "How is he?"

"Angry."

Trudy dropped her head.

"He said he would never love anyone as much."

Trudy's head shot up. "He said what?"

Jo repeated herself.

Trudy fell back against the porch post and said in a dreamy voice, "He said that?"

"He did."

"I don't deserve him, Jo. I'd be miserable for the rest of my life if he never spoke to me again, but I'd understand why he wouldn't want to."

"The two of you need to talk, but I've no idea how you'll arrange to with you being on punishment and all."

"Neither can I."

"Well, I want you to think on it because you're probably the only person I know who might be able to talk him out of going after Dred Reed."

"What!"

"Yes, Trudy. He believes it is his job to avenge your honor and his. He's planning on finding Dred and bringing him to justice."

"That's ridiculous. He could be hurt."

Jo didn't reply.

"This is all my fault."

"I hate to agree with you, but you're right."

Trudy crossed her arms and sat back again. "I've done some silly things in my life, Jojo, but this is the silliest. What if Bert is killed?"

"I doubt it will come to that," Jo countered, "but somehow, you need to speak with him."

"I'll work on it," Trudy vowed. "If I have to sneak out and ride my horse in the middle of the night, Bert has to be made to see reason."

"Oh, I almost forgot. He said to tell you that after he hands Dred over to the sheriff, he expects you to have on your wedding dress."

Trudy's mouth dropped.

"He said you two are getting married and he wants no more of your foolishness."

Trudy squealed with glee. She threw her arms around Jo and did a seated version of a jig.

The two friends jumped and laughed and Trudy had tears in her eyes. She said seriously, "If he's willing to forgive me, I plan on being the best wife anyone has ever seen. Oh, I love him so!"

Jo smiled. "I should hope so." Jo then told her about Bert's pledge to move out of the Dragon Lady's house.

For a moment Trudy could only stare. She finally said, "My goodness. What has come over him?"

Jo shook her head. "I've no idea, but it looks like the Dragon Lady might not be going on your honeymoon after all."

They both keeled over with laughter. When they finally came up for air, Trudy gushed, "Jo, this is all so exciting."

"Yes, it is."

"Well, I'm going to find a way to see Bert. Don't worry about him anymore."

Jo nodded but knew she would anyway, at least until the sheriff caught Dred and tossed him in the town jail.

They spent a few more moments talking about Bert, then Jo said, "Oh, I almost forgot. I met Bert's cousin Libby this morning."

Trudy made a face. "I met her once last year. Didn't care for her at all."

"Why not?"

"A bit fast for me."

Jo gave her a look.

"I know, I know. Who am I to be calling the kettle black after the mess I caused, but she's really fast, Jo. Bert thought she might be coming to stay here for a while because her parents can't control her. They're hoping Bert's mama might be able to put reins on her. I guess Libby was seeing a man her parents didn't approve of. Bert mentioned something about the man being old but quite well off, but Bert and I never discussed the full story."

Jo was impressed. "My."

"I know."

"Well, the Dragon Lady said Libby would be here through July."

"Lord, she'll have driven poor Bert around the bend by then."

"Maybe she's changed."

"Maybe Dred Reed's going to return the things he stole."

Jo chuckled. "Fine, I understand. At least now I'll know to avoid Libby as much as possible." Jo suddenly remembered something else. "Add this to the pot. Mrs. Waterman wants to introduce Libby to Adam."

"What on earth for?"

"Because he's handsome and may have money, and according to Libby, Adam is just the type of husband she's on the hunt for."

"I don't see Adam being fooled by her, no matter how pretty she is."

"Neither do I, but stranger things have happened."

"And how do you feel about that?"

"What do you mean?"

"How do you feel about another girl tossing her hat in the ring for Adam?"

"Why should I care?" Jo shrugged her shoulders but wouldn't look Trudy in the eye.

"Because you do, Josephine Best."

"I do not."

Trudy looked skeptical. "Fine."

"I don't."

Trudy remained silent.

"You don't believe me?"

"I'm the Sphinx."

Jo smiled. "All right, Miss Sphinx, it's about time for me to be getting home."

"I'll walk with you to the road."

While walking, the two friends spent a few moments talking about Mrs. Oswald's social tomorrow. Jo asked, "Is your mama going to let you go?"

"I really don't have the nerve to ask her."

Jo climbed up into the saddle. "Ask her, Trudy. Everyone in town will be there. I'd so like for you to be there, as well."

"Me, too. Maybe I can catch her in a good mood. If she says yes, I'll look for you when I arrive."

"Okay." Jo picked up the reins. "Bye, Tru. I hope you can come."

"Bye, Jo. Keep your fingers crossed, and I'll see Bert somehow."

They both waved goodbye, then Jo kicked the mare into a gallop toward home.

On the ride back to her house, Jo went over the conversation she and Trudy had shared about Adam and decided her friend's assessment wasn't worthy of even contemplating. If Libby Spenser wanted to throw herself at Adam's feet, it was none of Jo's concern. Yes, Jo was honest enough to admit she still had a tiny crush on Adam, but that didn't mean she intended to spend the rest of her life waiting to see if her feelings were returned. She and Adam had already settled the matter, so Trudy's idea that Jo might be bothered by Libby's quest didn't hold water. Or at least that's what Jo told herself.

Jo made herself conjure up George in hopes of keeping thoughts of Adam at bay, and it worked, but not in the way she'd imagined. Thinking about George only served to bring up all the doubts she'd been having about him lately. Yes, George was a decent young man. Yes, he was good company and a true gentleman. The woman he married wouldn't have to worry about him wandering off to pick flowers; George Brooks didn't appear to have a deceitful bone in his body, but in her heart of hearts, Jo knew George would never be more than a friend. Even if she had been looking to measure him for beau material, he would be found lacking. Growing up around her parents had shown Jo just how passionate and loving a marriage could be. There was no question that William and Cecilia Best loved each other deeply, and if Jo ever married she wanted that depth of commitment, too. There seemed to be no fire in George, however; no passion. Even though he was the very first male company she'd ever had over to the house, and the first man to bring her flowers, she didn't see herself arguing with George over substantive issues like politics the way her parents sometimes did. In his world such discussions probably weren't encouraged; women had a distinct place that a man defined. Jo had no desire to live in such a rigid world where she couldn't have her own place of business. Nor did she want any children she might have growing up with a parent unwilling to let them be who they wished to be. *So when are you going to tell him?* the tiny voice in her head asked. *As soon as I figure out how to do it without hurting him,* she answered herself, all the while knowing it might be easier said than done.

thirteen

when Jo rode up to the house, she was surprised to see the Waterman buggy parked out front. Jo thought Mrs. Waterman had gone home after her hair appointment, so why had she returned? It wasn't as if Corinne Waterman and Jo's mother were friends; the two never visited back and forth. Jo assumed the answer would be revealed once she went inside.

After putting the horse in the barn, Jo entered the house through the back door and heard voices coming from the front room. She passed through the deserted kitchen and came out into the parlor where sat her mother, Belle, Adam, Mrs. Waterman and Libby. The cow eyes Libby had fixed on Adam solved the mystery as to why the Waterman buggy was parked outside; Libby was on the hunt. "Good evening, everyone."

Jo's mother said, "Well, welcome home, dear. How was your visit?"

"Fine." Jo was glad her mother hadn't mentioned whom she'd visited. Jo had no desire to hear Mrs. Waterman attack Trudy.

Mrs. Best added, "Corinne says you've met her niece, Libby?"

"Yes, this afternoon."

Jo nodded a greeting to Belle, then said, "Evening, Adam."

"Jo." He inclined his head politely, but his eyes upon her

were so potent with intent, she had to focus her vision else-where in order to keep herself on an even keel.

Libby said to Jo, "We were just discussing tomorrow's ice-cream social. Are you planning to attend?"

"Yes, I am." Jo knew that Adam's eyes were upon her, so she forced herself not to look his way.

"Alone?"

Jo wondered why Libby wanted to know. "Uh, no. I'm going with a friend. His name is George Brooks. Belle's also going with us."

Libby turned to Adam and pouted prettily, "I wish I had someone to escort me."

Adam knew a fishhook when he saw one—or heard one. He saw no reason not to take the bait, though. He'd been cooped up in the house seemingly for weeks, and he welcomed any opportunity to get out of doors. Agreeing to escort the Waterman niece would also give him a legitimate reason to keep a discreet eye on Jo and her precious George.

The bold Libby asked again, "Will you escort me, Adam?"

"I'd be honored to," he offered. "That is, if your aunt would approve."

Libby smiled like a pleased cat.

Mrs. Best asked skeptically, "What about your ankle, Adam?"

"Mrs. Meldrum declared me well enough to graduate to a walking stick."

"Then it's settled," Mrs. Waterman announced. "Adam, thank you for offering. Libby doesn't know many young people here. I'm sure you'll see that she gets off on the right foot."

"As I said, it would be my pleasure," Adam replied, turning on the Morgan charm.

"I'm betting we'll have a wonderful time," Libby purred.

"I'm sure we will, too."

Jo could see Adam working his magic. She found the display so irritating, she longed to tell him all about Libby and then shake him until he came back to his senses. But since he was intent upon trying all the flowers in the field, Jo decided, she didn't care what happened to him. A small voice inside her head countered, *Yes, you do, and you're jealous to boot!* The voice surprised her. Was she jealous? Jo denied it vehemently, then announced, "Well, it's been a long day for me. I'm going to head up to my room. Nice seeing you again, Libby." Her eyes glanced toward Adam. His face was emotionless, but his presence touched her as if he'd spoken her name.

"It's been nice for me, as well," Libby cooed. "I'll be seeing you tomorrow."

Jo nodded. "Good evening, Mrs. Waterman."

"Good night, Jo. I'll have Bert bring Libby by in the morning."

Jo longed to tell her that she might have to make different arrangements if Bert went through with his plans, but Jo kept that to herself.

As Jo moved to leave, Belle stood hastily, and said, "Jo, let me go up with you. Wasn't there a hem you wanted help mending?"

There was no hem, of course, but Jo caught on immediately. "I pulled out the dress this morning. Come and take a look at it."

So the two sisters-in-law escaped, leaving Adam and Mrs. Best to deal with the Dragon Lady and her kin alone.

Once Jo and Belle were safely behind Jo's closed bedroom door, Jo asked, "How long have they been here?"

"Only an hour or so, but it's been an hour or so too long. The Dragon Lady said she just happened to be in the neighborhood and thought she'd stop by."

"Hogwash." Jo snorted, then told Belle about Libby's

desire for a wealthy husband, and what Jo had learned about Libby from Trudy.

Belle listened before saying, "Now that's mighty interesting. An older man, huh?"

"Trudy said Bert didn't get the whole story."

"Well, she certainly seemed set upon Adam."

"Yes, she did, and I didn't notice him trying to fend her off. Do you think he's really taken with her?"

Belle studied Jo for a moment before replying, "There's no accounting for taste, but I believe Adam's far too sensible to be hoodwinked by such a fawning twit. Why'd you ask?"

Jo shrugged. "No reason."

Their eyes met.

Belle asked gently, "Are you sure?"

"Positive. Just curious is all."

Jo knew Belle didn't believe her, but Jo also knew Belle wouldn't pry.

Belle then said, "Well, I'm going to my room. I'll see you in the morning."

"All right."

Belle slipped out.

Downstairs, while Mrs. Best walked her guests to the door, Adam sat in the parlor awaiting her return. Libby was admittedly lovely. He didn't know if his ankle would hold up under such an outing, but he supposed he would find out.

"So," Mrs. Best asked after returning, "what do you think of Libby Spenser?"

"She's a pretty girl. Seems nice, as well. Why?"

"Just wondering. Corinne Waterman has never stopped by to visit before, so I'm assuming it was so the niece could meet you."

"I'm glad she did. I'm more than happy to show Libby around," Adam lied.

Cecilia studied him for a long moment before declaring, "Well, I'm going up to bed now. Will you put out the lamps before you turn in?"

"Sure will."

"I'll see you in the morning, then."

"Good night."

Alone now, Adam was the first to admit he'd agreed only so he could be around Jo. His admission would anger her if she knew, but he couldn't seem to help himself. It was maddening really, because he didn't want to meddle in her life, but he couldn't seem to put a damper on his feelings for her. She and George seemed quite taken with each other, which Adam found equally as maddening because George wasn't the man for her. Brooks was too passive, too agreeable. Jo needed someone who would stand up to her and for her, and George didn't impress Adam as having that much inner strength. Adam had enough confidence in the old Morgan charm to know that if he really wanted Josephine at his side George Brooks wouldn't stand a chance, but Adam wanted Jo to come to him of her own accord. She was an innocent; Adam doubted she'd ever been kissed. A man of lesser character might take advantage of that innocence to try and influence her in her choice of a sweetheart, but Adam had no intentions of sinking that low. He wanted Jo to give her heart freely, and he admittedly didn't want that heart given to George Brooks.

So, what to do? He didn't know, and that was maddening, as well. In the end, he decided his only option was to concentrate on the willowy Libby Spenser for now and figure out what to do about his feelings for Jo later.

Adam stood and stretched. True to his word, he doused all of the lamps before heading upstairs. He agreed with Mrs. Best that the Dragon Lady had probably brought Libby by this evening for the express purpose of meeting him, but Adam didn't mind because to be forewarned was to be forearmed.

The morning of the ice-cream social dawned sunny and bright. With the war on, celebrations such as the one today were few and far between. The fighting down South had cast a pall over the country, and when people did come together, it was usually for a serious event such as raising money for the Union's efforts, or for rallies like the one being held next week in Detroit. According to the newspaper, the rally organizers wanted to alert folks to the plight of the thousands of escaped slaves who'd attached themselves to Sherman's armies and were following him across the South. Aid organizations both black and white were gearing up to send blankets, food and medicine in hopes of relieving the suffering.

Today's gathering would be strictly fun, however, and Jo planned to take in as much of the good time as a properly raised young woman could stand.

Dressed in her purple gown with the white lace inset, and with her hair done up just so, Jo took one last look in the mirror. Noting her reflection with approval, she left the room and headed downstairs to breakfast.

Everyone else was already seated at the table when Jo sauntered in calling, "Good morning. Isn't it a glorious day?"

Cecilia smiled. "Yes, it is, dear. You look lovely."

"Thanks, Mama."

Jo took a moment to bow her head and say a silent prayer before reaching for the plate of toast.

Adam held up the jam pot. "Jam, Jo?"

"Yes," she said. As she reached to take the pot from his hand, her fingers accidentally brushed against his and the spark of contact shimmied like lightning up her arm. Her eyes jumped to his. The knowing smile he gave her let her know that he'd felt something, too. Why was this happening? she wondered. The more she was around him, the less she seemed able to ignore him.

The voice of her mother broke the spell. "Pass me the jam when you're done, dear."

Jo dropped her gaze and refocused herself on her breakfast.

The festivities were to begin at ten in the morning, and George drove up in a rented buggy at precisely half past nine. Hoping she appeared and sounded cheerful, Jo called out, "Good morning, George."

"Morning, Josephine. You're prettier than the day."

In spite of his faults, George did know how to make her feel special. "Thank you, George. Where's your stick?"

"Doc says I no longer need it."

"Why, that's wonderful. Congratulations."

"Thanks. The leg still tires easily but it should get stronger. Is Belle ready?"

"Yes, but we can't leave just this minute."

"Why not?"

Jo explained how their original party of three had swelled to five, and that their departure had to be delayed until Libby Spenser arrived.

He said, "I don't mind waiting. The more the merrier, I always say."

Jo was grateful for his easygoing nature. He'd make some traditional woman very happy someday. "We'll have to take our wagon instead. Yours won't hold everyone."

"Fine with me. I'll park it here and take it back when we return."

"Good. Then shall we take a seat on the porch?"

"Never been one to turn down an invitation from a pretty girl," he replied with a smile, so he and Jo walked up to the porch to wait.

Adam stepped out and said coolly, "Morning, Brooks."

"Morgan."

Adam took a look at Jo in that lovely purple gown and felt his irritation with Brooks rise anew. If Adam could have sent the soldier packing he would have, but he had no right, so he went over to the bench, sat and tried not to glare.

When the clock read half-past ten and Libby still hadn't shown, a perturbed and now pacing Jo began to grumble beneath her breath. Adam met Jo's annoyed face with a shrug. Belle took off her hat and went back inside to wait. George continued to sit patiently but kept pulling out his pocket watch to check the time, which let Jo know that he, too, was becoming concerned.

Adam said to the pacing Jo, "Maybe something has happened."

"What's going to happen," Jo drawled back, "is, if she isn't here by the top of the hour we are leaving."

No one argued.

As more time passed, Jo wanted to stomp around and tell anyone who'd listen just how she felt about having her fun cut short by Libby's lack of timeliness. But in the words of her mother, such behavior would be neither Christian nor becoming, so she quit her pacing and took a seat.

Mrs. Best stuck her head out the door. "Are you all still here? I thought you'd gone some time ago."

Jo replied testily, "No, Mama. We're still here. We're waiting on Libby."

"Ah. Well, I'm going back to my book. If she's not here soon, I'd advise you to go on ahead."

"Thanks, we will." Jo was glad to hear her mother give them sanction to leave Libby behind. "I'll let you know when we leave."

Mrs. Best disappeared back into the house. Jo and the others resumed the wait.

Adam had to admit that he wasn't very happy with Libby's tardiness, either. He was a stickler for punctuality because he'd been raised not to keep others waiting. He would continue to give Libby the benefit of the doubt and hoped nothing was seriously wrong.

At five minutes before eleven o'clock, the Waterman buggy finally roared up. Bert was at the reins. Beside him on the seat sat Libby. Upon seeing them, Jo offered up a sarcastic sounding "Hallelujah!"

They all went down to meet Bert and Libby. Bert appeared to be as perturbed as Jo herself felt.

He nodded. "Jo. Sorry we're late. *She* couldn't decide what to wear."

Libby, her eyes only for Adam as he helped her down, said, as if wounded, "Bert, you make me sound like an addle-headed female who couldn't make up her mind, when in reality my indecision grew from—shame." She dropped her head dramatically.

Jo and Belle shared a look, then rolled their eyes.

Adam, his face filled with concern, asked, "Why shame?"

She said sadly, "I own only two dresses, Adam, and I had to decide which one would embarrass you less."

Adam wondered if she'd ever been on the stage, but said in as genuine a voice as he could muster, "You need not have worried about that. I'm not so shallow."

Jo wondered how much longer this saga would continue before everyone could get in the buggy and leave. Jo had to hand it to Libby, though; the performance was a good one, and the faded blue dress with its mended underarms and shiny frayed hem was just the right touch to elicit the sympathy of anyone who might care that Libby was so pinched by poverty. Jo didn't count herself in that group, however, so she said, "George, are you ready?"

He nodded. "Sure am."

Bert, patently ignoring his cousin, asked Jo, "Did you have a chance to deliver my message?"

"I did."

He nodded. "Then, I'm off."

Jo wondered if he meant he was going after Dred. "Bert, wait—"

But he drove away.

Adam asked, "What was that about?"

"Nothing," she lied, then asked with a false cheeriness, "Are we ready to go?"

George drove. Jo sat beside him while Belle, Adam and Libby sat on big hay bales in the bed.

Jo heard Libby say to Adam, "Thanks again for escorting me."

Then she heard Adam reply, "Again, you're welcome."

"What do you do, Adam?" Libby then asked.

"Right now, not much of anything. I just got discharged from the war. Once the Union Army gets everything settled down South, I'll decide."

"But how do you live without a means of income?" she asked innocently.

Jo turned so she could see Adam's face. He looked at Jo for a moment, then replied to Libby, "I have some funds at my disposal."

"It must be quite a sum."

Adam asked a bit coolly, "What makes you assume that?"

"Oh, the quality of your clothes, the way you carry yourself. I'm betting you're a very wealthy man, Adam Morgan."

"And that pleases you?"

"Of course, silly. Every lady wants to be on the arm of a well-to-do gentleman."

"I see."

Jo was pleased. Now maybe Adam would realize the flower he'd picked was really a stinkweed.

When Jo and her party finally reached the big field behind Mrs. Oswald's house there were vehicles and conveyances everywhere. In deference to Adam's limited walking abilities, George let Libby and Adam off by the festivities, then drove on to find a place to park. Jo had been correct; everyone in town seemed to be in attendance. Most of the attendees were young women, and many had their mamas in tow. Once again, Jo gave thanks for having Belle as a sister-in-law who could play chaperone. Not that Jo didn't love her mother, but Belle was younger and a whole lot more fun.

After leaving the buggy behind, Jo, Belle and George walked the short distance through a small stand of trees back to the grassy field where the main gathering was being held. As they entered the cleared glade, Jo spotted little girls jumping rope while their brothers and male cousins played marbles in the dust. She smiled at a group of adolescents squealing with laughter as they attempted to pull taffy that wouldn't cooperate on such a warm, humid day. One of the local farmers was giving pony rides to some of the toddlers in attendance. The soldiers were interspersed among the crowd, as well. The ones who were ambulatory were standing in groups talking to the ladies dressed in their Sunday best, while the men in casts and wheelchairs were waited upon hand and foot by everyone who passed them by. Jo was glad to see such a large turnout. The Dred Reed affair had made many of the townspeople wary of visiting with the men; that seemed to have changed.

Belle surveyed the large crowd and remarked, "This is wonderful. Look at all the people."

George nodded. "Glad folks figured out we soldiers are not all Dred Reeds."

Jo noticed Adam and Libby a few yards away talking animatedly with a small group of people Jo knew from school and church. Someone had fetched Adam a chair and he was seated while Libby hovered close beside him. When Libby glanced up and saw Jo watching, Libby's eyes glowed with such catty triumph, Jo turned away. "George, how about we find some punch?"

He held out his arm and she hooked it with her own.

"You two go on," Belle told them. "I'll see you later. There are a few of my friends I wish to speak with."

Neither Jo nor George argued, so Belle went one way and they went another.

In spite of the decision Jo had made about her future with George, she had a wonderful time with him. They ate sandwiches, drank punch and topped it all off with bowls of cold vanilla ice cream. He talked about his childhood and she told him what it was like being the little sister. "Oh, they treated me badly every now and again, tying me up, scaring me with snakes and things, but all in all, Dani and the Morgans were good big brothers to me."

George spooned up the last of his ice cream. "Well, I'm glad Libby came along to be with Adam. Keeps him out of our hair."

"Yes, it does," Jo agreed, even though she couldn't seem to stop herself from looking for Adam whenever she thought George wouldn't notice. Why she was so concerned about Adam's whereabouts and what he might be doing was beyond her, or at least that's what she told herself.

At half past two o'clock, everyone gathered in a corner of the field to marvel at the afternoon's main attraction: a man with a hot air balloon. He was a French Canadian named Maxwell Bordeaux and he made his living giving rides in his balloons at fairs, church picnics and any other outdoor gathering. Men were charged two cents to go up in the balloon; ladies rode for free.

"I want to go up," Jo told George excitedly, but he looked skeptical.

Mr. Bordeaux and his two male helpers were in the process of unfolding the yards and yards of material that made up the balloon.

"I don't know, Josephine. It looks to be dangerous." George voiced his doubt.

"So is crossing the road sometimes, George, but that doesn't make you hide out in your house."

The balloon was soon unfolded and the largest wicker basket anyone in Whittaker had ever seen was taken off the back of a wagon and set nearby. Jo thought it could easily hold two or three people. "Come on, George, please? Say you'll go up with me?"

While the helpers continued to work, the townspeople ringing the men tossed out questions to Mr. Bordeaux. "Is it dangerous?" one of the soldiers asked.

Mr. Bordeaux, who appeared to be in his middle years but still had a full head of jet-black hair, nodded. "It can be. One of the first men to ride was also the first man to die. His name was Pilatre de Rozier—but that was a long time ago. Mademoiselle, would you and your gentleman like to see the countryside as the birds do?"

Jo said eagerly, "I would."

George's reluctance was quite apparent, so much so that the crowd laughed good-naturedly. A male voice called out, "I don't blame you, George. Not even a girl as pretty as Miss Josephine could get me up in one of those contraptions."

The spectators continued to watch and marvel as the edges of the big red and white balloon were fastened to the basket with stout hooks and even stouter ropes. Mr. Bordeaux explained that the fire in the burner would fill the balloon with hot air and give it the buoyancy needed to rise and sail on the wind currents. He relayed to everyone that the first hot air balloon had been made in France, in 1783, by two brothers named Montgolfier. "Their first passengers were a sheep, a duck and a chicken."

Everyone laughed with disbelief, but Mr. Bordeaux swore the story was true.

Jo could see Adam and Libby among the curious crowd. To Jo it appeared as if Adam was trying to persuade Libby to go up with him, but Libby was shaking her head vehemently. He appeared frustrated and looked up just in time to see Jo watching them. He gave her a wave and a smile, then hobbled on his stick toward where she stood with George. Libby hastened to catch up to him.

When Adam reached Jo's side, he ignored the slight face George made and said to her, "Pretty exciting, don't you think?"

"I do."

The hot air was beginning to fill the balloon. It was now wavering upright and getting fatter. Thick ropes threaded around fat wooden stakes anchored the wicker basket to the ground.

Adam said, "Libby won't go up with me."

Jo confessed, "George turned me down, as well."

Adam grinned. "Then how about we go? The two of us."

Jo's eyes widened like a child's. "Really?"

Belle walked up.

Jo said excitedly, "Adam and I are going up in the balloon."

Belle tossed back, "And have your mother turn me to stone when I come back and tell her you're dead because you fell headfirst out of a balloon? Nope."

"Oh, Belle, please?"

"No."

George smiled. "Thank you, Belle. She wouldn't listen to me."

Jo shot him a quelling look, then declared, "Come on, Adam. I am seventeen years of age. I own my own business. I believe I am old enough to decide whether I can go up in a balloon or not."

Adam said with a smile, "Attagirl! Belle, I take full responsibility."

Belle drawled, "Remember that when you have to bring her lifeless body home to her mother."

Libby took hold of Adam's arm. "Adam, please don't do this. You could be killed."

Mr. Bordeaux countered easily, "Ballooning is safe, mademoiselle. Both the Union and the Confederate armies have been using them in the war to scout troop movements, and gather other intelligence. Nothing's going to happen."

George stepped in front of Jo and told her in no uncertain terms, "Josephine, you are not going up in that balloon. I forbid it!"

Jo raised an eyebrow. "Forbid? George, I'm going to assume your concern has made you irrational. I'll see you when I come down."

Upon hearing that, a triumphant Adam declared, "Mr. Bordeaux, you now have two willing passengers. What do we need to do?"

fourteen

when word went through Mrs. Oswald's glade that Josephine Best and Adam Morgan were going up in the balloon, everyone stopped whatever they were doing and came running. No one wanted to hear about it secondhand. They all wanted to boast that they'd seen the ascent with their own eyes.

Jo was too busy listening to Mr. Bordeaux's instructions to notice how much of a commotion she and Adam were causing. The French Canadian told them both where to stand and what to do in case of an emergency. "Pray," he said simply.

Jo didn't know if she liked that answer, but since he claimed to have twenty years of experience, she hoped he knew what he was doing. Knowing that Adam was going settled her nerves. No matter the outcome she trusted him to remain levelheaded, and she knew he trusted her to do the same.

Braced on his stick, Adam stood beside her in the basket, and asked, "You ready?"

She nodded. "Yes."

"Scared?"

"Terrified," she confessed.

"Good. Fear will keep you alive. Had you said no, I would've called this whole thing off."

"Are you scared?"

"Yes," he admitted.

Their eyes met and held. Jo wanted to know how she was supposed to resist a young man willing to ride with her in a balloon. Unlike Belle and George, he'd trusted her to make up her own mind. Jo had spent the last few weeks trying to keep the door of her heart shut tight against Adam Morgan. Now, as the voices of the crowd rose and she and Adam were observing each other so silently, that door in her heart began to creak open once more. She decided that if she wanted to pretend that she and Adam were keeping company for the short time Mr. Bordeaux said they'd be aloft in the balloon, she would. Only her heart would know. When the balloon came back to earth, they could revert to their agreed-upon role of friends.

Speaking of friends, Jo could see George standing as close to the balloon as Mr. Bordeaux's helpers would allow. He looked very put out; almost as put out as Libby standing beside him. Jo knew he was upset that she hadn't paid any attention to his ordering her about, but she didn't care; an opportunity such as this might never come again. Belle at least waved. Jo knew that if Daniel were here, he and Belle would be the next couple in line to ascend. In spite of Belle's stance as a chaperone, she liked adventure almost as much as Jo.

The balloon was now ready to go. It had fattened up nicely from the hot air rising from the burner. According to Mr. Bordeaux, most balloon accidents occurred during the ascent because of gas fires, explosions and such, so as the anchor ropes were undone and the basket lifted free of the ground, Jo held her breath.

Soon, however, she was too overcome with excitement and awe to remember to be afraid. They were now rising into the air on the wind's gentle currents. When Mr. Bordeaux increased the burner's flame the balloon rose higher, when he decreased it it would descend, but Jo wasn't paying any attention to that, either. The view was spectacular. Below the balloon, the trees stretched out like a magnificent green carpet, and the sky above was a beautiful crystal blue. Jo believed she could see to Canada if she only knew where to look. The steady wind and the warm sun felt good on her face. She looked over at Adam, who beamed back a grin. He seemed to be enjoying this just as much.

Jo saw the church pass below and then Trudy's house! Jo couldn't see anyone nearby on the ground, but she waved enthusiastically just the same. When she turned back and saw Adam was watching her, everything around Jo seemed to fade and disappear. The beating of her heart filled her ears. In an attempt to distract herself, she called out to him over the wind and the drone of the burner, "This is lovely, isn't it?"

"Yes, it is," he replied, but he was looking at her and not at the view.

Jo's heart began beating even harder; so much so, she forced herself to turn away and concentrate on the view, lest she shake into pieces.

As Adam watched Jo, he realized that all of the barriers he'd so carefully erected around his feelings for her were slowly melting away. How many young ladies were brave enough to sail above the countryside in a balloon? He knew of only one and her name was Josephine Best. She had fire, sparkle and, alas, his heart. Watching her enjoy this ride filled him with a happiness he wanted to feel for the rest of his life. Admitting that caught him by surprise. For a man bent upon picking as many different flowers as he could, he seemed to be fixated now on only one variety: the black-eyed Josephine.

The balloon sailed out of Whittaker and into nearby Ypsilanti. Jo couldn't stop grinning. When they crossed the

Huron River, she thought it looked like a fat brown ribbon snaking its way home. Jo had never done anything this exhilarating before. She wanted to sail on forever.

It was not to be. A short while later, Mr. Bordeaux announced, "It is time to set down, my friends."

Jo didn't veil her disappointment. "So soon?"

"Yes, mademoiselle. We don't want to get too far away from where we began. As it is, we will have to wait for my men to reach us by wagon before we can ride back."

Jo wanted to stomp like a petulant child, but didn't. Doing so might fulfill Belle's fear of Jo falling headfirst out of the basket, and Jo definitely didn't want that to happen.

Adam was disappointed, as well. He'd been savoring both Jo's company and the serene ride; he didn't want to relinquish either, at least not yet.

A rope pulley was attached to a small flap at the very top of the balloon's insides. The flap sealed a hole that could be opened and closed to vent the hot air and control the descent.

While Jo and Adam watched, Mr. Bordeaux doused the fire, then began to work the pulley. At first the passengers didn't notice any change in the altitude, but as the ground below slowly became larger and larger, they knew their adventure had come to an end. Jo and Adam shared a sad smile.

They landed with a jolt that threw Jo into Adam. He caught her, then, bracing himself, held her close while the basket bumped its way across the hard, uneven ground before mercifully coming to a stop.

Mr. Bordeaux asked, "You two all right?"

Jo, still being held by Adam's arms and eyes, murmured, "Yes."

Adam responded just as softly, "I'm fine, as well."

Mr. Bordeaux studied the two young people who seemed

so mesmerized by each other, and chuckled. "Come, I must secure the balloon."

Adam shook himself free from the spell of Jo's nearness, and reluctantly stepped away from her. "Certainly, sir."

The men helped Josephine out of the wicker basket. Adam offered to assist Mr. Bordeaux with the balloon but was turned down.

"I can do this with my eyes closed," the balloonist replied. "Enjoy your lady's company. As soon as the wagon arrives, we'll get you home."

Adam didn't argue; he'd offered his help merely as a courtesy. In reality, his ankle was protesting all it had done today. He looked around for a place to sit so he could rest it for a bit.

Jo could see the slight wince that crossed Adam's face each time he put his weight down on the still-healing ankle. She also found it hard to shake the way she felt hearing Mr. Bordeaux refer to her as Adam's lady. "You've hurt yourself."

"No. The ankle's just a bit tired. If I can sit for a moment or two, I should be fine."

Jo tried to mask her concern. "Then let's head for that tree trunk over there."

The downed trunk was old and weathered. Before sitting down on it, however, Jo gave it a quick visual inspection. Hornets and wasps liked to nest in old wood. Being stung in the bustle would certainly ruin a wonderful day.

Adam eased himself down beside her and let out a sigh of pure relief. He maybe shouldn't have been so eager to make this trip, but if he hadn't, he wouldn't be here with Jo. The verdant surroundings were quiet and still. Mr. Bordeaux was dismantling the balloon a few yards away.

Jo looked to Adam and said, "Thanks for coming along."

"Thank you, as well. That was fun."

Jo tried to forget the thrill of being held in his arms during the landing.

Adam tried to forget the thrill of holding her close enough to feel her heart beat.

They both failed.

Jo asked, "How long do you think it will take Mr. Bordeaux's men to arrive?"

Adam shrugged. "He mentioned his men being somewhere close by so it probably won't be a very long wait."

In reality, Jo hoped it would take the men hours to arrive; that way she and Adam could spend more time together. "I'd love to do this again sometime before I get old."

"Me, too."

Even though Jo had known Adam Morgan most of her life, the idea that they were out here together in such a quiet, beautiful place with so much unsaid between them made it difficult for her to hold his gaze for any length of time. She was nervous as a newborn colt.

"Jo?"

She turned. "Yes?"

When he looked at her, the world seemed to stand still. Jo didn't know if she was breathing or not. There was wonder and questions in his eyes, but she had no experience with which to answer.

He delicately stroked her cheekbone, then whispered, "Why did you have to grow up to be so beautiful?"

As he leaned closer, Jo's breathing accelerated, then quickened more. *Oh, my goodness! He's going to kiss me!*

And he did. He touched his lips to hers, closing her eyes and making her whole being sparkle. She'd had no idea a real kiss would be this marvelous. When he moved his hand up and gently cupped the back of her head, the kiss deepened, sending myriad wonderful new emotions rushing through Jo with such sweet force, she drew away from his lips in order to catch her breath. It took her a moment to find speech. "Adam—I—" Words failed her.

Adam had been moved by the short, sweet kiss, as well. He truly hadn't intended to kiss her, but she drew him in, in spite of his good intentions. "I'm sorry, Jo. That shouldn't have happened."

Jo finally recovered her ability to speak. "You don't have to apologize. I...could have stopped you."

Their eyes met. Unable to resist her, Adam said softly, "One more then..."

He leaned over and kissed her again, gently, potently. Jo began to spin. She was so outside of herself she couldn't tell whether she was sitting up or sitting down. "Oh my..."

"George hasn't kissed you, has he?"

"Of course not. George is a gentleman."

"And I'm not?" he asked, smiling.

She grinned. "No. What you are is trouble."

He picked up her hand and pressed it to his lips. "I'll take that as a compliment."

Jo thought he was at his charming best. "You are far too handsome for your own good."

"And you're too beautiful for yours. I want to court you, Josephine Best."

Jo searched his eyes for the joke. "Adam, that isn't necessary."

"It's very necessary. Shall I tell George, or will you?"

"Tell George what?"

"That he can find another hairdresser to be with. Your dance card is filled."

Jo thought he was being a bit presumptuous. "Adam, I'm not going to send George packing just because you kissed me." Even though thinking about it still made her tingle inside, and even though she had already decided to tell George the truth.

Adam knew what he wanted and was tired of fighting it. He tried again. "Maybe you didn't understand me, Jo. I'm done picking flowers."

"You say that now, but what about tomorrow?"

Adam stared at her as if he'd never seen her before. "Jo, are you turning me down?"

His incredulous tone made her chuckle. "I'm not sure, but I do know you well enough that I'm not going to hold you to anything you might say while we're here."

"You don't believe me." It was a statement, not a question.

"Frankly, no. Charming ladies is in your nature, Adam. I know it. You know it. What about Libby Spenser?"

"She's spent all afternoon trying to mine information about how well fixed I am."

Jo chuckled. "That's what you get for being drawn to beauty and not brains." She then said more seriously, "So, like I said, I'm not taking you seriously, but thank you for my first kiss. I'll always remember it. Always."

Adam tried again. "Jojo—"

Jo interrupted him with a gentled voice, "Adam, look. I'm a regular girl, and in spite of what you keep professing, I know I'm not beautiful, but I do have my pride. I refuse to turn my heart over to you just so you can add it to your trophy case."

Adam was not taking this well. He had all but declared for her, and she wasn't sure she wanted him? For a young man accustomed to having young ladies jump at his beck and call, this was a truly novel and, yes, humbling experience. Adam realized he could either be angry and turn his back on his feelings for her, or he could try and win her over. The latter was certainly more appealing and had the potential to be the most fun, so he set aside his bruised pride, and asked, "All right. What do I have to do to prove my feelings are sincere? Shall I spout Shakespeare under your window at dawn? Slay a dragon? What?"

"You—"

"Shall I bring you violets every morning, or shall I simply kiss you until you agree—?"

Jo blinked. Her heart began thumping with the speed of a runaway locomotive.

He vowed then, "You will be mine, Josephine Best—be it now or two years from now, but you will be mine."

That said, he got up to greet the men in the wagon who were just now coming over the hill.

Jo was so stunned by his verbal challenge, she sat frozen for a moment with her hand over her mouth, then she laughed.

The ride back to Mrs. Oswald's in the back of the balloonist's wagon took nearly three-quarters of an hour, and by that time the only people still in the grove were Belle, George and Libby Spenser.

Belle hastily approached the wagon. "My goodness, you two had me worried."

"We didn't mean to worry you," Jo replied, "but, Belle, it was marvelous. The next time Mr. Bordeaux comes to visit, you will have to go for a ride. The view was breathtaking."

Adam added, "My apologies, as well. We had to wait for his wagon to find us so we could ride back."

George had concern on his face as he helped Jo down. "Are you sure you're well, Josephine?"

"Positive. It was nice of you to wait."

"I couldn't have slept tonight had you not returned. Do you do this kind of thing often?" He didn't appear to be pleased.

Jo said simply, "I told you I was unconventional."

"You told me the truth."

As Adam got off the wagon, he and Jo waved goodbye to Mr. Bordeaux and his men.

A second later, a distraught Libby threw herself onto Adam. "Oh, Adam. I was so afraid for you."

He said easily, "There was nothing to fear. As you can see, I'm still in one piece."

"And it's a handsome piece, if I may be so forward."

He didn't reply to that, but said instead, "How about we get you back to your aunt's? I'm sure she's beginning to wonder where you are."

"She'll know I'm safe with you."

Jo thought she might be sick.

Belle said, "Since George is going to take us back, we can drop you by the Watermans' on the way."

"That sounds lovely," Libby replied.

George went to get the wagon.

Jo sat up front with George, while Belle, Adam and Libby rode in the bed. Jo did her best to concentrate on what George was saying about the work he'd been trying to find nearby, but Adam's kiss kept coming to mind. *Lord, what a kiss!*

Adam's voice broke into her reverie. "Jo?" he called out. "Are you listening to George?"

Shaking herself, she turned to Adam. "What?"

His eyes teased her. "George just asked you something. Is your head still up in the clouds?"

The secret in his smile was for her only. Unable to suppress the flutter of her heart, Jo turned away from him and back to George. "I'm sorry. What were you saying?"

"I said, I think I may have a job offer. One of the churches in Ypsilanti is in need of a sexton. I'm going over to see about it Monday morning."

Jo could feel Adam's eyes on her back. "That sounds very promising."

"Yes, it does."

"Will you let me know how it turns out?"

"You'll be the first to know."

The Watermans' house was the first stop. Libby cajoled Adam into walking her to the door.

"I had a wonderful—if too short—time with you today," she cooed as they stood on the porch. "Maybe we can have a longer time together soon? Bert said there's a play in Detroit on Saturday."

Adam thought it best he nip this in the bud now. Libby was lovely, but Libby was greedy. She also needed work on her punctuality. "Libby, you are a very beautiful young lady, but I won't be seeing you again."

Her expressive brown eyes widened. "Why not?"

"My heart belongs to someone else. I've tried to ignore my feelings for her, but I find I cannot."

"So you never want to see me again?"

"I can't. It wouldn't be fair to you, or to her."

"It's Josephine, isn't it?"

By revealing his feelings, Adam was attempting to be truthful with her; it wasn't his plan to tell her all of his business. "The lady's identity is of no matter to you."

She did not appear pleased. "I suppose you're right. Well, thanks for a lovely afternoon, anyway." And she stormed into the house.

"You're welcome."

Adam walked back to the wagon. Libby was indeed beautiful but his days of going from flower to flower like a pollen-seeking bee were over. All he wanted was Jo. The Libbys of the world would simply have to understand.

When they reached home, Adam and Belle went up to the house while Jo hung back to say goodbye to George. She tried not to watch Adam's progress to the door, but after the kiss they'd shared, she found it impossible not to. When she finally remembered that she was supposed to be talking with George, she turned back hastily. The tight set of his jaw let her know that he'd noticed her interest in Adam.

"I'm sorry. I didn't mean to stare at Adam, but his ankle—"

He didn't look any more pleased, so she dropped the subject and said, "Thanks for being our chauffeur today."

"It was my pleasure." He replied in the coolest tone she'd ever heard him employ. "You know, Josephine, if I get this job at the church, I hope to sit down with you and see what plans you and I might explore for the future."

Tell him! the voice in Jo urged, but she was chicken; she was also afraid he might not want to go and see about the job if she told him the truth. "How about we wait and see what Monday brings?"

He nodded. "I didn't mean to rush you, but I care very deeply for you, Josephine. I think I may be the man you need to tone down some of that wildness you seem to have."

It was the second time today he'd made reference to taming her and she didn't appreciate it any more now than she had before. "George, I'm not a piece of wood to be whittled into something you find more favorable."

He looked away. "I understand."

She didn't think he did. Not really. As she told her mother, maybe all he needed was to be around progressive women to see the errors in his thinking, but Jo doubted it would be that easy.

He asked then, "Are you angry with me?"

She shook her head, then said, "No, but I am who I am, George, and I make no apologies."

He nodded his understanding once more. "I should be getting back."

"You aren't angry with me, are you?"

"Never. You've given me something to think about though."

"Then I'll hear from you about the outcome on the sexton job?"

"You sure will."

"Good."

He climbed into the rented buggy he'd left at the house this morning, and with a wave drove off. Jo watched him until he was out of sight, then went inside.

fifteen

BEFORE Jo could tell her mother about the fascinating balloon ride, Cecilia took one look at Adam's slow movements and asked, "Are you all right?" Concern filled her face.

Adam couldn't lie. "It's a trifle sore from having to brace myself in the balloon, but I'll be fine."

Adam swore her ears perked up as she asked, "What balloon?"

Belle and Jo stiffened. Adam wondered if they were all about to get turned to stone, but he went ahead and told Mrs. Best about Mr. Bordeaux and the balloon ride.

"You and Josephine went up in a balloon?"

Jo wanted to run somewhere and hide.

Feeling very uneasy, Adam confessed, "Yes, ma'am. Mr. Bordeaux assured us it was safe, and he turned out to be correct."

"Belle, you let my child go up in a balloon?"

Jo sprang to Belle's defense. "Mama, she tried to forbid it, but—"

"You wouldn't listen."

"Something like that."

"So you went up with her?" Mrs. Best asked Adam.

"Yes, ma'am."

"Where was George?"

Belle waded in slowly. "He took my side and tried to stop Jo, as well."

"But she didn't listen to him, either?"

"No, ma'am."

Mrs. Best sighed. "I guess there's no need to fuss since you're both safe, but I'm too old to be worried about you doing something over-the-top every time you leave the house, Josephine Best."

"Yes, ma'am."

Cecilia's eyes then twinkled with excitement. "So what was it like?"

A happy Jo swooned. "It was fabulous, Mama! The view was spectacular."

"Well, maybe I'll get a chance to take a ride in one someday. Until then—Adam, to your room, and rest that ankle. If Bea finds out I let you go cavorting across the countryside and in a balloon, no less, she'll have my hide. I'll bring your dinner up shortly."

"Yes, ma'am."

She turned to the ladies. "Jo and Belle, I need help in the kitchen."

"Yes, ma'am."

Cecilia left them then and they all released sighs of relief. She hadn't chopped off their heads.

Adam said, "I'll see you ladies later." As he limped up the steps, Jo watched him. When he turned and met her eyes, he threw her a bold wink. She tried not to smile but failed. She turned back and found Belle watching her closely. "What?" Jo asked.

"Did something happen on that balloon ride?"

The memories rose and Jo relived the sparkling kiss. She could feel herself soaring and gliding all over again.

"Jo?"

Jo shook herself. "What?"

"Did something happen in the balloon?"

"Nothing happened. We went up. We came down."

Belle appeared skeptical.

"Nothing happened," Jo echoed. Of course, that wasn't the truth, but Jo wasn't ready to reveal the truth, not to Belle and not even to herself. Doing so would make Jo have to acknowledge that she was falling for Adam Morgan, in spite of her protests to the contrary.

"Well, let's go wash up and see what your mama wants us to do."

Jo followed her out.

When supper was ready, Mrs. Best sent Jo upstairs with a tray for Adam. When she entered the room and saw him seated outside, the memories of the kiss they'd shared came roaring back, making her remember the soft pressure of his lips, the warmth of his hand when he caressed her cheek. "I...brought your dinner."

He half rose from his seat. "Can you bring it out here, please?"

Jo did as he asked. In the awkward silence that followed she acknowledged how nervous she'd suddenly become. She wondered if the kiss had affected him as much as it had her. "How's your ankle?"

It was early evening, but because of the season there was still plenty of daylight on the horizon.

"Sore. I did too much today."

"I could have told you that," she replied gently.

She stepped over to the edge of the wooden railing and looked out over the green, lush Michigan countryside. Up above, the sight of the clouds in the blue sky took her back to all she'd seen and felt on the balloon ride.

Adam voiced softly, "I don't think I'll ever view the sky the same way again."

Jo agreed. "Neither will I. We shared something very special today."

"Yes, we did."

The tone of his voice made her turn to see his face. There were so many things that needed saying and clearing up, but neither seemed to know where to begin until Adam said quietly, "I meant what I said about my feelings for you, Jo."

The words thrilled Jo, but she still found it hard to take him seriously. "Do you need Mrs. Meldrum to come tomorrow and look at your ankle?"

"Stop changing the subject," he challenged softly.

To keep herself from succumbing to emotions she seemed unable to control or banish, she thought about George instead. "If George gets the job at the church, I think he's going to ask Mama if he can court me in earnest."

Adam couldn't believe she was still clinging to George. Forcing himself to speak calmly, he asked, "What do you see in him?"

"George is very nice. I wasn't really looking for a beau when we first met, but he's very special in his own way." Jo had no plans to marry him, but Adam didn't need to know that.

Adam didn't want to hear about George's so-called attributes. Brooks was not the man for her. "So, you think you may eventually marry him?"

Jo shrugged.

Adam couldn't take it any longer. "You're not going to marry him. You know it. I know it. Poor George doesn't, though, but that's his problem. The only person you're going to marry is me."

Jo turned on him slowly. Never mind that her heart was beating fast in reaction to his statement, never mind she could still feel his kiss. Her independent spirit—and the parts of herself afraid of Adam's penchant for heart breaking—tossed out, "You're awfully sure of yourself."

"Yes, I am."

"Arrogant, too, I might add."

"Look at the pot calling the kettle black."

Jo didn't appreciate that. Her hands went to her hips. "I wouldn't marry you if you were the last man on earth."

"If I kiss you again, you'd marry me *tomorrow!*"

The words pierced her so sweetly, Jo thought she'd melt right then and there, but to keep from swooning, she snapped, "It wasn't that monumental."

Their voices were rising.

"As if you have something to compare it with, brat."

"How dare you call me a brat! You—you *Casanova!*"

"Let me amend that—*spoiled* brat!"

Jo didn't believe him!

"Your precious George couldn't even keep you from getting in a balloon!" Adam threw back. "Some husband he'll be for you!"

"As if you'd be better!"

"Yes, I would!"

"Only if you drop dead first!"

Suddenly Belle and Mrs. Best appeared in the doorway, and Cecilia demanded to know, "What on earth are you two yelling about? Folks can hear you in Chicago!"

Adam groused, "Jo is under the impression that she's not going to marry me."

Mrs. Best's and Belle's eyes widened as if they couldn't believe their ears.

Jo couldn't believe her ears, either, and told Adam so angrily. "How dare you toss that out as if we were discussing the weather."

"Were you going to tell them?"

"Tell them what? That you're an arrogant, wooden-headed—"

"Josephine!" her mother snapped.

Jo's eyes were on fire. "Make him move out, Mama. Now!"

Before her mother could respond, Adam drawled, "Why? So you can make more time with that lapdog George?"

Jo drew up with indignation. "He is not a lapdog!"

"Yip-yip!" countered Adam, mimicking the high-pitched yap of a small, pampered dog.

Mrs. Best shook her head. "Stop this!" Both she and Belle were hiding grins.

Jo cried, "He called George a lapdog, Mama!"

"I heard him, dear. Now, settle down."

Jo wanted to sock Adam. How dare he have lips that could call George a lapdog one moment, and kiss her until she was left weak as water the next.

Cecilia said then, "Now, Adam, what is this all about?"

Jo spoke instead. "Why are you asking him first?"

Her mother glared. Jo dropped her head and grumbled to herself about the injustice of it all.

Adam looked over at Jo, but directed his words to Mrs. Best. "I want to court Jo, Mrs. B."

Mother turned to daughter. "And you don't want to be courted, I take it."

Parts of Josephine wanted to tell the truth, but other parts were afraid of being hurt. "No, Mama, I don't."

Adam said coolly, "Lightning is going to strike you for lying, Pest."

"Stop calling me that!" she yelled.

"All right, you two," Mrs. Best said. She directed her next words at her daughter. "Jo, would you wait for me in your room, please?"

Jo shot Adam a look. If she got into trouble because of him, she didn't know what she'd do to him, but she'd do something. "Yes, ma'am."

Cecilia then turned to Belle. "Would you give me and Adam a moment alone?"

"Sure."

So Belle and Jojo left Adam alone with Mrs. Best.

"Well," she opened.

He sighed. "I know. It wasn't my intent to start an argument."

"But you did."

"Well, *we* did. She got mad first."

Cecilia studied him. "Do you really care for her, Adam?"

"I do, and I really did try to take your advice about not meddling, but—" Adam wanted to tell her about kissing Jo, but he knew better and so said instead, "My feelings for her refused to listen. I want to court her with the intent of marrying her."

"But she's refusing your suit, Adam."

"I know." And he didn't know what to do about it, short of pulling Miss Sassy Mouth into his arms and kissing her until she agreed. "I plan to court her anyway."

Mrs. Best chuckled. "Oh, really?"

"Yes, ma'am, that is, if it's all right with you."

"I already told you I have no problems with the idea. Josephine's the one you have to convince."

Adam sighed with resignation. "I've never had a young lady throw my interest back in my face."

"A little humbling, is it?"

"Yes."

"It's good for the soul."

He replied grudgingly, "If you say so."

She came over and patted him on the back. "Just give her

time. You and George are the only beaux she ever had. This is all new." She added then, "One more item, then I'm going to talk to Josephine."

"Yes?"

"If you're intent upon courting Jo, that changes your status here. You're no longer just Adam Morgan, family friend."

"I realize that, and based on that friendship, I would never do anything to bring disgrace upon Jo, or compromise her in any way, if that's what you're asking."

"I am, but when you're young and in love, sometimes your thinking can be muddled. Do you remember Belle and Daniel sneaking out at night to meet behind the barn?"

Adam did.

"If there's any of that, you will follow your belongings right out of the front door. Do we understand one another?" Mrs. Best asked pointedly.

"Oh, yes, ma'am."

She smiled. "Good. Well, I'm going to talk with Josephine now. Do you need anything?"

"No. I'm in for the remainder of the evening."

"All right, then."

And she was gone.

Adam let out a breath he hadn't been aware he was holding.

When Jo heard the soft knock on her closed door, she called, "Come on in, Mama."

Mrs. Best stepped in and found Jo lying on the bed on her stomach with her chin in her hands. Cecilia closed the door behind her. "Still mad?"

Jo slowly sat up. "No, but why must life be so complicated? Here I am thinking I have the world by the tail and then—"

Mrs. Best came and sat beside her daughter. "And then—what?"

"Oh, Mama, I don't know."

Mrs. Best bent over and peered into her daughter's unhappy face. "Talk to me, Josephine. Are you really so opposed to Adam courting you?"

"I don't know. In a lot of ways, I'm ecstatic. I mean, who wouldn't be? He's handsome, intelligent, funny, and he says he wants to court me," she said, pointing at herself. "Me!"

"But?"

"But it's Adam, Mama. Who knows if he'll be singing the same tune tomorrow, or even an hour from now."

"You don't think he's being honest with you about how he feels?"

"I think he thinks he is, but—" Jo looked into the kind brown eyes of the woman who'd been giving her sound advice all of her life. "How can I be sure? And then there's George, of course. I've gone from having no one interested in me to too many."

Mrs. Best put an arm around her daughter's shoulder and hugged her affectionately. "Welcome to the world of love, dear."

"So what should I do?"

"I've no idea. This is your problem to solve, in your own way."

Jo looked perplexed. "You don't have *any* advice? That has to be historic."

Mrs. Best grinned. "I'm sure it is, but although you are still my daughter, you are now your own woman, as well. And it is that person who has to decide on George or Adam, or maybe even someone else."

"No more beaux, please. Two are more than enough." Jo then asked, "How did you know Papa was the one?"

"The day he took me for a drive and showed me the house he was building for me."

Jo's eyes widened. "This house?"

Her mother nodded. "Yes. Up until that moment, I felt a lot like you feel about Adam. Your father was a very handsome, well-to-do, *free* man from a good family. I couldn't imagine why he wanted to court me—a runaway living from hand to mouth cleaning houses and taking in laundry. I just knew his intentions weren't honorable."

"But they were?"

"Oh yes, and when he asked me if I would live with him as his wife in this house and raise a family and grow old together, I bawled like a baby."

"That's very romantic, Mama."

"Yes, it was. He's still quite the romantic, your papa is." Mrs. Best quieted then, and Jo knew her mother was thinking about her father being so far away.

Jo spoke softly, hoping to distract her. "If I ever marry, that's what I want. Someone who'll love me just as much and as proudly as Papa loves you."

"That's a worthy goal, but you don't think that could be Adam?" her mother asked her.

Jo quieted. "I don't know, Mama. He's fun to be with, he's witty and silly, but he can make me so angry sometimes."

"And what about George?"

"I'm pretty sure George and I will never be more than friends."

"No?"

"No. We weren't raised the same way. He thinks one way and I think another."

"Have the two of you talked about how you feel?"

"Not yet, but we will soon." She sighed. "All these different feelings. It's hard."

"I know, but time always clears things. Trust me."

"Well, regardless of what time brings, if a man can't support my goals for my business, he can't have me."

Her mother hugged her affectionately once more. "Now, that's the Josephine Best I raised. Stick to your guns."

Jo kissed her on the cheek. "I will."

In church on Sunday, Jo was elated to see Trudy slide into the pew beside her.

Trudy whispered, "What is this about you and Adam riding in a balloon?"

Jo whispered back, "We have to talk. Are you off punishment?"

"She let me come to church, so maybe, but I haven't had the nerve to ask her."

Jo understood. "How's Bert?"

"I'll tell you later."

As Reverend Harmony stood and opened the service, Jo and Trudy set their talk aside and began to sing the processional hymn.

As always after church, the congregation gathered outside under the trees for refreshments and fellowship. Jo's papa, William, often referred to the time as the Gossip Hour because it was an opportunity for neighbors to catch up on what had gone on in their lives since they had seen each other last. Unfortunately for Jo, today's gossip centered around her and the balloon ride.

Trudy broke the news while the two friends were drinking lemonade on the fringes of the gathering. "Mrs. Waterman is on the warpath."

"What about?"

"You."

"Me? Why?"

"Because you and Adam went up in that balloon."

"What does that have to do with her?"

"It isn't her, it's Libby. It seems Adam sent Libby packing. Now the Dragon Lady is telling everyone who'll listen that something must have happened in the balloon because up until then Adam was enjoying Libby's company."

"Someone should see if Mrs. Waterman is dipping in the sherry. I didn't have anything to do with Adam saying whatever he said to Libby. She ought to confront Adam, but I'll wager she won't."

"I'll wager she won't, either."

"Where is she now?"

"I saw her leaving just now."

"Good. Wonder who she'll blame if Bert does move out?"

"Me of course, but I'll be proud to be guilty."

Jo chuckled. "And I'll be proud that you're proud." Jo looked around to make certain they weren't being overheard before asking, "Have you had a chance to talk with Bert yet? I know it's only been a few days."

Trudy looked around before answering. "Yes. I snuck over to his house last night."

Jo's eyes widened. "You did not!"

"I did, too."

Jo shook her head with amusement. Whatever was she going to do with this girl? "Did you two talk?"

Trudy grinned. "We talked, a little."

Jo grinned in response. She was glad to hear that the two were on the road to reconciliation. "Is he still going after Dred?"

"Yes," Trudy said, sounding annoyed. "And no amount of logic could convince him to do otherwise. I even tried tears. Didn't work. He has his mind set and will not be moved."

Jo sighed unhappily. "So what are you going to do?"

"Nothing I can do. I can't tell his mother, and he made me swear I wouldn't tell the sheriff or anyone else his plans."

"Does he have a plan?"

"No."

"Trudy?" Jo asked with wide eyes. "He could be hurt."

"I know. I told him that, as well. He refuses to listen. I'm hoping that if he doesn't find Dred in a few days, Bert will simply give up. Bert's allergic to every plant the Good Lord made, so he won't be out beating the bushes for long. Hives will send him home, if nothing else."

Jo nodded. "I'll keep him in my prayers, though."

"Please do. He'll need them. Are you still planning on coming over later?"

"Sure am."

"Is this about Adam and that balloon ride?"

"Yes, and the fight he and I had last night."

Trudy's eyes widened knowingly. "You and Adam had a fight?"

"Yes."

"Well, where there's sparks there's always fire, Jojo."

Jo rolled her eyes.

"Has he kissed you yet?"

"Trudy!"

"Don't Trudy me. Answer the question. Has he?"

Jo knew she had to tell the truth. This was her best friend. She nodded affirmation.

Trudy lit up like fireworks and rubbed her hands with glee. "Oh, Jo. That's glorious. I can't wait. You must promise to tell me *everything!*"

Jo chuckled in spite of herself. "I promise."

The two friends embraced in farewell, then each went off to find their family members so they could head home.

sixteen

when Jo walked up to the wagon, her mother and Belle were already seated up front. "How's Trudy?" her mother asked.

"Doing well."

Adam stood beside the wagon and soundlessly offered Jo his hand so she could climb up into the bed. Jo accepted the assistance but avoided looking directly at him. After all, she was still supposed to be mad at him. But the warmth of his fingers was making her remember yesterday and how close he'd held her while the balloon bumped across the ground after their landing, so she found the anger hard to sustain. The emotions Adam's presence roused within her were much stronger.

Adam noticed she wouldn't meet his eyes, but he didn't say a word as he climbed in after her and took a seat atop one of the bales. When she did finally look his way, she simply raised her chin in a huff before focusing her gaze elsewhere. Adam supposed she still hadn't forgiven him for calling George a lapdog but he wasn't about to apologize. Instead, he leaned over and told her softly so that no one else could hear, "You can stick that chin up in the air all you want, but I'm still going to court you, Josephine Best." That said, he settled back.

Jo didn't want him to know how much the soft-spoken declaration had affected her, so to cover it, she opened her mouth to give him a stinging retort only to have her mother turn to Jo and ask, "You two comfortable back there?"

Jo smiled falsely. "We're fine, Mama."

When Cecilia turned back, Adam's amused eyes fairly glowed at Jo, who once again turned away in a huff.

Mrs. Best got the team under way and drove the wagon out onto the rutted gravel road that led home. "Mrs. Oswald has one of the Army doctors coming this afternoon to check on the men, so she doesn't think there'll be time for visiting," she told them.

Jo thought that good news in a way; not being able to see George today would give her more time to practice what she needed to say to him.

On the other side of the wagon, Adam thought it was good news, as well. He could have the black-eyed Josephine all to himself.

As the ride home continued and the landscape rolled slowly by, Cecilia said, "I heard some very disturbing news at church. Some homes were broken into yesterday while the owners were away at Mrs. Oswald's social."

Jo was very surprised at the news. "Really?"

"Yes. The thief took coins, plates, jewelry and food."

"Food?" Belle echoed.

Cecilia nodded. "One of the families lost a large cooked ham."

"Why would someone take a ham?" Jo asked.

"Hunger, maybe?" Adam pointed out.

Jo supposed. "Has the sheriff been alerted?"

Cecilia answered, "Yes, but he has no clues. There's talk that Dred Reed's still about. With the railroad conductors on alert, and all the lawmen looking for him, he'd have trouble leaving the area or boarding a train without being recognized, so some people think he may be hanging around, and responsible for the thefts."

The idea that Dred might still be lurking close by gave Jo a case of the willies. She hoped the authorities found him before he found Bert. "But where might he be?"

Adam shrugged. "There are many places to hide. Think of all the old farmhouses and abandoned barns in the area."

Belle said, "But I would think the sheriff would have searched all of those places initially."

Cecilia replied, "The sheriff is a good man. I'm sure he conducted as thorough a search as possible, but there are a lot of woods. Maybe he and his men missed a place or two."

Jo thought that possible. "Well, whoever the thief is, I hope he's captured and brought to justice."

Belle added, "Me, too."

As the ride resumed in silence, Adam set aside thoughts of the thief and focused instead upon Jo. What a spitfire. Would she still be as volatile when she reached her mother's age? Adam imagined she would. She most certainly would keep a man's life from being dull. How could he convince her that his feelings were true? If George Brooks planned to court her, would Brooks take her to the falls in Canada the way Adam longed to do so he could watch her marvel at its power and beauty? Adam didn't want George to be the one to escort her to the theater on Saturday evenings and to church on Sunday mornings; Adam wanted to be the one. Truth be told, Adam wanted to make her as happy as any man could make his sweetheart. But he had to get her to agree to be that sweetheart first, and so far, he hadn't made a lot of progress.

He continued his observance of her, though. The brown dress she had on had a lovely crocheted lace collar but the gown was plainly old. The slightly frayed hem and wrists attested to her support of Free Produce. Adam vowed that once the war ended and the embargo on Southern cotton was lifted, he'd buy her enough new gowns to fill a dozen armoires. After they married, of course.

While the wagon continued to bump along, Jo glanced over at Adam from beneath her lashes and wondered how long the memories of his kisses would haunt her. She was glad he couldn't read minds because if he could, she knew he would tease her unmercifully over her inability to set the encounters aside. Were all kisses the same, or different? Because of her inexperience and upbringing, Jo couldn't answer. All she knew for sure was that riding in that balloon with Adam Morgan had changed her in many ways. Before yesterday, she'd never been kissed or held close against a young man's heart; she'd never had anyone whisper to her that she was beautiful or slowly stroke her cheek. Being with Adam was like entering a strange new realm filled with all manner of wonders that were as tantalizing as they were scary.

She studied him covertly again. Lord, he was handsome. There was a solid brain behind all that male beauty, too; Adam was no featherhead. He would probably make some young woman very happy once he settled down a bit, but would that person be her? Jo didn't know and admittedly didn't trust him enough to let herself find out.

After dinner, once the dishes were washed and everything put away, Jo asked her mother about going over to visit Trudy.

Cecilia took off her apron and hung it on the peg on the kitchen wall. "Only if Adam goes with you. These break-ins are worrisome. I don't want you out by yourself."

"But I'll be back long before dark."

"Adam or home."

"Why can't Belle go with me?"

"She and I are off to Mrs. Lovey's. The organizational meeting for Saturday's rally is at her house this evening."

Jo sighed. She'd forgotten about that. How in the world were she and Trudy going to talk about Jo's Adam dilemma with Adam about? She sighed heavily again. If she hadn't already promised Trudy she'd come over, Jo would just stay home. Trudy would be expecting her, however. Were Jo in Trudy's shoes, she'd be dying for company and be very disappointed if company didn't show up. "Oh, all right. Let me go ask him."

Cecilia smiled maternally.

Upstairs, his door was open. He was at the writing table penning a letter to his brother, Jeremiah. Like the Bests, Adam hadn't had any contact with his brother since April before the fall of Richmond, and, like the Bests, was worried but kept praying he'd hear from Jere soon. Jo's entrance made him set the pen aside, however, and he feasted his eyes on her beautiful presence. "What can I do for you?"

"Mama won't let me go to Trudy's unless you come along. She's afraid Dred Reed or someone like him is going to jump out of the brush and grab me."

"Well, she's right to be careful. You'd be pretty hard to replace."

Jo told herself his words hadn't touched her heart, but it was a lie. "So will you ride over with me?"

"Sure. Horses or the buggy?"

"Horses. That's less trouble, but what about your ankle?"

"I can sit a horse."

"Good, then horses it shall be. You can ride Dani's stallion. I'll meet you in the barn."

"Thanks."

After her departure, Adam smiled. Yet another opportunity for him to plead his case. Maybe he'd be more successful this time around.

* * *

As they rode slowly side by side down the road, Adam quipped, "You must have been real desperate to agree to let me tag along."

"Belle and Mama have a meeting this evening, so it was either you or stay home."

"Well, I agree with your mother about having someone with you. Trudy doesn't live far, but anything might happen on the way."

Jo thought everyone was being overly protective but she didn't voice those thoughts. She and Adam could start an argument at the drop of a hat. She hadn't come out here to fight with him. It was still Sunday, after all.

Adam asked, "So, shall we agree not to fight today?"

Jo smiled. "I just said that to myself. So, yes, we can agree."

"Good. Truthfully, I'd much rather kiss you than fight you."

Jo's heart bounced. "Behave yourself."

"I'm trying. I really am."

Jo didn't believe that for a minute. To keep herself from succumbing to him, she said, "I'll race you."

Challenge sparkled in Adam's eyes and he grinned. "All right. On the count of three. One! Two!" And his stallion leaped forward. "Three!" he yelled out as he rode away, leaving her behind.

Laughter and outrage filled Jo's eyes. "Cheater!" she screamed. Bending low, she urged her mare to take up the chase. Jo's mare, Sassy, would run to Toledo if Jo asked her. The mare was fit, sleek and fast.

Adam rode hard, but what he didn't know was that his mount had a personality all his own. Dani named the horse Douglass after the famous Frederick, but unlike his namesake the stallion had no fire. Whenever Douglass tired of running, he simply planted his hooves and stopped. Unprepared riders were often thrown by the abrupt halt. Adam was one of those unprepared riders.

When Jo and Sassy rounded the next bend, Jo saw Douglass plant and Adam go flying over the horse's head.

Jo winced as Adam came to earth hard not too far from where the now-nonchalant Douglass stood grazing. Jo was relieved to see Adam move, even if it was gingerly. She waited to make certain that he hadn't broken his neck before she and Sassy strolled forward. "Well, well, well," she said, looking down at him picking himself up. "Fancy meeting you here."

He did not look happy. "That animal tried to kill me!"

Jo mimicked surprise. "Douglass? No!"

"He stopped right in the middle of the run!"

Jo chuckled. "That's what you get for cheating. And on a Sunday, too. Be glad you got off so lightly."

He glared up at her.

"If it will make you feel better, the stupid horse does that a lot. Dani says he's just temperamental. I say he's fat and lazy. Mama says if he ever does it to her, she's going to have Douglass turned into steaks and shipped to France where someone can have him for dinner."

"And I'll pay the transport fees," Adam groused while brushing his trousers free of twigs, grass and soil.

"Are you sure you're not hurt? How's your ankle?" Jo asked.

"I'm fine. Ankle's fine," he said, shooting daggers at Douglass.

"Good." Jo grinned and turned her mare toward the road.

"Where are you going?" Adam asked, concern on his face.

"This is a race, remember?"

"You're not going to just leave me here?"

"You have a horse."

"But—"

"See you at Trudy's," she called out. Sassy thundered away.

Had Jo looked back, she would have seen Adam throw his hat down in frustration.

Jo rode up to Trudy's gate. There was a note on the front door with Jo's name on it. She opened the square of paper and read,

Dear J.

Mama had to go to the meeting at Mrs. Lovey's and she made me go, as well. Hope to see you sometime before I turn thirty!

T.

Jo folded the note and placed it in the pocket of her skirt. Poor Trudy. Would her mother trust her home alone ever again?

Jo walked back out to the gate and sat on the ground to wait for Adam. As long as a rider didn't make Douglass do more than Douglass cared to do, he performed well. Jo figured Adam would show up soon.

He and the stallion arrived a few minutes later.

Jo got to her feet. "I see you made it."

"No thanks to you."

She grinned before asking, "Douglass give you any more problems?"

"No. He must have heard us talking about shipping him to France. He's been very well behaved. Haven't you, old man?" Adam patted him on the neck.

"Well, we came over here for nothing. Trudy's not at home. Her mother made her go to Mrs. Lovey's meeting."

"Do you want to head back?"

"I suppose we should."

"Let's take the long way."

"That's a great idea."

He got down to give her a boost back into her saddle. She

didn't weigh that much and so put no strain on his still-healing ankle. Once up, she looked down at him and said, "Thanks."

Adam found himself so taken by her beauty he didn't speak for a few seconds, opting to drink in her loveliness instead. He finally said, "You're welcome, but I'm going to get you for leaving me back there."

Jo had no defense for the attraction she felt building up between them. "You're just mad because you lost, you cheater."

"Pest."

She playfully stuck out her tongue in response.

While Adam mounted Douglass, Jo adjusted her skirt over the trousers she wore beneath for modesty's sake, then she and the mare followed Adam and Douglass back to the main road.

The "long way" incorporated the backwoods paths they often took during their childhood: tracts and trails that led to lush, hidden glades; small, fish-filled creeks; and over hills and dales that would eventually lead home. But Adam and Jo rode slowly, enjoying the silence of the beautiful green countryside, and each other's company. They spied hawks and deer, beavers and butterflies. They eyed untouched stands of multicolored wildflowers, then stopped and ate their way through a small patch of wild strawberries. Mounted again, they passed the tree where the boys had tied Jo up and used her as bee bait. The river nearby seemed an ideal place to water the horses and rest them for a moment, so they dismounted.

After seeing to the needs of the horses, Jo and Adam sat silently on a felled log near the riverbank. The silence around them was total.

Jo threw a few pebbles into the water and said, "I wouldn't come down here for a long time after you all tied me up back there. Every time I did, all I could think about was how mad I was after being honeyed and then rubbed raw."

He smiled. "You're not still mad now, are you?"

She shook her head. "I should be, but no, I'm not."

Suddenly Jo saw a large brown trout jump up out of the river and into the air to catch an insect for a late-evening snack before diving sleekly back into the depths. She smiled. When she was a little girl, her father once told her that nature always supplied gifts if one waited and watched. Jo took the sight of the magnificent fish as the day's gift, and silently sent up a prayer for God to watch over her father and Dani and keep them safe. "Do you think the war is ever going to end?"

"I think it will. According to the papers, General Sherman is bringing the South to its knees. Shouldn't be long now."

Jo certainly hoped he was right.

"Worried about your father and Dani?"

She nodded. "I try not to, but it's hard."

"I know. I worry about Jere, too—all the time. I tell myself he can take care of himself, but it would be better if I could see him and know for sure how he's faring."

Jo agreed.

Silence settled between them and Adam found himself unable to look at anything but her. He admired the way she'd styled her hair. "I don't think I've ever seen your shop. Can you give me a tour sometime?"

"Sure." Jo realized that George had never expressed any interest in seeing her place. Yet another reason why they weren't suited?

"What does George think of your enterprise?"

The innocent question threw her. She searched for a way out without having to reveal the truth.

When she didn't respond right away, Adam peered at her, but she wouldn't meet his eyes. "Would you rather not talk about it?"

Jo nodded tightly.

"All right." It didn't take a genius to deduce that the question made her uncomfortable. Adam wanted to know why, but didn't press her for an explanation. He sensed something wasn't right, however.

Jo realized she should have given Adam an answer, but she didn't want to tell him the truth and then maybe have to listen to him crow about how right he'd been about George not being the one for her. She knew Adam wouldn't intentionally hurt her feelings, but he was a boy, and boys liked to win and brag no matter what, or at least that was her assessment of how they acted.

The silence was suddenly pierced by a woman's cry for help. Adam and Jo got to their feet and looked around.

"Which direction?" Adam asked.

Jo was already running to Sassy.

The cry came again.

"That way!" Jo yelled, pointing east.

She and Adam mounted up and rode in that direction.

They found, of all people, Old Lady Donovan. Jo hadn't seen her since the day she refused to pay Jo for doing her hair and then bragged about her hair to a friend. Now was not the time to hold grudges, Jo told herself. Mrs. Donovan was lying on the ground. From the scratches and scrapes on her face, she appeared to be hurt.

"Oh, thank goodness." The woman gasped. "He tried to take my buggy."

Jo saw the buggy and the mule standing a few paces away.

"Who?" Adam asked with concern on his face.

"A man. I've never seen him before."

Jo helped Adam get Mrs. Donovan into a seated position and Jo asked, "Are you hurt?"

"He pushed me from the buggy seat to the ground and I injured my ankle in the fall."

They assisted her to her feet, then guided her over to a large boulder where she could sit and recover.

Jo passed her the canteen she'd just filled at the river. Once Mrs. Donovan calmed, Adam said, "Now, tell us what happened."

"He was there in the middle of the road. He appeared nice enough. I thought he was lost or needed some assistance, but when I stopped, he jumped for the reins and produced a big kitchen knife."

She looked up at Jo and Adam. "He told me if I didn't get out he'd cut me into little pieces." Old Lady Donovan began to cry. "I've never been so afraid in my life. Never. But Lady over there refused to move. She must've known he was a bad man. You can't make a mule move if they don't wish to go."

Jo said gently, "Can you describe the man? The sheriff will need to know what he looks like."

"Oh, yes. I'll remember that face until I'm placed in my grave." She went on to describe him. Jo got the willies again. The man was Dred Reed.

Adam said gently, "Let's get you home, Mrs. Donovan."

She blew her nose into a handkerchief. "I don't know what I would have done if you and Josephine hadn't happened along. It seems like I was lying there for hours."

Jo was glad they'd happened along, too. Not even Old Lady Donovan deserved to be terrorized and left to fend for herself.

They tied Sassy to the back of the buggy, and while Jo got Lady the mule and the buggy under way, Adam rode beside them, scanning the countryside for any signs of the knife-wielding Dred Reed.

seventeen

JO had never been to the Donovan home before, so when they reached the house she was surprised to find the place so run-down. Mrs. Donovan had always sashayed around as if she owned gold mines. *Apparently not,* Jo thought to herself as she eyed the sagging porch and the badly patched roof.

The inside of the small two-room house was empty but for a table and chair, a small hot plate and a pallet on the floor. There were no knickknacks or prints on the walls, no cloth on the warped wood table. Poverty lived here—poverty and its companions hunger, loneliness and despair. Jo wondered if her mama and the other ladies at the church knew of Mrs. Donovan's desperate straits.

When Jo turned back, Mrs. Donovan was seated on the room's lone chair, and she was staring Jo right in the face. "You and your young man are the first people I've let inside in many years. I'm sure you can see why."

Jo did. She also wanted to tell Mrs. Donovan that Adam was not her young man, but decided that didn't matter, not right now.

Mrs. Donovan was speaking. "You may have saved my life today, and because you did, I owe you at least the truth."

Jo was confused. "About what?"

"That day in your shop. In reality, you did a beautiful job on my hair despite what I said afterward."

"Then why—"

"Because I have no money."

Jo's heart broke. "Why didn't you tell me that, Mrs. Donovan?"

"Pride, my dear. Terrible pride." Tears filled her eyes.

Jo looked over at Adam. He appeared to have been affected by the revelation, too.

Jo asked with deep sincerity, "Do you have family anywhere, someone you could write to for assistance?"

She shook her head. "I've a daughter. Last I heard she was in St. Louis but that was before the war. We don't speak, so I doubt she'd come even if I could find her."

Jo thought about her own mother and couldn't imagine anything coming between them that would be disastrous enough to cause such a rift. "Well, I'm going to have Bea Meldrum stop in and look at your ankle."

"There's no need. Bea has enough to do. I'll soak it for a couple of days. It'll be fine."

Jo asked her pointedly, "Do you want me to send my mama instead?" Jo refused to let Mrs. Donovan suffer alone a moment longer.

Mrs. Donovan smiled for the first time in Jo's memory. "You are just like that formidable mama of yours. Do you know that?"

Jo smiled in reply. "Thank you."

"All right, send Bea by. She's probably the lesser of the two evils."

Jo agreed. "I'm worried about you being here alone, though."

"Don't be. I'll be all right."

"But you have no neighbors, Mrs. Donovan," said Adam

in a reasonable voice. "Suppose you fall or need help with something else?"

She shrugged. "I've managed up until now."

Jo still didn't like the idea of the old lady being so isolated. "Are you sure you'll be all right here by yourself?"

"Yes, Josephine. Now go on home before that mama of yours calls out the sheriff to find you."

"Yes, ma'am."

Jo sensed that Mrs. Donovan's pride was returning, and Jo didn't want to start an argument, so she asked instead, "Do you mind if I come by and visit with you every now and again?"

Mrs. Donovan smiled. "I'd like that, Josephine. Very much," she replied softly.

"Then I shall see you soon, and your next hair appointment is Friday. I'll be coming here to do it."

Mrs. Donovan said softly, "I don't need your pity."

"But you need your hair done, right?"

Mrs. Donovan chuckled. "Yep, just like your mama. All right. I'll be expecting you on Friday."

"Good." Jo looked to Adam. He seemed reluctant to leave, but they had no choice. In fact, he said, "Mrs. Donovan, you make sure you let Mrs. Meldrum help you when she stops in."

"I will," she replied.

"Promise?"

Mrs. Donovan grinned. "Who could resist such a handsome young man? Josephine, he's the one for you. I can feel it."

Jo rolled her eyes. "Thanks, Mrs. Donovan."

Jo and Adam left shortly after.

On the way home Adam asked, "Do you believe she'll let Bea Meldrum into the house?"

"Nope. That's why I'll be telling Mama about her as soon as we get home."

Adam smiled at Jo's astute assessment of Mrs. Donovan. He didn't believe she would let Mrs. Meldrum in, either. "I was hoping you'd say that."

"Don't worry. Mama will take care of everything." Jo wondered who would take care of Bert, however.

Dusk had fallen by the time they returned to the Best home. When they rode up, Mrs. Best was seated on the big swing in the yard, enjoying the evening quiet.

"How was the visit?" she asked, rising to meet them.

While they dismounted, Jo told her about Mrs. Donovan's frightening encounter with Dred Reed.

Cecilia's hand went to her mouth. "Oh, my goodness. I'm so glad you found her. I know you don't like Mrs. Donovan, Josephine, but—"

"No, mama, I like her fine now. She told me why she didn't want to pay me that day." Jo then revealed the conditions Mrs. Donovan was living under, and the bad times the elderly woman seemed to be having. "She doesn't have any money. I don't think she even has food in the house."

Cecilia shook her head sadly. "I wish she had let someone know."

"Apparently she didn't want to. Her pride, I suppose, but she needs help. I worry about her being by herself."

Cecilia's eyes shone with love for her second child. "You have a heart of gold. Bea and I will go over and see Mrs. Donovan first thing in the morning. If Bea's busy, I will go alone. We'll figure out a way to help her, don't worry."

Jo was glad to have such a caring mama.

Adam wanted to help out, as well. "Mrs. Best, if there's a need for funds, I'd like to pledge mine. Purchase whatever Mrs. Donovan needs, and bring the bill to me."

Jo turned and stared.

Mrs. Best said, "Adam, I don't think that will be necessary—"

Adam wanted her to hear him out. "You told me that you and Mr. Best have been saving money for years in anticipation of the war and him being called away to fight, am I right?"

"Well, yes, that's true."

"So the money you have saved is finite?"

"For all intents and purposes. Yes."

"You need your money to keep this household going and to do your work. My mother left me quite a large inheritance when she died, and I'm sure she'd insist that some of it be used to help my fellow man. In this case an old lady."

Cecilia smiled.

Adam added, "You shouldn't have to beggar yourself to do a good deed, Mrs. Best, when I have so much at my disposal."

Cecilia studied him. "Handsome and mature," she noted. "You have grown up, haven't you?"

Adam nodded, pleased by the compliment.

"All right then. I'll bow to your request." She then added in a serious voice, "Somewhere your mother is very proud of you, Adam Morgan."

Jo was proud of his giving spirit, as well. Having to add generosity to his already glowing list of attributes only made it harder for her to keep her feelings for him at bay.

"Jo?"

Jo turned her eyes from Adam and trained them on her mother. "Yes?"

"Did you hear me?" Cecilia asked gently.

Jo shook herself back to reality. "No, Mama. I'm sorry. What did you say?"

Cecilia smiled knowingly. "I said, go and bed down the horses, and I'll see you in the house."

An embarrassed Jo hadn't meant to be caught staring at Adam. "Yes, ma'am."

Cecilia walked toward the house. Jo and Adam led their mounts to the barn to remove the saddles and put the horses in their stalls.

Once that was done, Jo headed toward the barn door, only to have Adam gently capture her hand. The contact made her resonate like the peal of a bell. "I have to go in, Adam."

"I'll keep you only a moment. I promise."

Jo trembled like a leaf in a gentle wind. "All right."

"I know that in a few days George is coming over to tell you how he feels, but I have something to say, as well. No one—and I do mean no one—in this whole world cares for you as much as I do."

Jo went instantly still.

"No one has more respect, more admiration, or will feel more passion for you than I, Josephine."

Jo's barriers began melting away.

"I know you're having a difficult time with the thought of us being together, but imagine how I feel. Do you honestly believe I'm looking forward to the interrogation I'm going to receive at the hands of your father and your brother?"

She smiled slowly.

"Dani will probably hit the ceiling when I tell him I want to court you, and Lord knows what your father's going to say. But for you—" his voice softened, yet seemed to intensify "—I'd face a thousand William Bests, and ten thousand Daniels."

Jo couldn't speak.

"When the war ends, this country is going to be filled with new opportunities for folks like you and me. It's going to be an exciting time, and I want to see those times with you. No one else. Trust me, Jo. If I ever break your heart, I swear I'll cut out my own and give it to you on a platter."

His declaration had been so unexpected and so moving, tears were standing in Jo's eyes.

He reached out and gently thumbed away a tear from her dark cheek. "Don't cry."

Jo dashed away the water with her palms. "I...don't know what to say."

Adam told her then, "I don't want you to say anything right now. I just want you to think about it. All right?"

Still wiping at the dampness on her cheeks and in her eyes, Jo nodded.

Adam looked at the young woman he planned to love far past the time when he became old and gray and smiled softly. "Go on back to the house. I'll see you at breakfast."

As Adam watched her walk away, it came to him that for the first time in his life, he might not get the young woman he'd set his cap for.

Lying in bed that night, Jo looked up at the dark ceiling and thought back on Adam. Never in her wildest dreams had she expected to hear such a passionate declaration directed her way. The words had been so moving, they made the hair on the back of her neck stand up and gooseflesh run up and down her arms. Even now, remembering the soft timbre of his voice made her a bit breathless.

So, what to do? In all fairness, she had to speak with George first. He deserved to know that his feelings weren't reciprocated. Jo wouldn't mind being friends with him because he was a very nice young man, but he hadn't engaged her heart the way Adam seemed to have done. Jo hadn't wanted a beau when all this began, but Cupid's arrows seemed to have pierced her anyway.

Everyone was seated at breakfast the next morning when a knock sounded on the door. It was followed by Trudy calling excitedly through the screen, "Mrs. Best! Jo, come quick! I've something you need to see!"

Everyone put down their napkins and hurried to the door. Sure enough there stood Trudy looking happy as a child at Christmas.

Mrs. Best asked, "Trudy, whatever is the matter?"

Trudy could hardly contain herself. "Look!" she squealed while pointing at the road.

The Bests and Adam stepped out onto the porch. They saw a mounted Bert, and beside him on another horse sat the trussed up and gagged Dred Reed. Jo's jaw dropped.

"Oh, my goodness." Mrs. Best gasped.

Adam whispered, "Well, I'll be." With a smile on his face, he and his stick hobbled fast down the steps to congratulate Bert.

Jo met Trudy's eyes. The two friends grinned, embraced and did a jig. Trudy cried, "He did it, Jo! He did it!"

Jo and Trudy left the porch to join the others now talking with Bert. As Jo neared, she could see the smile beaming on Bert's puffy, swollen face. Evidently the hives Trudy had talked about had found him. He had scratches on his cheeks, and the hands holding the reins were swollen and scratched up, as well.

"Son, you look awful," the always candid Mrs. Best told him.

Bert nodded. "I know," he said thickly from between his hive-covered lips, "but I'm going to be a hewo."

Everyone smiled. Except Dred, of course. To Jo, he looked fit to be tied and she smiled to herself at the terrible pun.

Adam asked, "How did you catch him?"

"Walked up on him just befowe dawn. He was asweep at the base of a twee a few miles fwom Mrs. Donovan's pwace. Used an old twee bwanch to make certain he stayed asweep, then tied him up and gagged him so he'd know how my Twudy felt."

Trudy took up the story. "Then he brought him over to my house, so I could see him."

Dred's eyes were furious, but with his hands tied behind his back and the rag stuffed in his mouth, there was nothing he could do but sit and fume.

Jo was so pleased everything had turned out well. "So where are you two headed now?"

Bert said proudly, "To the sherwiff."

Everyone laughed.

Trudy added, "Then straight to Mrs. Meldrum's so she can give him a salve for his hives."

Jo's heart melted at the tender look the two sweethearts shared. It appeared as if Trudy and Bert would now live happily ever after; that is, if they had their way. There was still the Dragon Lady to take on. But Bert seemed to have discovered his inner strength in his quest to redeem his true love's honor, so Jo didn't think Mrs. Waterman would be much of a factor from now on.

Trudy mounted her mare, saying, "Jo, I'll see you later on."

Jo said, "All right," then added genuinely, "Congratulations, Bert."

Adam added, "Well done, Bert."

As the Best women and Adam waved, Trudy, Bert and their prize rode away.

Bert was indeed a "hewo." There was talk of giving him a plaque for his bravery, but the ceremony would have to be postponed until he recovered from his hives.

On Wednesday morning, Jo gave Adam a tour of her shop before she opened for business. Adam looked around at the small, neat establishment and was impressed. "I like this."

"I've been doing more and more business lately, so I'm

thinking of asking Papa and Dani to enlarge this place if they can when they return. As it is now, one can hardly turn around in here."

"Well, if you're looking for an investor to help with your expansion, let me know."

"Really?"

"Sure. I know you are an astute woman, so why not invest in a growing enterprise?"

"Is that your only reason?"

"I admit my feelings may be involved somewhat, but my business sense is at play, as well."

Jo didn't know what to say except, "Thanks, Adam."

"You're welcome."

And once again, Jo could feel herself being drawn to him. "Suppose it doesn't work out between us?"

"I'd be hurt, but I wouldn't let it affect whatever business relationship we may establish."

Jo found that encouraging. She was just about to ask him what other business opportunities he might wish to pursue after the war when George knocked on the screened door.

"Josephine, may I come in?"

"Of course. How are you, George?"

Jo opened the door and he entered saying, "I'm well. And you?"

"I'm doing well, too."

George saw Adam then and the two rivals eyed each other. George asked Jo, "May I speak with you privately?"

Jo glanced at Adam, who said, "I'll wait outside."

Jo was pleased by his graciousness.

When Adam left, George looked out to make certain Adam wasn't hanging around just outside the door, then asked again, "It's good seeing you again, Josephine."

"Good seeing you again. I'm glad you came by. There's something I—"

"I'd like to speak first, if I may?"

Jo studied him a moment. He looked uncomfortable. She shrugged. "Go right ahead."

"I hear Trudy's intended caught Dred."

"Yes, he did. Everyone in town is so proud of him."

"The men over at Mrs. Oswald's are happy, too."

Jo didn't think George had come over to talk about Bert and Dred. "What did you wish to speak with me about?"

George fidgeted a moment, then said, "I got the job."

"That's wonderful. Congratulations."

When he didn't offer anything more on the subject, Jo peered at him. "George?"

"I'm sorry. I'm—I'm trying to pick my words."

"Take your time." Jo didn't want to rush him because the sooner he declared his intentions toward her, the sooner she would have to tell him his feelings weren't returned.

George started to speak. "Josephine, you know that you're one of the most special young ladies I've ever had the pleasure to know, and—well."

Jo asked softly, "Well, what, George?"

"Well, I met a young woman over at the church where I'm going to be working. She's the secretary there. And, well, she's real nice. Just as lovely and gracious as you, but where you're boisterous, she's quiet. Where you're adventurous, she's cautious. We suit well. Much better than you and I will."

Jo realized that after all her agonizing over this meeting, she was the one being shown the door.

He continued. "I'm sorry if I led you to believe otherwise."

"That's quite all right," Jo told him. Even though this conversation would result in what she'd wanted, this was not the way she'd envisioned it happening. She was admittedly outdone. Happy, but outdone.

George met her eyes. "I'd like us to remain friends. That is, if you care to after this."

"I think that would be nice," she said genuinely.

"You're not angry?"

"No, I'm not angry. I fully understand your thinking. We wouldn't suit."

He smiled wanly. "Are you certain?"

"Yes."

"Good then."

Silence settled between them.

George said, "Well, I guess I should be going. I start work today."

"All right. Make sure you bring your sweetheart over for a visit so we can all meet her."

George nodded. "Sure will."

He walked to the door. "Thanks, Josephine."

"You're welcome. Goodbye, George."

And he stepped out into the sun.

As Jo stood there, she waited until he rode away before lifting her voice to the heavens and shouting, "Hallelujah!"

Adam had positioned himself on a tree stump situated between the house and Jo's shop. He had no idea what had taken place between Jo and George, but the smile George had on his face when he rode away, coupled with Jo's unexpected shout of hallelujah made Adam think she'd accepted the lapdog's suit, and that Adam's own chances of making Jo his own were gone.

eighteen

when Jo saw Adam walking toward the house, she wanted to go after him and let him know what had happened, but her first customer of the day drove up at that same moment, and Jo had no choice but to greet the woman and get to work.

Adam brooded alone in his room most of the morning. When Mrs. Best came up to ask if he wanted lunch, he told her he'd prefer to take it on a tray in his room so as to further rest his ankle. In reality the ankle was well on its way to full recovery, but Adam didn't want his unhappiness to be seen.

By dinnertime, Adam decided brooding only made him feel worse, and locking himself away in his room accomplished nothing. The sooner he gave Jo his congratulations, the sooner he could get on with his life; a life he had hoped to share with Jo, but George had put an end to that dream.

When Adam saw Jo seated at the table, he plastered a false grin on his face and took a seat.

"Ankle feeling better?" Mrs. Best asked.

"Yes, ma'am. Just needed to rest it."

Jo passed him the bowl holding the mashed potatoes. "Has it been bothering you today?"

"Yes, a bit." He took the offered bowl, but avoided looking into her eyes.

"I'd like to talk to you later on, Adam," Jo said.

"Sure."

"Mama, Adam says he might want to invest in my business if I decide to make my shop larger."

"Really?" Cecilia asked.

Adam replied, "Yes, ma'am. Of course, I'd have to see her ledgers first, but she assures me she runs a good solid enterprise."

Belle nodded. "That she does. She and I talked of finding a larger piece of property that would house my seamstress shop on one side and her hair shop on the other. But we figured all that smoke from her hair irons would ruin my fabrics, so we decided against it."

Adam thought that made sense. He glanced Jo's way and the happiness in her eyes made his spirits drop even lower. Convinced George's news had given her that glow, Adam spent the remainder of the meal trying to conceal his gloom.

Jo could see that Adam had something on his mind and wondered if that ankle of his was giving him more problems than he'd wanted them to know. She didn't put it past him to be in enough pain to lay himself low again. Maybe once they had their talk he'd tell her the truth about his ankle.

The talk was delayed, however, by the arrival of Barbara Carr. She and Mrs. Best went into the parlor. A few moments later, Jo was called away from washing the dinner dishes to join them.

When Jo entered the parlor, the worry on the faces of the two women made her ask warily, "Is something the matter?"

Mrs. Carr answered, "Yes, Jo. Trudy and Bert have eloped. At least according to this." And she handed Jo a note. Trudy's scrawled writing stared back as Jo read:

Dear Mama,

 Bert and I are off to be married. It is what we both want.

 Your loving daughter, Trudy

"Oh, my," Jo whispered. She handed the note back to Mrs. Carr.

Mrs. Best asked, "Did you know anything about this?"

"No, Mama. Not at all."

Both mothers studied Jo so intently she felt like an ant under a glass magnifier. "I didn't," she repeated. "Bert mentioned to me that he planned to move out of his mother's house, but neither he nor Trudy ever mentioned eloping." Jo hoped they were all right.

Barbara Carr sighed. "Well, I suppose there's nothing to do but wait until they surface."

Mrs. Best agreed. "I suppose so."

Jo didn't say a word.

"All right, Jo," Mrs. Best said, "you can go back to the dishes. Thank you, dear."

"You're welcome."

Mrs. Carr's voice halted Jo before she could leave, though. "Jo, promise me you'll let me know if you hear anything."

Jo nodded. "I will."

As she finished up the dishes, Jo thought about Trudy. Apparently she and Bert had decided to take their lives into their own hands. Jo couldn't fault them. They'd done what they felt was necessary, and as their friend she would support them in whatever way she could.

Jo hung up her apron and decided it was now time to talk with Adam. How in the world do you tell a young man you are ready to accept his suit, she wondered? What if she had put him off so long, he'd changed his mind, a small voice inside her head asked. *Then I will be left looking like a fool,* she answered herself, but Jo didn't let that deter her. She took a page out of Trudy and Bert's book. It was time to take charge of her heart and her life, so she left the kitchen and went outside to find Adam.

He was seated on her mother's swing. He gave her a bittersweet smile as she approached.

She asked, "It's still fairly early. Do you want to go riding with me?"

Adam didn't really. He simply wanted to hear the bad news about her and George and go back to feeling sorry for himself. "Didn't you want to talk with me about something?"

"I do, but I have to go and take some food over to Mrs. Donovan's and I thought we might talk on the ride over."

Adam's heart sunk lower. Josephine Best had toppled him from his Casanova throne and turned him into an ordinary mortal. He didn't need the beauty of the countryside to cushion the blow.

"Adam, is something wrong?"

"No. Can we talk here? My ankle, you know."

Jo shrugged. "All right. I suppose Mama and I can ride over to Mrs. Donovan's tomorrow."

She took a seat on the far side of the swing. The motion of the bench propelled them both for a moment while Jo tried to find the words for what she'd come to say. "The funniest thing happened to me today."

Adam steeled himself.

"George showed me the door."

For a moment, Adam wasn't sure he'd heard her correctly. "Say that again, please."

"George showed me the door, and if you start teasing me I will sock you in the nose, Adam Morgan."

Adam was speechless. All day long he'd been laboring under the misconception that his heart was broken, when all the time— He began to laugh. It started as a chuckle. Then as he relived the day and watched himself moping and whining, the chuckle gained strength, and soon Adam was laughing like a child at the circus, not at Jo, but at himself.

Jo punched him in the arm, hard, then flounced off the bench and began striding away. "I told you not to laugh!"

That made him stop. Well, almost. "Jo, come back. You have it all wrong."

"The only thing I have wrong is that I thought you cared for me, you woodenhead!"

Adam hastened off the bench. "Sweetheart, wait. I'm not laughing at you. I'm laughing at myself."

The sincerity in his voice, and hearing him call her sweetheart, made Jo stop. She turned back. "Explain."

When they were facing each other, Adam spent a few silent moments just drinking in all that she was. "Do you know how beautiful you are to me?"

The timbre of his voice made her anger dissolve.

He picked up her hands and then slowly kissed the fingers of each. "Forgive me if I hurt your feelings, but the joke was on me. I was convinced George had won your hand and I've been pouting about it all day."

"What made you think that?"

"The smile he had on his face this morning when he rode away and the hallelujah I heard you shout."

Jo understood now and she smiled. "So you've been tortured by that all day?"

"I have."

She shook her head with amusement even as her heart sang. "He found someone else."

"I'm glad."

"So was I. That was the reason you heard me shouting."

Adam looked down at her and thought himself the happiest man in the world. "So, your dance card is empty, I take it?"

"It is."

"May I pencil in my name, then?"

"Yes, you may," Jo responded with a twinkle in her eye.

Adam hooted, grabbed her around the waist and swung her around. Jo screamed happily, "Put me down, you loon!"

And then he kissed her right there in front of God and all the birds in the trees, and Jo practically swooned with delight.

He asked then, "Is that ride offer still available?"

"It is."

"Then let's go."

"I have to go and tell Mama."

"All right. I'll meet you at the barn."

Under the auspices of doing a good deed, Jo and Adam rode away. They took the main road to Mrs. Donovan's and grinned at each other the entire way. When their task was done, Mrs. Donovan thanked them sincerely for the foodstuffs, and Jo and Adam headed home. They took the long way so they could enjoy themselves and their newfound happiness.

They were sitting by the river when Jo said, "You know, Adam, I agonized over how I was going to tell George we didn't suit without hurting him, only to learn he'd set his cap on someone else. I'm still trying to decide whether to be offended or not."

Adam chuckled. "Fate has a wicked sense of humor sometimes." He tossed a stone out into the water. "You didn't want to marry Brooks anyway. The minute he demanded you go shoeless and stay in the kitchen, you would have gone after him with a broom."

She laughed. "I know. He told me where I was boisterous, she was quiet, and where I was adventurous, she was cautious. I haven't decided if I'm offended by that, too, or not."

"I wouldn't be too hard on him. I'm one of the few men around willing to take on a boisterous and adventurous woman."

"Who are some of the others?"

"Your father—your brother, Daniel."

"Hey!" she challenged with mock outrage. Reaching over, she punched him in the bicep. "Are you casting aspersions on the females in my family?"

"Every boisterous and adventurous one of them," he confessed with a chuckle.

Jo was so glad she'd opened her heart to Adam. In addition to all of his other sterling qualities, he was a great source of fun. "Well, stop it."

Adam shook his head with amusement. "You have no idea how miserable I've been all day."

"Humility is good for the soul."

"You sound just like your mother."

"Thank you," she replied proudly. "Oh, I didn't tell you. Trudy and Bert eloped last night."

"They did!"

"Yep. Mrs. Carr showed me the note."

"She's pretty worried, I'll wager."

"Yes, she is, but Bert has a good head on his shoulders. I think they'll be all right."

"Would you elope with me?"

Jo shrugged. "As long as I didn't have to live with Mama afterward."

He found that surprising. "You don't want to live with your mother?"

"Not forever. I love her, but the house is her house, and I want my own. Belle is content living there, but I'd want a house that had *my* china in the cupboards, *my* silver on the table and *my* vegetable garden outside." She looked at him seated beside her. "Is that so selfish or wrong?"

He whispered, "No."

"Good. I mean no disrespect to Mama."

"I know. Do you think you could live in a hotel?"

The question confused her. "Why would I choose to live in a hotel?"

"Because, my boisterous pest, that's where I'll be living. I'm thinking of building one."

"What? Where?"

He shrugged. "Not sure yet. I want to wait until the war ends before deciding."

Jo didn't know what to say. Finally, she asked, "Will there be room for a hairdressing shop?"

"I already have your space incorporated into the design in my head."

She was more than a bit pleased. "Really?"

"Yep. You don't have to live in the kitchen to be with me."

She grinned. "I'm beginning to like this, Adam Morgan."

He replied with all confidence, "I knew you would."

Adam then asked something he had been meaning to get clarified. "Isn't your birthday in January?"

"Yep, the twenty-fifth. Why?"

"Just trying to figure how long we may have to wait before we can marry."

The words took her breath away. She calmed herself. "I have to be at least eighteen, that I know."

"So, roughly six months?"

"Yep."

"Do you think your parents are going to make us wait longer?"

"I don't know, Adam." Then she added shyly, "I hope not."

He grinned. "Me, either." He reached out and traced a finger down her silken cheek. "Today has turned out to be the best day of my life, Josephine Best."

"I think it's been awfully nice, too."

He gently coaxed her closer until they were no more than a breath apart. When he lowered his head, she closed her eyes. The kiss was so sweet and so tender. He gathered her into his arms and she lifted her lips so the kiss could continue. Jo felt as if she'd been touched by magic. He made her feel treasured. She wanted nothing more than to be held by him in just this way until the seasons changed, but knew her mama was expecting them home. She murmured over her pounding heart, "Mama's going to come looking for us...."

His lips left hers to place light, fervent kisses on her jaw, her cheek and little soft ones against her eyelids. "I know, but Lord, you're lovely..."

Jo thrilled to the sound of his husky declaration. Her whole world seemed to have come alive in response to his kisses. Now she understood how a girl could become over-whelmed and allow a boy to take liberties he shouldn't. The soaring sensations and rising emotions were so exciting, Jo didn't want to stop.

They had to, however, and they both knew it. To that end, Adam literally picked Jo up and set her down a few feet away. "Sit over there," he directed in a firm but soft voice. He fought to calm himself and to catch his breath; she attempted the same. It took them a few minutes.

Adam told her, "Now, let's get back on those horses. If we don't, I'm going to kiss you again."

Jo responded with a knowing smile. "Is that so bad?"

His eyes sparkled. "Yes, because if your mother finds out what we've been doing, she's going to fry me and broil you."

Amused, Jo dropped her eyes for a moment, then said grudgingly, "Okay."

"But one more…"

This time the kiss was firmer, more potent and when he finally drew away from her lips, her eyes were closed and every inch of her body seemed to be singing.

"Let's go," he whispered.

Still entranced, Jo stood and mounted her mare.

Up in her room that night Jo thought about Adam. The memories of the feel of his lips on hers lingered within her much in the same way the fading scents of a fine perfume lingered in the air. She wondered where he'd learned to kiss so well. Did boys go to a secret school somewhere to be taught the intricate nuances? She knew the thought was silly, but Adam was very good at it. She gingerly touched her lips. They felt puffy and tingly. She wondered if all boys kissed the same. That was still an unanswerable question, but Jo didn't worry about it. She certainly had no desire to go around making comparisons. She wondered if Trudy felt like this when Bert kissed her. Thinking about Trudy made Jo hope the two were all right and would return home soon. Their adventure had more than a few people worried, but Jo was convinced everything would turn out fine. As Jo turned over to go to sleep, she said a prayer for the safety of her father and Daniel, then wondered what her father would say when he found out about her and Adam.

Saturday morning, the Best family with Adam in tow parked their wagon among a sea of other vehicles, then walked the short distance to the gathering spot where the day's rally was being held. The spot, a parklike area in the center of Detroit's downtown, was also the place where the men of the First Michigan Colored Infantry had paraded before mustering off to the war. Jo remembered the multi-colored banners, how smart her papa and Daniel had looked in their uniforms and how many of the families had cried when the men marched by.

That had been then. Today, people of all races and denominations had come together to aid the fight in a different way. Fugitive slaves were fleeing their masters in droves and seeking shelter with the Union soldiers now campaigning across the South. The Army had made no provisions for such an overwhelming number of refugees, so the Union was establishing camps for the people to live in until a more permanent solution could be found. Because housing was only one of the needs, the rally attendees were being asked to donate whatever they could spare in coin, clothing and other essentials.

While Cecilia and Belle went off to help the organizers, Jo and Adam threaded their way through the large crowd listening to speakers, adding their names to various petitions and generally enjoying the festivities. They saw some people from the church, and Jo recognized other faces in the crowd from the rallies and lectures she'd attended in the past. Another familiar face made Jo stop and say to Adam, "There's a friend of yours over there."

When he turned to look across the crowd, he spotted a laughing Libby Spenser draped on the arm of a well-dressed young man. Adam said, "I see it didn't take her much time to find someone else."

"Apparently not."

"Do you know who he is?"

"Yes, his name's Jasper Gleason. His father is a coal distributor. The family's very wealthy."

"I wish Jasper luck."

"He'll be fine. His mama is a very intelligent lady. She'll have no trouble seeing through Libby and showing her the door."

Adam hoped Jo was right.

As they continued their stroll past vendors hawking everything from popped corn to freshly caught fish, Adam reached down and folded his hand over hers. When he looked back at her, Jo felt like swooning. She'd never held hands with a gentleman publicly before, or even privately for that matter. The idea of what it represented made her feel very special and a little giddy.

Lunch was provided by the churches in attendance, and the bountiful fare included chicken, coleslaw, pound cakes, coffee, lemonade, potato salad and pies and cobblers of all sizes and flavors. Jo cut herself a wedge of a delicious-looking cherry cobbler, to accompany her chicken and coleslaw, then followed Adam over to a grassy spot where they could sit and eat. Adam gently set his plate down, then removed his brown suit coat. He spread it on the ground. "Have a seat."

Jo didn't protest. She knew how stubborn grass stains could be and she didn't want any on her dress, even if it was old.

While she and Adam ate in silence, they savored each other's nearness and company.

Adam asked, "What do you think would happen if I leaned over and kissed you?"

Jo quickly looked around to see if he'd been heard by any of the people milling about or seated nearby. "You'd better not. Mama will kill us both."

"I could do it real quick so no one will see me."

Jo giggled. "Eat your lunch."

"No, really, watch—"

Before Jo could blink he leaned over, gave her a quick, deep kiss on the lips, then leaned back. While she sat there stunned and seeing stars, he very casually resumed his meal. He shot her a wink, and she shook her head in disbelief and wonder. She also moved herself just a bit farther away from his side. The incorrigible Adam Morgan was a handful.

nineteen

At the end of the rally Jo, Adam, Belle and Cecilia headed back to the wagon for the long ride home. Adam had volunteered to drive and so maneuvered their wagon into the long line of vehicles threading their way up the road. It took him a while to get clear of all the traffic, but once he did they became one of a smaller group of people traveling west. It was a warm July evening and there were many hours of daylight left to see by.

Cecilia, seated on the bench next to Adam, said to Jo, "I have something for you."

"What is it?"

Cecilia held out a letter. "It's from your father."

Jo's eyes widened and her heart began to pound. She took the letter and asked in a voice filled with wonder, "Where did you get it?"

"From one of the men in their company. I saw him today at the rally. He's been discharged and said William asked him to carry the letters home." She turned to her daughter-in-law. "Belle, here are two for you. One from Daniel and another from your father."

Belle had tears in her eyes as she took the letters from Cecilia's hands.

Mrs. Best said emotionally, "I've already read mine."
Jo eagerly tore open the missive and began to read.

My dear daughter, Josephine,
   Are you staying out of trouble?

Jo smiled. It was her papa's special greeting.

   I hope you are, as I am not there to rescue you and
Trudy from any mischief-making. Your brother and I
are doing well and we both miss you very much. How's
your hair-shop business? I am so proud of you and the
goals you have set. So proud. I tell the young men here
just how lovely and intelligent you are, and all wish to
make your acquaintance. The food here is terrible, the
hours long, the insects ravenous, but for freedom we
endure. I received word from your mother that Adam
Morgan is there. Daniel and I find that comforting
news. We were surprised to hear about this courting
business, though, but because your mother is there—
and I am certain she will roast Adam like a turkey
should anything untoward happen—I do not worry.
Adam is a fine young man, but tell him I will be speaking with him when I return. Stay well, my dearest Josephine. You are in my prayers each night.
   Love, your father, William

Jo had tears in her eyes when she was done.
Adam asked softly, "Is he well?" but couldn't help wondering when he'd hear from his own kin.
Jo nodded and her heart swelled in response to the love
now beaming from her mother's eyes. "They're faring well,

Mama," Jo stated happily. Today had been an absolutely perfect day.

"Yes, they are."

Belle relayed the news that both her own father and Daniel were doing well, too. Hearing from the men filled the women with such joy and relief, they all smiled the rest of the way home.

That evening, Jo stepped out onto the porch to find Adam sitting alone on the bench. He looked as if his thoughts were miles away. "Would you like some company?" she asked.

He gave her a soft smile. "Sure."

Jo sat. She could sense his melancholy. "Is it anything I can help with?"

Adam wasn't surprised that she had read his mood so well; after all, she'd known him her entire life. "No. Just thinking on Jeremiah. Wondering how he's faring, is all."

Jo had been so elated to hear from her father, she'd all but forgotten that Adam was still waiting for word from his brother. "I'll keep him in my prayers."

"Thanks."

"So how can I cheer you up?"

"Just sitting here is enough for me."

Jo smiled. It was enough for her, as well. "My papa mentioned you in his letter."

Adam turned her way. "He did? What did he write?"

"That he was glad that you were here with us, and that he and Daniel weren't so sure about us courting."

Adam's spirits sank. "Oh."

"But," Jo added.

"But what?"

"He went on to write that he thought you were a fine young man, and that he wasn't really worried because he knows Mama will roast you like a turkey if anything bad happens."

Adam chuckled. "That's an endorsement, I think."

"Papa also said he'll be speaking with you when he returns."

Adam nodded. He had no qualms about facing William Best. Were Jo Adam's daughter he'd want to quiz her young man closely, too. Adam had no doubts about being able to convince Mr. Best that his feelings for Jo were true, though; if he could convince Jo, he could convince anyone. "You think me kissing you out here will turn me into Thanksgiving dinner?"

Jo giggled. "Probably."

"Do you want to go for a ride?"

His bold request made her tingle with excitement. "I have to ask Mama."

"I know."

"Suppose she says no?"

"Then we'll ride another time. But suppose she says yes?"

Jo smiled and hurried into the house.

She returned promptly and the gleam in her eyes told all. "She said yes!"

Adam grinned.

"But she says be back within the hour because it will be dark soon."

"Then let's go."

Because Jo and Adam were now more than just friends, Jo was certain it would have taken her several hours to convince her father to let her ride unchaperoned like this with Adam, but her mama was a bit less old-fashioned and trusted Adam and Jo to behave themselves. For once, Jo was glad her papa wasn't around.

Seated astride Daniel's stallion, Adam rode beside Jo and said, "You know, an hour is not going to be nearly long enough."

Jo grinned. "I know, but I promised Mama we'd be back by then."

"Well, I'm selfish."

They found a quiet spot beside the river, then dismounted and picked out a shady spot to sit. After a few moments of silence, he asked her, "Did you ever think back in those days when we played along these banks that you and I would be here like this today?"

"No," Jo said truthfully. "Never. You were just one of my brother's friends."

"And you were just his little sister."

Jo met his eyes. "Both of those things are still true."

"Yes, they are."

Adam reached out and softly stroked her cheek. "Little Jojo, all grown up."

He kissed her. The past quickly vanished to be replaced by the sweet, fresh love of today. Adam had awakened this morning wanting to kiss her this way, wanting to hold her in his arms. Her lips were as sweet as honey, and the smell of her vanilla perfume filled his nose and muddled his senses.

The male in Adam wanted to do more than kiss her, much more, but the man in him knew doing so would be wrong. Jo wasn't a fast girl, she was an innocent, and because of that, pressuring her wouldn't be fair. Adam contented himself with feeding on her thrilling kisses; he loved her enough to wait.

Being a gentleman was difficult, however, and she was as tempting as a piece of sweet potato pie. So to make certain he didn't overstep any bounds, he reluctantly drew away from her lips. Upon doing so, he saw that she had her eyes closed. He kissed each lid delicately. "We have to stop."

Jo felt like a shimmering ray of sunshine. "Why?" she whispered.

He chuckled and touched his finger to her beautiful lips.

"These lips are the reason. They're about to push me over the brink."

Jo grinned saucily. "Really?"

"Don't gloat."

"I've never had anyone tell me that before."

He kissed her again, soundly, softly. "Now put your lips away."

"No," she countered with a teasing voice and boldly kissed him again.

Adam groaned and pulled her onto his lap. "You are such a pest."

The kisses began again, and when they finally came up for air, Jo asked dreamily, "What time is it getting to be?"

Adam kissed her ear. "I don't know or care."

His voice sent a ripple through her skin, and Jo somehow found the words to say, "Mama will...."

Knowing she was right, Adam reached down and opened up his pocket watch. "We've got just enough time to get back and beat the witching hour, but we have to leave right now."

"I don't want to."

"Neither do I, but I want to be alive on our wedding day."

Jo had her arms placed loosely around his neck, and all she could do was marvel. "You really do want me to be your wife, don't you?"

His eyes were affectionate. "You're just figuring that out, are you?"

"Well, no, but yes. I mean—I don't know what I mean."

"As long as you agree to be my wife, it doesn't matter. How I feel about you is hard for me to explain sometimes, too."

She kissed him again, infusing it with all that was in her heart. When she drew away, he had his eyes closed. He opened them and said, "That, my pest, was a kiss."

She smiled. "Good."

"You're a quick study."

"I've a great tutor."

He laughed. "Up. Otherwise we'll not make it back in time."

Jo stood, but Adam had to have one more kiss. She obliged him happily, and only afterward did they mount their horses and ride home.

Mrs. Best was standing in the doorway when they rode up, but she couldn't fuss. They'd made it back with five minutes to spare.

On Monday morning, Belle filled the wagon bed with the last tissue-wrapped trousseau items for her client in Ann Arbor. She was going to drive over and deliver them. Since Belle wouldn't be returning until after dark, Mrs. Best asked Adam to ride with Belle and he was more than happy to do so.

As Jo stood on the porch watching Adam and Belle load the gowns, Jo thought back to yesterday's kisses on the riverbank and smiled.

Her mother stepped out onto the porch, took one look at her dreamy-faced daughter and asked. "And what has you so happy, Josephine?"

The voice jolted Jo back to the present. "Uh, nothing. It's just a beautiful day."

Her mother looked skeptical. "Mmm-hmm. The Lord will get you for lying, Jo."

Jo's eyes sparkled. "All right. I was just smiling watching Adam."

"That's what I thought."

"He wants to marry me, Mama. Adam Morgan really wants to marry me."

"You sound as if that's hard to believe. You're quite a catch yourself, you know."

"I know, but I keep waiting to wake up."

Her mother smiled. "It's real, Jo. I promise."

Mrs. Best went down to see if she could help with the loading. Jo went back to smiling.

Jo spent the rest of the morning sweeping the floor in her shop and making sure all of her supplies were up to snuff. She didn't have many appointments this week, but she wanted to be ready for walk-ins. The last person she expected to see was Trudy, but it was the person Jo most wanted to see. Jo squealed with delight, and the two friends embraced as if they'd been separated their whole lives.

"How are you?"

"I'm fine. Mama wasn't real happy at first, but she's starting to come around."

Jo stepped back and asked, "So you really, actually did it?"

Trudy nodded. "Yep. I am now Mrs. Bertram Waterman."

Jo was impressed. "That's wonderful, Trudy."

"Yes, it is. I am so happy, Jo. Just wait until you and Adam get hitched."

"That may not be for a while. We'll have to wait until Papa returns before we can talk about a date."

Trudy stared with shock. "I was just joking, Jo. You mean to tell me you and he are sweethearts?"

Jo nodded. "Yep, and, Trudy, being with him is so wonderful."

"Oh, my goodness!"

"Enough about me, tell me about you and Bert."

So Trudy did, beginning with the elopement and ending with the reaction of Mrs. Carr and Mrs. Waterman. "The Dragon Lady says she's cutting him out of her life, but Bert's being strong. He told her she can't run the Waterman brick-laying business without him, so she could either accept the marriage or not."

"He told her that?"

"Yes, so we're living with Mama right now, but we're going to look for a house sometime next week. I had no idea Bert had so much money saved."

Jo was glad to hear Bert had prepared himself financially for the newlyweds' future. "I wish you all the happiness in the world."

"Thanks, Jo. Mama is giving us a reception on Saturday. Will you come?"

"Is Jeff Davis a Reb? Of course, silly. An army couldn't keep me away."

"Good. Now, I want to hear all about you and Adam!"

Jo grinned. Trudy was back and Jo was happy.

Jo was even happier two days later when Adam received a long letter from Jeremiah, who wrote that in spite of the challenges of the war, he was doing just fine.

Jo and Adam had a wonderful time at Trudy's reception. Trudy looked beautiful in her new blue dress, and Bert stood beside her looking like the proud bridegroom that he was. Mrs. Waterman attended the affair with the intention of stopping the festivities, but was summarily shown the door by both Bert and Barbara Carr before she could start any serious trouble. Mrs. Best and Belle went home after the main festivities ended, but Adam and Jo had been given permission to stay for the dancing and party games Trudy had planned for their set.

Now Adam and Jo were driving home, as well. It was dark and the stars were out. Jo had her arm linked with Adam's and her head rested cozily against his shoulder while he drove. "Did you have a good time?" Jo asked him.

"I did. How about you?"

"Marvelous. I hope our wedding party will be as much fun." He chuckled. "Let's not invite Mrs. Waterman, though."

"Don't worry." Jo was sleepy and she yawned. "It's been quite the week."

"Yes, it has. First Bert captures Reed, and then he and Trudy elope."

"George gives me the boot, and I get you."

Adam leaned down and placed a soft kiss on her forehead. "And I get you. Now that Trudy and Bert are back and married, I'm jealous."

Jo leaned back so she could see his face. "Are you?"

"Of course I am. They're married and we aren't."

Jo snuggled close again. "But we will be, and it will be before you know it."

"Promise?"

"Promise."

"Promise me you'll love me until we're both as old as Old Lady Donovan?"

Jo grinned. "Promise."

Adam looked down at her and said genuinely, "I love you very much, Jo Best."

She whispered softly, "I love you, too, Adam Morgan."

The drive home continued, and they were both content.

epilogue

IN April of 1865 when General Ulysses S. Grant and the Union Army forced General Lee and the Confederacy to surrender, the citizens of the north celebrated the end of the war. Church bells rang from Massachusetts to Kansas, but the celebration soon turned to mourning as news of President Lincoln being shot and killed spread around the world.

With Adam handling the reins, the Best women traveled to Ann Arbor to pay their respects at a memorial service being held by one of the city's large churches. Everyone for miles around had turned out, it seemed, and the traffic was horrendous, but Adam managed to find a spot to park the wagon not too far away from the church, and the four of them joined the large crowd of all races slowly entering the sanctuary.

Once inside, Jo wondered if she and her family looked as somber and sad as the others in attendance and thought they probably did. Mr. Lincoln had kept the Union together, set in motion the emancipation of three and a half million slaves, and now his life had been snuffed out by the actor John Wilkes Booth.

The memorial was a moving mixture of hymns, testimonials and speeches touting the president's greatness and strength of character. The finale was an emotional singing of "The Battle Hymn of the Republic" that reduced every man, woman and child to tears.

A few days later, as the country continued to grieve and thousands of Americans lined the route to witness Lincoln's funeral train make its way from the nation's capital to his hometown in Illinois, Jo and the citizens of Whittaker set about resuming their normal routines. Jo reopened her shop and Adam began looking over drawings for his hotel, but the gloomy mood was hard to shed.

After dinner as the two young lovers sat side by side on the swing, Jo said, "I never knew one death could inspire so much sadness, Adam."

"I know. It has hit our people particularly hard because of all he did for us, even if some of it was done reluctantly."

"But it is done."

He nodded. "And hopefully not to be undone. Many are worried about the direction President Johnson will take and what it might mean for the newly freed."

Jo had been following the debate in the newspapers. Some editors were taking a wait-and-see attitude, while others were sounding the alarm and warning that Johnson was in bed with the defeated Confederacy. Jo had no idea what the future might hold, and for the first time in her young life saw clouds on the horizon. She supposed it was because she no longer viewed the world through a child's eyes and could see the many nuances. She wasn't sure if she cared for this new maturity.

As if reading her mind, Adam took her hand in his, looked down into her eyes and said, "No matter what comes, we'll face it together, be it good or bad."

She squeezed his hand and felt better than she had in days.

Early the next morning, breakfast was interrupted by a

knock on the door. Cecilia got up from the table. "I wonder who that could be?"

"Bea, maybe?" Belle answered.

Cecilia went to the door, and when she screamed, Belle, Jo and Adam ran to her aid, but she needed none. There in the doorway stood Mr. Best with his wife in his arms rocking her in a joyous, tearful welcome. Beside them stood Daniel. Belle shrieked and ran to Daniel, who caught her up and held her tight. Once she seemed assured that her husband was alive and well, she moved from him to share a strong hug with her father, who entered next. Jo felt she might burst from so much happiness and looked over at Adam with happy tears blurring her eyes. Then Jeremiah inched his way into the room and Adam gave a shout of surprise as the brothers hastened to embrace for their own long-awaited reunion.

At dinner, Jo looked at the four war veterans. She didn't know who was happier, but counted herself amongst the happiest. They'd all lost weight, and although they looked less weary than they had upon arrival, exhaustion was clearly reflected in their faces and eyes.

"So, Adam Morgan," William Best said as Jo set out the dishes of ice cream for dessert, "what makes you think I'll agree to you marrying my daughter?"

Jo stopped in midreach.

Adam froze as all eyes turned his way. He straightened, looked at Jo for a moment, then replied, "I love her, sir, and plan to do so for as long as I have breath."

A slightly embarrassed Jo smiled at the soft-spoken declaration and a grinning Jeremiah lifted his coffee cup in tribute.

Daniel asked pointedly, "And how many other ladies have heard you say the same thing?"

"Daniel!" Belle fussed.

"I know him, Belle."

"But do you know his heart?"

Adam met Daniel's skeptical gaze coolly and without flinching. "Weren't you pledged to another when you fell in love with Belle?"

Cecilia hid her smile behind her napkin.

Belle folded her arms. "Well, Daniel, what say you now?"

"I just don't want my sister hurt."

William added, "And neither do I."

Ignoring the fuming Daniel, Adam said to Mr. Best, "Sir, I have already told Jo that if I ever break her heart I'll cut out my own and hand it to her on a platter. I love her, sir, truly. I will support her, protect her and pledge to be the best example of a husband and a son-in-law you or anyone else has ever seen."

Mrs. Best said, "If I might interrupt, I will say this. Adam has been nothing but a gentleman to Jo. He's been respectful to me and to Belle. He's carried his weight, helped me in ways that have endeared him to me, and if there is a vote, he gets mine."

Jo came over and gave her a hug. "Thank you, Mama."

William looked to his daughter. "I suppose you have something to say?"

She replied, "Only if I'm asked, Papa."

"I'm asking."

"I love him, Papa. I didn't take him very seriously at first. He is a Morgan, after all."

"Hey!" Jeremiah said, taking mock offense.

Everyone smiled, even Daniel.

"And he is still a woodenhead sometimes," she confessed as she looked into Adam's eyes, "but I'd like to be Mrs. Woodenhead because I love him, Papa, very much."

William glanced over at Belle's father, who gave him a shrug of his shoulders in response.

William sighed. "Okay. I'm willing to say yes."

Jo ran to him and hugged him for all she was worth. "Thank you, Papa! Thank you!"

He laughed and returned her embrace with all the love he felt for his spirited, unconventional daughter.

Adam looked over at Daniel and stuck out his hand. "Pax?"

Daniel clasped it firmly and nodded. "Welcome to the family."

On June 1, 1865, Josephine Best, beautifully clad in the flowing white dress made for her by her sister-in-law, Belle, became the lawfully wedded wife of Mr. Adam Morgan. Jeremiah stood up with Adam, and Trudy stood up with Jo.

As Jo held Adam's hand and looked out at the smiling faces filling the parlor, she knew that regardless of what lay ahead, she would always be Mrs. Adam Morgan, the happiest young woman in the whole wide world. "I love you, woodenhead," she said to him over the congratulatory applause.

He looked down and grinned. "I love you, too, pest."

And with that said, the newly married couple led the way into the dining room for the wedding dinner and the start of their life together.

AUTHOR NOTE

Josephine Best made her debut in *Belle,* and she was such a force of nature I knew she had to have her very own book. Although *Josephine* takes place five years later, Jojo still possessed the same spunk and spirit that made her so well loved in *Belle.* I hope you enjoyed her story.

For anyone interested in more on the historical background, please see *We Are Your Sisters: Black Women in the Nineteenth Century,* edited by Dorothy Sterling, and for more on the key role played by African–Americans in the Civil War, please see *Black Abolitionists* by Benjamin Quarles and *The Negro in the Civil War,* also by Benjamin Quarles.

In closing, I'd again like to thank Glenda Howard and Linda Gill at Harlequin/Kimani for their faith and support. Without them, Belle and Josephine would never have been brought back to life. Thanks also to all the readers both young and old who e-mailed me, sent letters and stopped me at signings to let me know how much they wanted the books to be reprinted. I hope you're pleased—I know I am!

Be blessed.

B

QUESTIONS FOR DISCUSSION

1. How is courtship different now than it was in Jo's day?

2. Do you think Jo would have gone ahead and said yes to George had Adam not come back into her life?

3. Besides his good looks, why did Jo find Adam to be a better match?

4. Trudy said she loved Bert, yet Dred Reed made her forget that. Why?

5. Why was it important for Jo to have her own business?

6. Mrs. Best and many of the other women in Jo's life can be called strong women. Who are some of the strong women in your life, and why do you think they are the way they are?